# Patapsco Spirits

*Eleven Ghost Stories*

ADDISON HODGES HART

# Patapsco Spirits

## Eleven  Ghost  Stories

 Angelico Press

First published in the USA
by Angelico Press 2023
© Addison Hodges Hart 2023

For information, address:
Angelico Press
169 Monitor St.
Brooklyn, NY 11222
angelicopress.com
info@angelicopress.com

ISBN 978-1-62138-929-3 pb
ISBN 978-1-62138-930-9 cloth

Cover design: Michael Schrauzer

For my son and daughter,
Addison and Anna

# CONTENTS

# A (Superfluous)
# Note to the Reader

I AM A HAUNTED MAN. Haunted, that is, as many of us are, by memories. Some of the most persistent of those memories are of growing up in Howard County, in the State of Maryland, and especially of my childhood years living in Ellicott City during the late fifties and early sixties.

The Patapsco River Valley and the surroundings of Ellicott City in those days were still mostly rural, not much changed in many respects from the place H. L. Mencken could nostalgically and evocatively describe, referring to an even earlier era (the eighteen-eighties), with extraordinary charm: "I roved the woods day after day, *enchanted* by the huge aisles between the oaks, the *spookish*, Grimms' Fairy Tale thickets, and the cool and singing little streams."[1] I have italicized the words "enchanted" and "spookish" above for obvious reasons. Mencken, it seems, felt that very same *something* that I had always felt there, which supercharges (or once did) the entire region—an ambience of lurking mystery in its nature, its ruins, and its very atmosphere. In one passage, Mencken portrays a favorite spot where a brook flowed: it "seemed to me to encompass the whole substance and diameter of romantic adventure... The trees along the brook belonged to the original forest, and some of them were immense. Great vines clung to their trunks, and between them was a jungle of saplings and shrubs. There we made acquaintance with brambles and poison oak, and learned to detect the tracks of possums, coons and foxes..." In other words, things wild and unsettling, maybe even uncanny, roamed that river valley and among its hills.

---

1. Mencken, *Happy Days* (1880–1892), Chapter Six, "Rural Delights."

The sort of enchantment and "spookishness" that Mencken describes and that I also experienced in those same locations have, to an unfortunate extent, been erased by development and suburbanization since my boyhood. I confess that I experience a sense of loss whenever I visit the area today; the county is virtually unrecognizable to me now. Such is life, however, and impermanence is the one constant. But Mencken reminds me that the deep, forbidding woods were never far away there in earlier times, and still during my childhood they were everywhere. (At least, though, Patapsco State Park has protected a great swathe of that ancient forest land.)

My haunted memories of that time and place supply the soil from which the eleven stories in this book have grown. The overall setting for them is a region at the southern bend of the Patapsco River, where that thirty-nine-mile-long waterway borders Howard County to the south and Baltimore County to the north. The two towns most frequently referred to in the tales are Catonsville and, of course, Ellicott City. The latter, as it happens, is considered by some to be one of the two most haunted towns in Maryland (the other being Frederick). Whenever I speak of "the town" in these tales, with the definite article, it's Ellicott City that I mean. But it's not the Ellicott City of today, but of that other, older time, when the town was still surrounded by the woods, the waterways, and farmland, and when an atmosphere of impenetrable mystery still lingered on the edges and in the corners of it, a ghostly "presence" that usually—but not always—remained concealed from our direct view. I have no doubt that that presence, which could be felt by those born and bred there, was the result of centuries of history, much of it tragic and much of it strange.

I also need to confess that my fictional picture of Ellicott City, as presented in these pages, strays from facts both geographical and historical at times. I make no apology for inventiveness where telling a tale is concerned. Anyone at all familiar with the town and the surrounding region will spot the inaccuracies, even as they also might recognize this or that house or location in a story. For example, both of the "haunted houses" described in "The Debunker" and "Henry" are based on actual houses, and the hauntings in both stories are exaggerated fantasies that have for their creative kernels

2

actual lore about the originals. The cottage in "The Grisly Pond" is based on one in which an uncle of mine lived briefly. The house in "The Two Boys" is the house of my childhood. "All Souls Convent," which appears in two of the stories—"From All Ill Dreams" and "Bone Fire"—is based on an actual convent near Catonsville. "All Souls" isn't its real name, however. Once an order of the Episcopal Church, it is today a Roman Catholic convent. The church, train station, and former hardware store, mentioned in "They Fly Forgotten," still stand in Ellicott City. But there—as far as I recollect—the verisimilitude ends; the rest is fantasy, the fruit of imagination, memories, and vivid dreams.

All the tales take place during the period of 1960 to 1964. The reason for it is that those years are deeply impressed on my own memory. It is perhaps not irrelevant that this period also saw the beginnings of the rapid changes that were coming to the region. By the end of the decade, Howard County had become a quite different place than it had been at the outset, some of it necessary (advancement in racial justice, for example) and some not (over-development, gentrification, and environmental loss). "Time, like an ever-rolling stream…" I set my stories, then, in that brief period just before many of the local ghosts would face eviction.

These tales are intended to entertain and not be taken too seriously (always a danger in our querulous age). Which isn't to say that there is absolutely nothing in them of a serious nature. The ghost story is a genre that sometimes deals with serious matters indeed. To cite three classic examples, *A Christmas Carol*, despite its humor and color, was written by Dickens as an intentional chastisement of the rich and miserly; Henry James, in "The Turn of the Screw," clearly didn't shy away from the (at the time) disturbing suggestion that the children in the story might once have been menaced by some undisclosed "corruption"; and many a great ghost story since has deftly explored the psychology of its characters—Shirley Jackson's *The Haunting of Hill House* readily comes to mind. A handful of the stories in this collection likewise touch on serious issues. These include the issue of racism ("The Conjuring Song" and "They Fly Forgotten"), Post-Traumatic Stress Syndrome and depression ("Bone Fire"), and one story involves child kidnapping and murder

("The Spot on the Bridge"). For those who have no wish to deal with that last topic even remotely, it's easily skipped over.

Despite their setting in modern times and along an identifiable waterway in the United States, these eleven stories can be said to be medieval in inspiration. The "worldview" in these pages comes deliberately, unapologetically from the past. The spiritual entities teeming these pages are the demons, faeries, ghosts, goblins, fetches, tricksters, sprites, elementals, and angels that have occupied our phantasmal folklore for millennia. Two specific church traditions provide, for good reason, a contextual element in these stories. These are the Roman Catholic and Episcopal (Anglican) churches. Both traditions have historically retained belief in a spiritual realm that includes entities of all kinds, from the most malignant to the most exalted. It's no accident that some of the best writers of ghost stories in English have been practicing Roman Catholics and Anglicans. One of my desires was to tell medieval tales in modern guise.

Finally, these are not gory tales. Some blood is spilled, but I'm not attempting to stir up horror so much as a presentiment of mystery. When reading or writing about the supernatural or (better) the preternatural, I prefer stories that don't, on the one hand, merely disgust or, on the other, try to "explain" anything, but instead captivate and *suggest*. Most real-life stories of hauntings and the like leave us unsettled and unclear, with the veil still in place between one plane and the other. And supernatural fiction is better when it doesn't expound but rather leaves us in a state of wonder, even perplexity. The explicit ruins such fiction, in my opinion. A modicum of subtlety is something I try to maintain, as much for psychological effect—and psychology is key, I believe—as for verisimilitude. I don't often provide clear explanations or a "back story" or a neatly packaged conclusion. I don't like them, and they're not needed.

With all that said and gotten out of my system by way of introduction, I hope the reader will find enjoyment in these tales, "enchanted by the huge aisles between the oaks, the spookish, Grimms' Fairy Tale thickets, and the cool and singing little streams."

A. H. HART

# The Grisly Pond

W HEN MY UNCLE purchased the property, he did so because of the pond. It had captivated him the very first time he saw it as a small boy. It was owned by his first cousin once removed, and it was a gathering place for members of the extended family. He had always loved the spot and, whenever he could, he visited it, sometimes alone or with his dog. The thickly wooded property, on which the pond was located, with its picturesque cottage was situated some ways above the town just off the old Church Road. When he was in his thirties, it was put up for sale by his then-sixty-seven-year-old cousin. My uncle snapped it up. He bought it, he declared forthrightly, not for the old cottage which both he and Mary found charming and (as Mary called it) "magical," or because the property had been in the family for many years, or because he had nostalgic memories of playing there as a boy, but because of the pond. It drew him. It beckoned to him. He loved it. He said that it summoned him.

One must understand that my uncle was an artist and an occasional poet, a consummate romantic. This, despite the fact he fancied himself a Beat—it was, after all, the very early Sixties. Although he resided in Maryland in the hills above the Patapsco River, I believe he saw himself as a sort of spiritual brother of Kerouac and Ginsberg. His artwork in those days was reminiscent of Edward Hopper's, although he could use his paintings to shock at times. He wasn't afraid of making the occasional political statement. His notorious painting of a Klan rally (which the gallery on Main Street refused to hang among his other exhibited works there), depicting a colossal cross luridly aflame against a night sky, dark-hued parked cars and pickups in the foreground that looked like so many orb-eyed behemoths, and white-robed Klansmen beyond them cavorting like fiends from hell engaged in a black sabbath, was miles away from Hopper's film-noirish depictions of solitude and loneliness.

5

That said, most of my uncle's works at that time were subdued in their subject matter, visually "quiet," verging—like Hopper's—on the melancholic. His poetry, on the other hand, was execrable and best left unremembered.

My uncle's name was Roger Scott Parlette. I called him "Roger" and not "Uncle Roger" because he was only nine years my senior and more like an older brother to me than an uncle. Indeed, we bore a striking resemblance to one another, although he was bearded Beat-style and I was clean-shaven. He had a head of unruly black curls, cut long for the time. He looked a bit like a satyr with his goatee. I suspect he self-consciously affected a louche appearance, which he enhanced with a constant pipe. In those years, I was teaching math at Howard High and looking for a good woman, and he was getting himself established as a mature artist—and succeeding, I should add, to get noticed and sell paintings. Luckily for him, he had inherited some money from his father, and in marrying Mary he had been able to supplement that small fortune with the equally modest one with which she had been provided.

Mary was a stunning beauty, with her long blonde hair that looked like it belonged on the head of a folk singer and her ballerina's figure. She was only two years my senior. I have always suspected that Roger married her as much for her potential as a model as for anything else. Being the sort of free spirits they were, they showed absolutely zero embarrassment displaying before me the nudes he had painted of her. I don't blush easily, but I know I blushed whenever a new one was unveiled before my eyes, with the model herself sitting or standing just inches away observing me as I viewed it with my thinly disguised discomfort. I don't doubt the scene probably amused them both. I would have charged them then and there with cruelty, but I couldn't bring myself even to acknowledge that the pictures affected me. I played along, in other words, pretending to be more sophisticated and relaxed about these things than I was.

Their newly acquired property was, like most of the properties along Church Road, practically situated in a forest. Trees and flowering hedges were everywhere. Vines, especially dark ivy, were seen to cling to virtually every house and every stone wall along that ancient winding lane—reputedly once an Indian trail. Mosses grew thick and plush on tree trunks and rocks and roofs. Roger and Mary's cottage had been built circa 1900, was single-storied, white with dark green shutters, and seemed to emerge organically through the ivy that covered so much of its exterior. It wasn't large, but it was comfortable, and Roger had ample space for his studio. It was thickly overshadowed by the foliage of oak, maple, birch, and beech. It had something about it that reminded me of a fairy-tale cottage, and Mary's description of its atmosphere as "magical" seemed apt.

But it was the natural pond that he loved most about the property. It wasn't large, but it wasn't tiny, either; maybe ninety-four or ninety-five feet in diameter, roughly circular in shape, about thirty feet across from one side to the other at whatever point one stood along its circumference. It was the greenest spot I've ever seen. Even in winter, if there was no snow on the ground the moss remained visible and flourishing on the surrounding dark stones and rotting logs along the bank, and the thick masses of ivy that clung to the boles of the huge trees were darkly green. In the summer, the foliage of the trees spread out above the pond in such profusion that the location always looked as if it lay under perpetually overcast skies. The light of the sun on the clearest day couldn't pierce that canopy. In Maryland, summers can be hot and unpleasantly humid, but the shaded spot where the pond was located stayed comfortably cool always. The pool itself looked like ebony-colored glass with faint flickers of emerald and gold in its depths. It was rare to see movement in the pond. Usually, it appeared viscous and unnaturally still. No fish moved in it and insects seemed to flit over it but never alight upon it. At one end, a great willow hung over it, with its branches drooping and partly sinking into the dormant water. If you were to peer into that water, you might dimly see your reflection looking back at you, but it would invariably appear blurred and distorted. I always felt ill at ease looking at my reflection there for reasons I could never have explained. Roger, however, looked into its waters often and seemed to find it alluring to do so. Just how deep that small body of water was I've never known, and I don't believe Roger or Mary knew, either. I had always heard it referred to as "The Grisly Pond" or just "Grisly Pond," but I never knew why. I recall that I asked my uncle about it one summer morning as we sat at his kitchen table smoking and drinking coffee, as we often did, and looking out through the wide-open top half of the Dutch door at falling rain.

"I don't think anybody really knows," he had replied. "Some say a coven of witches used to gather around it in the sixteen-hundreds to do whatever unspeakable things witches do. Which is baloney, of course. I've also heard it said by some of the old-timers around here that a couple of children were murdered there about a hundred years ago and their bodies were thrown into the pond, and their bones are down there still, and that's why it's black as pitch to this day. But there's no record of anything of that sort ever happening, and there certainly would be if the story were true. Which it isn't. I checked it in the records at the public library, in fact, 'cause I was curious. No child murders, no witches, just a pond. So how that dear old pool got the name 'Grisly' is anybody's guess. Probably somebody with an overwrought imagination came up with it or made up the scary stuff to keep the neighborhood urchins from swimming in it."

I remarked that maybe someone named "Grisly" had named it.

"Hell of a name," my uncle had replied, restuffing his pipe. "Although I've got some paperbacks with covers sketched by an artist I like named 'Gorey'—that's 'Gorey' with an 'e-y,' not just 'y,' but still."

The first time he took me to see the pond, I was enchanted by it. I use that word "enchanted" in its full sense. The place struck me both as beautiful and yet somehow eerie, as if we weren't alone in it. It was a foggy Saturday morning in mid-May when he took me there to see it, which made the naturally shaded clearing appear even murkier than it would look during later visits. From somewhere among the wet limbs of the trees there could be heard the melancholy moaning of a mourning dove, a sound which I've always found lovely, yet haunting. To get to the pond, one had to follow a disheveled path which was little more than an indentation in the high-grown grasses and weeds between the trunks of trees, always watching not to trip over roots underfoot or get oneself caught by the outstretched claws of a thornbush. When we came out into the

8

clearing it was delightful to the eye and yet, as I said, it felt uncanny. It struck me as somehow poignant, lonely, and strangely alive. Dimly, I could comprehend how it might "draw" my uncle to it. It wielded a natural spell, or—I thought with some hesitation—a preternatural one, that might well conjure a response from someone with his sensibilities. If Roger or anyone else had told me then and there that this spot was haunted or that some "genius of the grove" abode there, I might have believed it. It occurred to me at first that perhaps it was only the call of the mourning dove that aroused the sense of uncanniness in me. But, later, when I had visited the spot quite a few times and no dove was cooing dolefully, and yet I still had the sensation that this secluded area was *alive* and *aware* and *watching*, I came to believe it was due to something intrinsic to the location itself. Mary said she felt it, too, and Roger… well, this is really his story, and for him it became a passion.

"What do you think?" Roger asked me on that first occasion. We were standing beside the dark waters of the pool.

"It's arresting," I said. "Beautiful, really. Mysterious, too, I'd say."

"Mysterious it is," he agreed. "Timeless. Like it's been around, just brooding since the world began. Some say it's spooky here. Mary does, for instance. Not that she doesn't find it beautiful, but it kind of scares her, too. Don't know why. Can't say I find it spooky myself. I love it. It's the reason I bought the place. It feels like home to me in a way."

"Home?" I asked, my curiosity stirred. "How so?"

He was looking off into the trees as he answered me. "I can't really explain it—just a feeling I've always felt here, ever since I was a boy. Like it's a part of me or I'm a part of it, whatever *that* means." He laughed. "Hell, I don't even know what that means. It's just how I feel. Completely subjective. My granduncle used to bring me here when I was a little boy. He was very old, and it was his son from whom I bought the place. He was a dear old fellow. He died when I was eight."

As he talked, he appeared to become mentally distant, reliving his memories. He lapsed into silence. Melancholy—which, for him, was never very far away—set in for a moment or two, it seemed, but then he shook his mind free of it.

9

"I mean," he went on after collecting his thoughts, "it's sort of like loving someone and being loved in return, these feelings I have for this place. Crazy as it sounds, I feel like something here connects with me with real affection. It reflects me and I reflect it. Sounds nuts, I know. But when I'm here, I become a mirror of these surroundings. This place possesses a *thou* that reflects my *I*… I'm not making any sense, damn it. Have you read any Martin Buber?"

"The philosopher?"

"Yeah, the philosopher. He wrote a book called *I and Thou*. I can't say I understand it all, but wow, man, Buber was really cooking when he wrote that thing. It gave my head a jolt. It made me think we don't live in an *I–it* world, but in an *I–thou* world, or at least that's how we should look at it. Whatever Buber might've meant, I feel it's like what I experience *right here*, right on this spot."

"You're an artist, Roger," I replied. "You write poems. You're allowed to think like that. I'm just a math teacher. My sensitivity is pretty retarded."

He laughed. The mourning dove cooed. Roger turned to me and gestured toward a stretch of grass off to our right.

"I'm going to put some Adirondack chairs and a table over there—green ones. Everything here should be green. Mary and I— and you when you come visit—can sit out here this summer and drink iced tea and gab. I intend to come here daily with my easel and paint, too. I'm going to erect a canvas lean-to there, too, so that when it rains, I can take shelter under it and keep on painting. I always wanted to paint this place—do a whole series that catches its moods. It's a living entity. That's how I see it. It deserves portraiture. Photography could never capture its essence the way me and my oils could."

"I'm sure you're right," I said. "I'm sure you'll pull it off admirably."

That was my introduction to "The Grisly Pond."

During that first summer I could see that my uncle's affection for the pond and its surroundings was unusually fervent. I took his enthusiasm in stride in those early months, chalking up his effusiveness to an artist-poet's temperament. I gave it little serious thought during that time because the normality of his behavior in all other respects didn't allow it to trouble me. I was a frequent guest of Roger and Mary's. They were my closest friends, the family tie with Roger merely augmenting our natural camaraderie. Roger enjoyed introducing me to wines he had recently discovered, Mary liked cooking for me (I displayed heartfelt appreciation for her culinary skills), and the three of us shared a wide range of interests—literature and art chief among them.

And yet, as happy an association as it was, a subtle *something* began to creep into our conversations, an unexpected tension, *something* that I could tell was troubling to Mary whenever it came up. I could see that it troubled her, but Roger evidently couldn't, or else chose not to notice. It was the subject of the pond, which Roger came back to again and again in nearly every conversation. As early as July of that first year, I could see he was obsessed with it. It was odd, I began to think, for him to be so occupied with the place. And Mary's reaction, it seemed to me, was verging on jealousy. It was as if, in her mind, Roger's preoccupation with the pond was becoming a rival to his love for her.

In the early days in their new home, she would involve herself in the conversation, commenting on the exquisite beauty of the pond, praising Roger's first efforts to portray it on canvas, telling how much she enjoyed just sitting there beside it on one of those Adirondack chairs Roger had purchased, watching him labor away with his paints and easel while she read or knitted or simply relaxed. But, as the weeks went on, her contributions to the exchanges dried up. Before long, when the subject of the pond came up, as it invariably did, it was her signal to get up from the table and start clearing things off it or silently slip off into another room or outside to tend her rose garden. Roger seemed oblivious to her reactions, although I could "feel the vibes" like static in the atmosphere. He didn't—or pretended not to—notice her reaction. I would then become his captive audience, sometimes for an hour or longer.

I don't deny that, at times, he was mesmerizingly eloquent about the matter. He could describe the "moods" of the enchanted spot in terms of colors and chiaroscuro, sounds and silences, pungent fragrances and traces of fragrances, and how all these sensual impressions commingled and corresponded with his own moods, producing in him variously wistfulness, melancholy, rhapsody, quietude, longing. He employed language more poetic than his actual poems, telling how the thread-slim veins of a leaf might astound him as he observed it, how the noises made by treefrogs sounded to him like echoes from an alien world, how the winking lights of fireflies at dusk enraptured him, how pleasurable was the feeling of soft moss or cold mud on his bare toes. He was not only painting the pond area, but he was also drinking it in, absorbing it and being absorbed by it daily. It was, as Mary intuited, a love affair. Whether or not it was something psychologically unhealthy, I wasn't prepared to say at so early a stage. Perhaps in time he would grow out of his state of fixation.

But he didn't grow out of it. Instead, there came—I recall it so vividly—what I consider now to have been the inevitable breaching of a hitherto tightly guarded barrier. I wasn't meant to see the rupture but saw it I did. The guard was down. We had consumed quite a lot of wine that evening. Mary said to Roger in exasperation, right in front of me at the table, that they should try for a baby. A moment of silence ensued. I didn't move. Roger broke the spell and said she was right, that it was a good idea, they should have a child. She replied, with an unusually cold tone in her voice, that he needed to make time for it, then.

Roger instantly became self-conscious. His face fell. He looked rebuked and hangdog. He went from wincing to trying to smile it off. He glanced at me with a "What can you do?" wide-eyed expression on his face.

I made some excuse, said my goodnights, and left them to work it out between the two of them. But that incident lingered in my mind and heightened my growing unease regarding Roger's obsession. I had little doubt by this time that whatever Roger's difficulty pertaining to their intimacy and Mary's wish to start a family, it was his feelings about the pond that lay at the heart of the problem.

# The Grisly Pond

Summer turned into autumn. I was back at school teaching now and so my visits with Roger and Mary were fewer, but I still saw them for dinners and conversation a few times a month. One evening just before Halloween, while Mary was in the kitchen carving a jack-o-lantern for the few trick-or-treaters that were bound to show up even out at this remote place in the woods, Roger and I went for a walk around the property. The sun was sinking into the west, and we had stopped at the head of the path that led through the trees to the pond. Roger had just lit his pipe and, blowing a few smoke rings into the air, he said he had seen something out by the pond that afternoon that had taken him aback.

"In fact," he went on, "I've seen them before. And, in fact, I've been seeing them every day for the last few days—but I haven't told Mary. I'm not sure I should. Not sure I *can*, really."

"Them?" I asked. "What do you mean by *them*?"

"An old man and a little boy," he replied.

"Just wandering through the area there?"

"I *suppose* you could say that," said Roger. "At any rate, there they were again today."

I casually tossed a stone into the surrounding woods.

"Any idea who they were?"

"Yes," he said, rather mysteriously. "It surprised me, but I think I do. Anyway, they both just stood at a distance on the other side of the pond, over near the willow tree. I just watched them come out of the woods the first time I saw them. The old fellow was dressed in a tweed overcoat and had a scarf and cap. The boy was in jeans and a red-checked coat with a hood. But his hood was down, and his head was bare. They waved and then went back into the woods, like they were just continuing their walk and didn't want to disturb me while I painted."

"You said you think you know who they are," I said, "and that you've seen them more than once—today, in fact. And that it surprised you."

"Well, here's where it gets unsettling," he said. "You might think I'm crazy when I tell you, but here goes. You have to promise me you'll suspend your disbelief."

"Sure, but I already know you're crazy," I said, with a smile. He didn't smile back. He just looked at the trees and the sunset and puffed on his pipe.

"I thought I recognized them on all the previous occasions, but I also thought my imagination was going haywire. Up till today, they had kept their distance, so I couldn't be entirely sure. But today I called out to them, and they came closer than they ever have before. They came over and stood just a few feet from me. They didn't say anything. They didn't have to. They just smiled at me—*knowingly*, I thought. But *knowingly* about what? I also got the strangest sensation that they were on one side of some invisible partition, and I was there on the other side, and we were just looking at each other. And I got a good look at them, and I knew who they were."

"Well, then, who the devil were they?" I asked, feeling a chill in my spine, though I had no idea why I should.

"The boy was no older than six or seven. And all of a sudden, I realized he was *me*, exactly as I looked at that age. And the old man was, without any shadow of a doubt, my granduncle. There's no mistaking that face."

I couldn't say anything at first. It was as if my brain had been put on hold. All I managed to get out was: "Then what?"

"Then they waved and left just like they've done each time before. Friendly like. But," and he turned to me in the descending darkness and I could feel his eyes on mine, "that boy was me, or the spitting image of me, and that old man was my granduncle."

"What do you make of it?" I said, hesitant to suggest he might have been hallucinating or else fallen asleep in one of the Adirondack chairs and dreamed it.

"I think something or someone is trying to tell me something," he said. "I don't know what or who or why. You're more than a relative. You're a friend, and so I'm confiding in you. I'm not crazy, man, and I was wide awake. I did see what I saw."

"Won't it scare you to go back there again, then?" I asked. "I mean, that's a very weird experience—and you say you keep seeing them there." I was halfway hoping he'd consider discontinuing his daily visits to the pond as a result.

Roger shook his head. "On the contrary, it makes me want to go out there more than ever. I want to understand what it means."

He paused and for a few moments neither of us spoke. Then he said, "Let's go see how Mary's getting on with that pumpkin."

I didn't visit Roger and Mary again for about four weeks after that. It was an unusually long gap between visits, but I had been swamped with work. But then I had a few free days at my disposal, and I paid them a visit. I had avoided the subject with him over the phone during the past few weeks, but as soon as I got Roger alone, I somewhat reluctantly brought up the old man and the boy. Had they come back? Had they spoken to him?

Roger shook his head. "They haven't been back since I told you about them. But something else has happened. I told Mary about it, but I think I probably shouldn't have."

"What was that?" I asked. We were outdoors walking again in the early evening.

"Well..." He began tentatively, seemingly unsure whether he should go on or not, but then deciding to trust me. "Even if Mary is starting to doubt my sanity, I swear it actually happened. Lots of things happen in that spot, to be honest, but most of them haven't been so tangible as this. The old man and the boy—the facsimiles or whatever of my granduncle and me—they were separated from me, and I couldn't touch them or speak with them. This new thing that happened, though, was—*tangible.*"

"I'm listening," I said.

"You remember our dog and cat, when you were young...?"

"Back when you were in your teens, you mean?"

"Laurie, our collie, and our cat, Gray," he replied.

"I remember them," I said.

"When Laurie got old and died, I was miserable," he said. "You might remember that. I really loved that old girl. And Gray—he was a lovely charcoal gray with a white nose and a white triangle on his chest and white paws, you'll recall. He used to follow Laurie and me through the woods on all our walks..."

"Yeah, I remember that, too. He was a special kind of cat."

"He wandered off one day and we never saw him again. I loved that cat, too. I missed them both when they were gone. Living out in the country, I didn't have a lot of friends to hang around with, but they were a good substitute. Anyway, I've seen them—alive. Both of them. By the pond."

"Roger…" I began. The worry must have been evident on my face, even in that diminishing light.

"Hold on," he interrupted, holding up his hand. "Let me finish the story before I regret bringing it up. I'd been standing and painting all morning long, and I'd sat down on one of the chairs for a few moments to rest. I was staring across the pool toward the willow tree. It was another misty day—early November, very somber. The trees were going bare. And as I watched, from out the underbrush under the trees, there came Gray. It was definitely Gray. I'd know that fellow anywhere. He came trotting over to me just like he used to—right over to my legs and he rubbed himself against them. He wasn't ghostlike at all—he was solid and warm-blooded. I picked him up and he was purring like he always did. Tears came to my eyes. I'm not ashamed of it. But that wasn't all. I dropped my right hand limply over the armrest of the chair while I held Gray in my left, and as I did, I felt a familiar cold snout nuzzling my right palm. I looked over and there was Laurie, happy and excited just like when she was in her prime. I don't know how long I scratched and petted them both. And, hell, I was an emotional mess, laughing and crying all at once. It's no wonder Mary thought I was nuts when I described the scene to her. I was just so excited I couldn't bottle it up, so I told her like an idiot. Stupid me. She was furious—told me I should go see a shrink."

I didn't respond to that. Instead, I asked, "Where did Laurie and Gray go after you saw them?"

"They went back into the woods after a while," he said. "Somehow, I got the impression that's where they live now. Where they're waiting for me… Or something like that. I can't explain it, but it was *comforting*. Not at all terrifying or upsetting."

"I don't doubt it," I said. "It must have felt good to know they're happy and not truly gone."

"They're innocent," he replied, then he stopped. He couldn't continue the thought, and it hung there in the cold air unfinished. I could see he was moved at the memory of the encounter. I wasn't going to contradict it. His feelings meant too much to me to hurt

16

him. But, still, I was more perplexed and worried than ever about his state of mind. I could, in other words, understand Mary's dismay.

When we went back indoors, Mary served us pumpkin pie and coffee.

Throughout the winter and into the spring, Roger seemed to grow more and more remote and distracted. Conversations became more strained, as if he couldn't stay connected for long on any given topic, unless that topic had something to do with his preoccupation. He went daily to the pond, in rain or snow or shine. On wet days, he painted under the canvas lean-to he had erected. He labored passionately to render the surroundings there in exquisite, but eccentric, detail. Canvas after canvas he completed, and soon most of the rooms of the house became storage for them. He no longer told Mary or me much about his experiences at the pond; at best, he was allusive. He wasn't, it seemed, trying to hide anything; rather, these were matters so precious to him, so personal, that I believe he couldn't articulate them without somehow betraying himself. At least, that was how it came across to me. His secret was his own. He could still be friendly and even talkative on occasion, and sometimes he would mention The Grisly Pond in matter-of-fact terms rather than passionate ones—when this was the case, it was simply "the place where he was currently working." He would talk now and then about the exhibition he was planning. He knew a gallery in Baltimore where he had an in, he said, that would provide the perfect atmosphere for displaying his "pond portraits."

And the artwork was indeed the best I had ever seen him do. It was frequently breathtaking. But they were also unusual and mysterious works. Each canvas was arresting and evocative, revealing his imagination to be as lively as his attention to literal detail was precise. A few examples might suggest what I mean. In one piece we see the willow tree at the far end of the pond and the other trees closest to it. It's early spring, the green buds are wispy, and the interlacing branches are visible. And almost, but not quite, veiled throughout that woodland scene, one sees eyes peering at the viewer. No whites of the eyes can be seen, everything is in shade. Yet one still glimpses eyes in the shadows, and one can just make out the shapes of hidden watchers. But it's only a suggestion that something more lurks there. Even looking intently at the painting, one can't entirely be certain that his own eyes aren't playing tricks on him. Another example: we see the pond in winter. It's dark, the water black with its veins of emerald light glimmering in its depths. But the shape of the pond has altered. It's no longer its actual nearly circular configuration, but instead it has the hourglass figure of the female form— it has been transformed into a dark, opalescent woman. The hair of the head is the willow, the facial features that are one with the tree's bole are dusky, the dark waters become an undulating body. A third and final example: another winter scene, this one with snow. The surface of the pond is frozen hard. Roger captures the texture of the ice with a mastery I've never seen in his work before. It's gorgeous, it's threatening, it chills the blood to look at it. A gray column of vapor seems to be rising from the icy surface, but it's a vapor in which one can make out human faces. One of the faces is Roger's own. It's a piece of art that verges on the surreal, strangely captivating. It seems to sing in polyphony, the swirling faces forming a choir. Above this vaporous throng shines a star, looking somewhat like the crowning ornament on a Christmas tree.

Occasionally, I paid Roger a visit at the pond as he worked. He was responsive, but also sometimes withdrawn and curt, obsessed with his efforts. Always the sky appeared to be overcast directly above us, as if there perpetually hung a cloud over the area, obscuring the sunlight. As the months wore on, Roger spoke less and less during my visits, sometimes voicing little more than perfunctory grunts. As this became the situation more often, I found myself not staying for long there, and I would go to see how Mary was doing and talk with her instead. I could see that she wasn't happy, that their marriage was under strain, and that she had come to loathe the merest mention of the pond. She had long since given up visiting Roger when he was at work there.

And then, one summer afternoon, the full gravity of the situation crashed in on me. Mary and I were drinking coffee at the kitchen table. Roger was, of course, at the pond. I had just come back from seeing him and little else. He had barely said a word to me. He had been there all morning and he would be there until evening. Mary was left alone, as she had been day after day for months.

"I think I've lost him completely," she told me. The statement seemed to come out of nowhere. So far, we hadn't so much as mentioned Roger.

But I didn't need her to explain. Still, I asked anyway, "How so?"

"You know what I'm talking about," she replied. "He's out there day-in, day-out. I see him for dinner, and that's it. When he's here with me, he's mentally still *out there*. We never talk, except when you drop by, and it's not a hell of a lot even then. We don't share any kind of life." The sadness in her eyes as she said this affected me more than I could have wished. I felt a sudden urge to embrace her. I didn't.

"We used to have shared interests," she continued, "and a shared vision of what we wanted together. That's all gone. He and I are on completely different wavelengths now."

She leaned slightly forward, casting a fleeting, furtive look in my direction. I was examining the half-empty mug of coffee in my hands, but I registered the glance out of the corner of my eye. It sent an unanticipated charge through me.

She looked down at her own mug and went on. "We have no marital life to speak of, no… you know. I want children. I know he still finds me attractive. He says he does, at any rate."

"Mary…" I started to say, beginning to feel uneasy.

She ignored my interruption, or else it didn't register.

"He hasn't asked me to model for him for months," she went on. "It's been a long time. That used to lead to something else pretty regularly in the old days. We might actually get somewhere if he just started back doing the nudes again." She smiled coyly as she said it, looking away demurely. I knew it was feigned. She touched my hand with hers. I looked resolutely down at my three-quarters-empty mug.

I said, wishing the conversation would move on to some other topic and fast, "I'm worried about him, too. That pond is always…"

"Do you know what he said to me the last time we talked about it?" she said, cutting me off, her hand now laid gently on mine.

"No," I said, tension building within me. "What did he say?"

19

I didn't dare look at her. I didn't want our eyes to meet.

"He said we shouldn't have children because he might not be here for them."

That hit me hard. I looked at her then and saw that her eyes were shining with tears.

"What did he mean by that?" I asked.

"I asked him that," she said.

"And...?"

"I think he meant he might go away or... die, I guess."

"That's... well, that's just incredible." I was agitated. I said, "It's crazy. It doesn't sound like Roger at all. Has he lost his mind?"

"I think, if I could just get him to... get him to get me pregnant... If I could get him just once to... you know... well, then, he might not talk like this anymore. He might come to his senses, start wanting a family again..."

Her hand was gripping mine tightly. We were looking at one another directly now, and she seemed to be imploring me, and she never looked more lovely. My body was doing things I didn't want it to do. I began to get it, where this was going, and I was adamant that it shouldn't. I took my hand away—jerked it away actually. In that instant I was acutely aware of the fact that I resembled my uncle physically. Mary had said so many times. She was only two years older than I was. There was a simultaneous pull toward the transgressive and an acidic sensation in my stomach, a dull pain below even that and my head was filling up with shame and guilt—I had to get out of there. My Catholic conscience had kicked in big time.

I shot to my feet, knocking over the kitchen chair as I did.

"I'm sorry," I said, my voice shaking noticeably. I picked up the chair and set it back on its legs. "I've got to go see Roger. Maybe I can talk him into pulling his head out of his backside."

Mary blushed crimson. She turned away.

"No," she said. "I should be the one to say I'm sorry. Of course, you go and talk to Roger. If he'll listen to anybody, he'll listen to you."

I left quickly and didn't look back.

# The Grisly Pond

I made my way through the trees toward the pond, profoundly shaken but determined to talk sense into Roger.

"And it would've been *his* fault," I said furiously to myself as I went, "if something had happened back there. Damn him for that." But even as I muttered railings and regrets, my head was still full of thoughts of Mary, her vulnerability, her pathos, her beauty... and something wicked in me wanted me to turn around, not lose the opportunity, head right back to her while there was still some chance. And I hated myself for harboring the idea.

I was now in the strip of woods surrounding the pond. A zephyr stirred the ivy on the tree trunks. The leaves seemed to rattle as it did, and the air seemed filled with whispers. I was certain I heard voices, susurrant and murmuring. They seemed to be all around me and moving along with me. Moving along with me toward the pond.

It was late in the afternoon. Who, I wondered, would be out here in these woods at this hour besides Roger, besides me? I pressed on under the towering, spreading beeches, with their foliage so thick above me that no ray of sunlight penetrated. The path was a narrow strip of dirt. Now I could swear I heard children's voices somewhere nearby, and soft laughter. I heard a dog barking ahead of me, where I knew the pond lay. Then I heard Roger's voice. He was singing.

Then it all stopped, just as I stepped out into the clearing where Roger stood. He was looking off toward the woods on the other side of the pond, his easel and paints beside him. His back was to me. He turned slowly around to face me. His eyes looked sad and a bit glassy, but he smiled at me. There was no one else in sight and that fact only increased my apprehension. Surely those voices, that barking, had indicated that others had been here mere moments ago. I had heard them distinctly. I felt a keen sense of dread—this perpetually uncanny place, this pond, these surroundings sent chills through me.

"Where are they?" I asked him.

He didn't answer. He gestured toward the canvas he had been working on, and my eyes turned in that direction. I came closer. The painting was unfinished, but I could see it was a masterpiece already. The colors were vibrant, the shadows deep, and everything in it seemed to move—the pond seemed to ripple, the trees seemed to stir, the grasses seemed swept by the wind. The painted ivy clinging to the painted tree trunks appeared to move like the living ivy I had passed on my way here. And all around the pond were figures, unfinished figures, faceless and sketchy, standing or dancing or reclining. A dog sat in the foreground, a red-haired collie, its mouth open, its tongue hanging out. A gray cat was off to one side, rolling in the grass. Behind the gathering of faceless people was the foliage, and I realized as I looked more closely that the foliage formed the features of a man—a man composed of green leaves and twisting limbs.

"What does it mean?" I asked, looking at him. He stood at my right elbow.

"It means what it is," he said slowly. "I can't *explain* anything. It's a dark enigma, this place. Its full purport is beyond me."

It sounded to me like something out of a book, not like Roger. It aggravated me.

"I'm sure I heard voices just now," I said. "And a dog barking. Did I? Who were they?"

"You heard them, too, then?" He looked as if the news cheered him a bit. I nodded. "Ah, good."

I pointed to his painting. "Are these the people and the dog I heard?"

"Yes." He spoke evenly, soberly.

"And the face in the trees…?"

"A metaphor," he replied. "Think nothing of it. This is a thin place. You've heard of thin places, haven't you? Nature, memories, the past, the present, you, me, *them*—it's all intertwined here. Everything."

"Them?"

"You heard them," he said. "You said so. They're all around us. Around us right now, in fact. You can feel them."

I looked around, apprehensive, then I looked back at him. Despite my newly awakened dread, my temper also flared. I grabbed Roger suddenly by the shoulders and made him look me in the face.

"Damn it, Roger," I said, a note of pleading in my voice. "I don't know what's going on here. I don't know who 'they' are. I don't know who or what's haunting you out here or what's got you—I

22

don't know—*bewitched* or whatever you are. But, right now, I don't care. I mean, I do care—but we can talk about all that some other time, somewhere else—but *not here*. More importantly—much more importantly—do you have any idea—*any idea whatsoever*—what you're doing to your wife? Do you know how close you are to losing Mary right now?"

He winced.

"Yes, I know," he said. "I know she's very upset. I know it's my fault."

"Well, then, what do you intend to do about it?" I let go of him. "It's either her or this obsession you've got. That's how serious it's gotten. It's her or this… this dreamy-assed *hang-up* you've got stuck in your brain where this goddamn pond is concerned."

Before I knew what had happened, I found myself on my backside in the grass, Roger standing over me. He had shoved me backward violently. At the same instant, the wind whipped up and the trees writhed wildly. He looked like a wild man, his black hair tossed by the gust, his fists clenched, his face contorted. Then just as quickly, his features softened and showed remorse. He leaned down, took me by the hand, and raised me to my feet. The wind died down as he did. Roger began making effusive apologies.

"Quit it," I said, raising my hand and waving him off. "Just stop. I'm concerned about Mary. I'm concerned about you. *That's all.* You've got someone special there you don't want to lose. You need to go home. You need to go home *now.*"

Without another word, he covered his canvas, folded his easel, and put them and his paints under the lean-to. We left the pond together. We didn't speak as we made our way back to the cottage. We parted ways at the Dutch door. I couldn't face Mary yet, so I made some lame excuse to Roger and took off "hell-bent for leather."

It was a few minutes after six the next morning when I got the phone call. It was Mary, upset, nearly hysterical. I got her to calm down and tell me what was wrong.

"Roger's disappeared," she said. "He's gone. I can't find him anywhere."

23

"What about the pond?" I asked, thinking, surely, he would have gone there.

"I went out there," she said, her voice rising unsteadily again. "He's not out at the pond. The spot's empty. He's just nowhere to be found. The car's here, right where we always park it, but he's gone."

"Did you call the police?" I asked.

"I just did," she said. "They're coming now. I want you here, too, if you don't mind coming..."

"I'll be over in a few minutes," I assured her.

I dressed and got to the cottage in record time. The police had already arrived. They had a dog with them, and, after sniffing some of Roger's unwashed clothes that Mary provided, the dog led them straight through the trees to the pond. There he stopped, by the water's edge. Mary stood by me, holding my arm. I could feel, rather than hear, her sobbing.

"It's gloomy as hell here," said one policeman to another within earshot of us.

"I once heard a story about some kids getting murdered up here a long time ago," said the other. "Something about witches doing strange stuff here, too."

"That's all bunk, but it's a weird place," said the first policeman.

The police radioed in and requested a diver to investigate the pond, it being too deep to dredge. I walked Mary back to the cottage, where we sat silently and watched the police outside. We had answered all their questions and they had done a thorough search of the premises. They had been looking to see if Roger might have written an overlooked note or left behind some other clue. Nothing turned up.

The canvas he had been working on the day before had been uncovered by one of the policemen at the pond.

"Strange picture," he had remarked. "Who're all the spooks in it?"

"Spooks?" Mary had asked.

"Well, they sure look like ghosts," said the policeman.

"No idea who they are," Mary had replied. I said nothing.

And now Mary and I watched the police work and only had the barest of conversations between ourselves. She was no longer weeping; instead, she looked shellshocked. A diver finally arrived a little after noon, and we all went out to the pond again. He searched it as well as he could for the better part of two hours.

"It's black as ink down there," he reported, sitting on the ground beside the pond and removing his flippers. "Too deep to drain, that's for sure. Nothing down there I could see, and I looked around pretty good. There's no body in there. Completely empty—not even any fish. Maybe he went in there, lady," he said to Mary, "but he's not down there now. So, you've got reason to think he's still alive, in other words."

The search stretched on for days, but there was to be no sign of Roger.

A year passed.

During that time, Mary sold as many of Roger's paintings as she could. She also put the property up for sale. I visited her now and then, but we were growing apart without Roger's presence in our lives. Neither of us ever spoke about what had happened between the two of us on the last day that either of us had seen him alive. It was something I wanted to forget, and I believe the same was true for her. But we stayed in touch for a while.

When the property finally sold, she got herself another place in town. In time, she remarried and moved out of state. We lost touch completely then.

That summer, with the cottage empty, right before the new residents moved in, I decided to go up and look around the property one last time. It was a melancholy visit. The place was, of course, deserted. Mary's roses were in sad shape. The little house stood lonely and forlorn, where so much love and laughter had once been the order of the day.

On a whim, I walked to the pond, although I confess that I felt a thrill of dread run through me as I did. But I strengthened my resolve and headed into the trees. I made my way through the familiar wood, down the narrow dirt path among the grasses, and finally came out into that dreary clearing. The pond was, as ever, its glassy black-shot-with-emerald self. The atmosphere hung heavy. The lean-to was still there but collapsed on one side. I glanced inside and saw some strewn brushes and paint tubes. The Adirondack chairs, covered with leaves and other debris, had also not been removed.

I stood motionless there for some minutes, just gazing at the pond and the willow on the far side of it, lost in my memories. Then, shaking my head to clear my thoughts, I stirred myself to move along and return to the cottage. As I did, I saw the foliage at the other end of the pond stir, then begin to shake. I knew something was over there, approaching the area through the underbrush. I didn't move. I just stood and watched to catch a glimpse of whatever was pushing its way through the branches and bushes and vines.

Out into the clearing they came. Two persons. They stopped and looked across the pond in my direction. They spotted me and both waved to me. The old man wore a tweed overcoat, a scarf, and a cap. The boy had on jeans and a red-checked coat with a hood. The hood was down. His head was bare.

I turned and ran.

26

# The Two Boys

O
N THE DAY the boy was born, his grandfather saved his life. It happened like this.

The grandfather, ecstatic, keyed up, had come to set his eyes on his very first grandchild, born just a few short hours earlier at the "Women's Hospital" in Baltimore. No sooner had he arrived and visited his daughter's bedside, where he found her fast asleep, than he had—after vigorously shaking the hand of his son-in-law, seemingly as an afterthought—dashed directly down the hall to get a good look at the boy. Arriving at the window that separated visitors from the newborn infants, he had quickly spotted his grandson among the rest. The baby's crib was tagged with his last name in bold black caps and decorated with a powder-blue ribbon. But even as he took in these details, he observed something else, something that sent an electric shock of horror straight through him and shoved him instantly into action. The distracted nurses were oblivious to the fact that his grandson—*his grandson*—was turning blue. The baby was choking and gasping for air. With no regard for protocol or etiquette and cursing so thunderously and unselfconsciously that the nurses on the other side of the window shot him startled looks of dismay, he shoved his way through the door just as one of the nurses was coming out to shush him. He pushed past her, nearly knocking her over, and went directly to the baby, picking him up from the crib and shouting to the flustered women for help.

The rest of the story, told many times in the family circle ever after, is simple enough. The baby was instantly seen to, and the newborn's grandfather was a hero. It even merited a short piece in *The Baltimore Sun*, with a photograph of him holding his grandson. In fact, so grateful were the parents that they named their boy "George" after him, and not after his father as they had originally planned to do. They also went so far as to call their son by the same unusual nickname that the grandfather had always gone by, even in

27

his adult life—"Boy." And, as the child he had saved grew in years, nobody venerated the old man more than young "Boy" did.

The house in which they all lived—parents, Boy, and his Grandpa (the elder Boy)—had been built in 1905. It was a commodious brown shingle house of three stories with an expansive basement and a long, broad porch that wrapped around its eastward-facing front and along the north side. At the porch's far end on the north side hung a bench-swing on which three or four persons—depending on their sizes—could sit side by side in a row. It was painted dark green and was suspended from the porch's ceiling by a pair of sturdy chains. All around the house were lush trees and verdant bushes, and the property stretched for some acres into the surrounding woods. Grandpa had bought the residence in 1924, the year he had married, and he and his wife had raised five children in it—four boys and one daughter, the last being Boy's mother. When his wife had died of pneumonia thirty years later and two years before his grandson's birth, Grandpa had turned the home and its property over to his daughter and son-in-law. He moved upstairs to the third floor, which was a self-contained apartment, complete with a kitchen and two bedrooms. He had only just turned fifty-one.

He owned and oversaw two filling stations in town until a few years before his death, though every few days he would still drop in on them to make sure things were being handled properly. But he trusted Tommy implicitly, the man he had left in charge to run the stations and whom he had known since childhood. Grandpa's life had not always been a happy one; in fact, most of it had been anything but happy, though he wasn't one to complain about things. His father had committed suicide when he was only nine, and it had fallen to him soon after—as the oldest among his siblings—to earn a living for the household of five.

It was also upon his father's death that he discovered alcohol by way of the cooking wine in his mother's kitchen, and it soon became a daily habit that he was helping himself to it. His drinking grew and developed as he did, and he realized he had the capacity to hold his liquor well. He could be intoxicated and yet perform his duties without his condition being detected. The only telltale sign was that he was more prone to lose his temper when drinking than when he was sober, but one had to know him well to recognize it. Later in life, his alcoholism was supplemented with an addiction to morphine—the town doctor being the one who had gotten him hooked and then become his supplier. Consequently, his wife and children often lived under a dark cloud, never knowing when his addictions might render him unusually angry, possibly violent, depressed, or broke. Nevertheless, the family made it through the Depression better than many others did, sustained as they were by the public's need for fuel and auto repair.

No doubt, it was the combination of liquor and chain-smoking (yet another addiction—the one he never kicked) that brought on Grandpa's lung and throat cancer later in life. By the mid-1940s, he had given up drinking and using morphine. As Boy's mother admitted to those in whom she confided such things, during the years of her growing up living with him could be hell, but after he stopped drinking, he became a pleasure to live with—an utterly transformed man. Far from being prone to the violent displays of anger he had exhibited during her young life he was now the gentlest of men. It was this changed man, this mild and tender grandfather, that Boy knew and loved so well.

And Boy had much to sustain that love as he grew in years. While his father was at his office in Baltimore, working for the Koppers Corporation, and his mother was busy maintaining the household, it was often the case that the two Boys kept close company. Grandpa taught Boy such priceless secrets as how to pull the stem of a honey-suckle blossom so carefully from its back end between thumb and index finger that the single drop of sweetness it contained could be put to his tongue. He showed Boy where the blackberry bushes were in the woods and how to pick them without getting pricked. He instructed the child in the lore of snakes—blacksnakes were "good" because they killed the poisonous copperheads, so he must never harm a blacksnake or a milk snake either. He also made sure that Boy could recognize poison ivy so as to avoid it. He taught him how to distinguish between types of trees. In winter, he let Boy shovel the snow with him. And he initiated him in the mysteries of what lay under the hood of the family car, often taking him into town to

visit the gas stations and Tommy. And there were many other practical things he explained to the child. He also read to him and told
him stories and sat and listened to Boy as the child expounded on
his own special interests—like dinosaurs, for which he had an
unflagging passion. Often these exchanges of information happened on the big green swing on the porch, a place of wonder in
spring when the scent of lilacs and other flowering bushes filled the
air, and in summer when a thunderstorm was brewing and the trees
were reeling wildly (and Boy liked to imagine that a Tyrannosaurus
Rex was passing by just behind them) and the fragrance of impend-
ing rain permeated the atmosphere, and in autumn when the gold
and red and russet leaves were falling—which they all, parents,
grandfather, and child, would later rake up into piles and burn in
the crisp air on some happy Saturday morning.

And there were other, more arcane and hoary truths that
Grandpa imparted to Boy. He told the child about "the little people," whom he said were a mixed race of those who had come to
American shores from the old world and had mingled with their
indigenous counterparts of the new world. Grandpa called them
"Pukwudgies"—that's "the Indian name," he said—and claimed he
had seen them once when he was Boy's age. Boy was five at the time.

"They're very wary—'wary' means 'cautious'—where big people
like us are concerned," he told Boy. "Sometimes children can see
them, but grownup people usually can't."

"Why not, Grandpa?" Boy asked. It was a sticky summer afternoon, and they were both sitting on the porch swing in hopes of
catching a breeze when they had had this particular conversation.

"Because grown people are usually *too* grown up and have lost
the ability to see anything outside of their own ideas and worries,
and that's sad. But," he cautioned the child, "if *you* ever see any, you
better watch out. The little people are tricky and a lot of times they
steal things, and they tell lies and they set fires and *sometimes*..."
Grandpa paused for effect. "*Sometimes* they even steal children who
aren't careful and who believe whatever they tell them. Never, ever
believe anything one of the little people tells you if you should ever
meet one. Sometimes what they say might be true, but most of the
time it's not. And they like to confuse you by telling you something

30

true but mixed with lies, just to catch you. The little people in these parts are especially wild and they tell lots of lies, so don't trust them. You can recognize them if you see them."

"What do they look like?" asked Boy.

"Well, they're about your size," replied the old man. "They have long black hair as a rule, and their skin is a pale gray color. And they have short, bent legs."

"What do they steal? Do they steal *toys*?" Boy's face became hard. "They better not steal mine!"

"I don't know if they steal toys," said Grandpa. "They never took any of mine when I was a boy. Well, maybe a marble or two. They like shiny, colorful things. But you know what?"

"What?" said Boy.

"You may not believe me if I tell you."

"Try me," said Boy.

"I really believe they may have made off with my straight razor." Grandpa looked grave about this suspicion of his. "Here. Feel my chin." And he rubbed his chin against Boy's forehead.

"Yee-ouch!" exclaimed the child, pulling his head away.

"Couldn't shave this morning," said Grandpa. "I'm sure they took it. I looked everywhere and I can't find it and I'm sure nobody else moved it. And I always keep it in the same place. And nobody else seems to know what happened to it."

"I didn't do it," said Boy.

"I know you didn't. But it's not good and it worries me. They can do all sorts of mischief, those pukwudgies, especially with something like that—and especially if they took some of my hairs along with it. They can work magic, you know. They have secret knowledge. They could put me in a trance, if they wanted to, and then one of them could disguise himself to look like me. That sort of thing. All it would take for them would be a few hairs from my chin."

Boy looked frightened, and the old man noticed it.

"Well," he said, his features brightening, "at least they didn't steal *you*." And he poked Boy in the side to dispel his fear.

But Boy still looked concerned. "Where do they take the children when they steal them?" he asked.

"Oh, underground, I guess," said Grandpa. "To their own country. They're made to be servants and dishwashers and suchlike down there."

At another time his grandfather also told Boy about the ghosts, in particular about the ones who lived across the road in the big house there and, even more particular still, about the ones who lived with them in their own house. About the latter, he said, "You needn't be afraid of them. They're our relations."

It was autumn when they had this conversation, when matters ghostly are more significant than at other seasons of the year.

"Like Grandma?" asked Boy.

"Yes, especially Grandma," answered his grandfather wistfully. "She's waiting for me to join her, you know. That's all."

"Waiting for you?" asked the boy. "Where?"

"Where we all must go someday..."

"You mean," the boy's voice dropped to a whisper, "when you *die*?"

"Yes," said Grandpa gently. "We all have to do that someday. Can't really be avoided. There's nothing to be afraid of about death, though. It's just a bigger kind of life."

"But I don't want *you* to die, Grandpa," said Boy. "If you go, I want to come with you."

"Well, you'll catch up with me one day," said his grandfather, "but let's hope that's not going to happen for a long time yet. Like I said, we'll all have to die someday. But I sure would like to see your Grandma again."

"Can you see her sometimes, Grandpa?" whispered Boy. "As a ghost, I mean...?"

"I have seen her," said Grandpa with a sigh. "Just once. It was in the early morning, right before dawn, not long ago. It was two days before the little people made off with my straight razor, in fact... Curious. But as a ghost is not the way I want to see your grandmother. I want to see her where we can hold hands again. You'll understand that one day."

He looked down into his grandson's troubled but wondering eyes. "And I've seen other ghosts, too, and even heard their voices sometimes. Some of them are your great aunts and great uncles, so you shouldn't be frightened of them. It's a big family you're part of.

## The Two Boys

They're all *your* family. So, there's nothing to worry about or be afraid of. They're just keeping watch over us here—and, of course, they love you. So, if you ever hear their footsteps at night in the hallway or upstairs, it only means they're checking on us to make sure we're all right."

"That's good," said Boy. "Do they know about the little people?"

"Oh, sure, they do," said his grandfather. "That's one of the reasons they keep a lookout on us down here. Can't let the little people bother us, now, can they?"

"I s'pose not," said Boy.

He scratched his nose, and Grandpa could see he was still troubled by something. At last, Boy said, "But the little people did steal your straight razor…"

"Yes, that's true," said Grandpa thoughtfully. "Well, sometimes even the ghosts miss some things, I guess." And the conversation that day moved on to dinosaurs and other germane topics.

Conversations such as these were not to the liking of Boy's parents. Being neither children themselves nor old enough to have learned some important things about life and the nature of reality, being still in that indeterminate state of young adulthood, they reacted to these tales when they were related to them by Boy with mild condescension and—in the case of Boy's mother—irritation. His father was only slightly disdainful, his mind being on other, job-related matters. He didn't like it, but he didn't find it terribly worrying, either. But his mother said to Grandpa in Boy's hearing, "Daddy, you shouldn't fill his head with nonsense like that. Tell him you're making it all up, so he won't have nightmares…"

At this, Grandpa only winked solemnly at Boy, who understood it—correctly—to mean: "Every word of what I've told you is true."

Then, to the child his mother said, "Don't pay attention to his stories, Boy. They're just stories. Your grandfather likes to tell stories. They're just made-up stories like on TV. Just stories to amuse you, like on *Captain Kangaroo.*"

At this, Boy winked solemnly back at Grandpa, and the two of them understood each other without a word spoken between them.

Meanwhile, the mystery of the missing straight razor remained unsolved.

It was the following year, when Boy turned six, that Grandpa was diagnosed with cancer of the lungs and throat. The results of the tests were made known to the family precisely on the child's birthday. After he had spoken with the doctor and put the telephone receiver back on its cradle, Grandpa looked up at his daughter and son-in-law from where he was sitting and, with a wan smile, softly broke the news. Boy was outdoors at the time, playing in the snow.

"We'll tell him tomorrow," said Boy's father. "We'll just let him have a happy birthday today."

They were a family that possessed an old-fashioned stoical character and tended not to hide the truth, no matter how difficult the truth might be, even from their child. When they finally did bring themselves to tell Boy—not the following day, but two full days after that—he burst into tears and ran upstairs to his room. All he could understand was that his grandfather was terribly sick and that very possibly he wouldn't be alive much longer. But after he had recovered his composure, he came back downstairs and for a long while sat silently on his grandfather's lap, who in turn held him close.

In the weeks that followed, his grandfather's condition worsened noticeably. He was in and out of the hospital. He lost so much weight that Boy thought he looked like another person, no longer the robust man with a full head of gray hair, who had taught him so many things and taken him for long walks in the woods and whom he had often observed, his sleeves rolled up and his arms muscular, energetically laboring over the family automobile. Now the clothes sagged on a skeletal frame, he was shedding his hair, his chin was perpetually grizzled, and he coughed a lot—and sometimes he coughed blood. And then, on one particularly horrible day, he returned home from some days away in the hospital with a hole cut into his throat and a strange-looking contraption attached to it. Boy's parents explained to him about the tracheotomy and why Grandpa had to have it done—that it helped him breathe and that he could still talk through the contraption, but maybe not so much as he had before, and that Boy needed to listen more closely when he spoke and be patient if he wanted to understand what he was saying. Grandpa's voice now sounded "funny" to Boy, though not

34

"funny" in an amusing way. It was raspy and harsh, reminding him a little of Donald Duck's (he was an avid viewer on weekday afternoons of *The Mickey Mouse Club*), only lower and gruffer than Donald's. Grandpa, of course, made light of it and tried his best to relieve the child's anxieties, but that only worked to a limited extent.

Eventually, Grandpa became too weak to climb the stairs to the third floor, so it was decided that he move down to the second floor and occupy the master bedroom, his daughter and son-in-law moving into the south-side guestroom. The master bedroom was a spacious room, with three windows looking out onto the enormous catalpa tree on the north side, the closest branches of which were mere inches from the panes. His daughter had always said that to be in that room was like being in a tree house. Grandpa had planted that catalpa in 1924, and among the many things he had taught Boy was that the word "catalpa" was an old Muscogee Indian word that meant "a head with wings." This, of course, had intrigued the boy, who from that moment on associated the tree with a mysterious living winged head that watched protectively over the house night and day.

And there the dying man remained, mostly bedridden, visited by his doctor every few days, a local nurse daily, family members and friends on occasion, and—as often as he could be there, which was every day—his grandson. On the other side of summer, however, Boy started attending elementary school, which in turn meant that he wasn't home during the week until mid-afternoon. But he would come up to see his grandfather right after school and share with him each day's events and what he was learning. And on weekends he could visit Grandpa at any hour of the day, and he did. In this way life went on until November.

One Sunday evening before bedtime, his teeth brushed and in pajamas and bathrobe, Boy visited his grandfather. He had no idea, of course, that this would be the last time he would see the old man alive. It was pitch-black outdoors and the sound of rain drummed on the windows of the bedroom. In the room itself only a dim golden light came from the lamp on the bedside table, near where Grandpa was propped upright on pillows. Boy climbed up onto the bed next to the emaciated figure, laid his head on his now bony

shoulder, and said matter-of-factly, "We don't learn anything interesting in school."

"Oh?" rasped the old man.

"Just arithmetic and spelling and stuff like that," said Boy. "Nothing about trees or dinosaurs or ghosts or the little people... I told
my teacher about the ghosts and the little people, but she said they
aren't real."

"Teachers don't know everything," said Grandpa.

"Are they real, Grandpa?" asked Boy.

"Teachers?" asked Grandpa.

Boy laughed. "No. The ghosts and the little people. Mama and
Daddy don't believe in them either."

"Well, now, I'll tell you what," said Grandpa. "Your mother just
doesn't want you getting scared. And your father doesn't want your
mother getting upset about you getting scared. But your mother
knows better because I brought her up right. But grownups sometimes forget—until they get old themselves. But I told her you won't
get scared. Right?"

"Right," said Boy resolutely.

"So, that's that. But listen now." Grandpa became quite solemn at
this point, and he looked through his filmy eyes into Boy's bright
ones. "Soon I'm going to be a ghost myself and I want you to know I
won't be very far away from you when I am. I'll go on up to heaven
when I think everything's okay down here and the time's right, but
until then I'll be keeping an eye on you—with your grandma and
the others. You understand me?"

"Yes," whispered Boy.

"I was there on the day when you were born, and I'll be with you
as long as you need me around. If you get in trouble, just remember
that."

"Mama and Daddy told me you saved my life," said Boy.

"That was God," said his grandfather. "It wasn't your time to die.
I just happened to be around at the right moment, that's all. And
I'm glad I was. You're a fine young man and I love you very much.
I'll be watching out for you."

"Because of the little people?"

"Sure. Because of the little people and anything else that tries to harm you. So," he gave the boy a wink, "if you hear footsteps at night or see a shadow pass you by in the hallway, don't be afraid. It'll probably just be me or your grandmother. The little people won't bother you while we're around."

"They did steal your straight razor and get away with it," Boy reminded him.

"Well, they won't steal you. So, goodnight. Get some sleep now. School tomorrow."

The boy slipped down off the bed and said goodnight and went down the hall to his bedroom. When his mother tucked him in, she asked him what he and his grandfather had talked about.

"Oh, nothing," he replied. "Just school and dinosaurs and stuff."

It was the following day that Boy came home from school to a scene of horror. His mother and father met him at the front door and, telling him the news as tenderly as they could, they tried their best to keep him from going upstairs. But he ducked beneath the arms that would have restrained him and virtually flew up the stairway to the master bedroom, barely touching a single step. Upstairs he found a gathering of strangers in white with mops and buckets, at work scrubbing down the bathroom. But Boy could already see the blood—lots of it, as if it had been sprayed against the walls the tub, the toilet, and the sink with a hose, the tiled floor covered with dark red puddles and drying red-brown stains. The trail of blood extended from the bathroom to the master bedroom, where still other strangers were similarly engaged in cleaning up the mess. Grandpa's body was gone. It had been conveyed from the house to the mortuary less than an hour before. Boy's parents caught up with him and gently led him, sobbing, downstairs. Once they had him seated at the kitchen table and ready to listen, they told him that they hadn't wanted him to go upstairs and see things in the state they were, that they were sorry he had, and they explained to him that his grandfather had had what's called a hemorrhage, that it looked appallingly ugly, but that he had died quickly and hadn't suffered long.

The funeral took place on a bleak, drizzly November Saturday at

St. John's churchyard. Through it all, Boy felt numb. The body in the coffin was barely recognizable to him. It looked to him like a wax dummy. But, as the days became weeks, the boy's initial numbness gave way to bouts of inconsolable weeping, followed by a lengthy period of gloom. Every inch of the house, the yard, the trees outdoors, the furniture in the home, and, of course, his grandfather's clothes and personal effects presented him with a sharp sense of absence where before there had been a vibrant, loving presence. Only gradually would he, bit by painful bit, day by lonely day, adjust to a dismal, hollow home that his grandfather had before made so cheerful. At night, in his bed, he listened to the creaks and groans of the old house and to the clanking sounds that the radiator made, and sometimes he did think he could hear footsteps outside his door in the dark hallway. Perhaps, he thought, it was his grandfather making the rounds to keep an eye on him. This period lasted for some weeks.

And then something changed in Boy's behavior all at once. He seemed to his parents to have suddenly and inexplicably snapped out of the doldrums and accepted the loss. He appeared happier, more content. His parents were relieved that the worst seemed to be over for him, although they couldn't help but notice how sudden this transformation had occurred. But his observant mother also began to notice that every afternoon, as soon as he came home from school, Boy gobbled down his customary cookies and milk and then headed directly up the stairs. His father was at the office during weekdays, of course, but both parents noted that Boy made for the upstairs on the weekends as well and would remain there for hours. They assumed he was up in his own room, playing or reading or coloring. But this was a new behavior in their only child and—like most watchful parents of an only child—they began to wonder what was going on. However, not wanting to compromise his privacy, they didn't ask him about it.

But then Boy began to say things that at first sounded to them merely like a six-year-old's active fantasy. But, when these occasional comments continued to slip out over a lengthy period of days, their content began to nag at them. What could they mean, they wondered?

"I think Grandpa wants me to come and visit him," he announced one evening over supper. "He says it's wonderful up there where he lives now, and I'd like it if I came and saw it."

"What on earth makes you say that?" his mother asked him, looking surprised.

"Oh, nothing," he replied. "It's just something I thought about." And the subject was changed.

Another time, he told them, "Grandpa looks well again. His hair has all grown back."

And yet another time he said to them, "I told Grandpa he can move back to the third story, and we can visit there, but he likes it better in your bedroom."

At this, both his parents looked alarmed and glanced at one another wide-eyed.

And then, one late Saturday afternoon, Boy came down the back steps from the second floor into the kitchen. His mother said, "You've been up there for hours. What have you been doing all this time?"

And he answered, "I've been up in your room talking to Grandpa. He doesn't talk funny anymore, and his neck doesn't have a hole in it neither."

His parents just stared at him blankly at that, and Boy could see that he had said something that worried them. Being only six, though, he didn't know what it was. Maybe they were worried about Grandpa.

"It's okay," he said quickly. "He's all well now. Don't worry."

But he could tell that that wasn't it. Something else was bothering them. Then he thought maybe it was that other thing he had said to them a few days ago that had seemed to upset them. So, he said as brightly as he could, "You don't need to worry. Because I'm not going to go see where he lives. I told him I can't right now."

"Son," his father said, kneeling down so that they were face to face, "you know that Grandpa died, right?"

"Yes," said Boy, "'Course I know that."

"Okay, then," said his father. "So, it's playing, right? You're playing that Grandpa is still alive. Well, that's okay. And I know you know he isn't coming back... Right?" His son was looking either inattentive or impatient, he thought. He tightened his grip on Boy's shoulder. "You'll see him again someday in heaven, but for right now, you have to understand..."

"I *know* he's not *coming back*," Boy interrupted. "But he didn't leave for good yet. He's a ghost now, so he's back and forth. I talk to him upstairs."

"All right," said his father, standing up, but keeping his hand on Boy's shoulder. "I understand. You need to believe he's still with you. Just don't get carried away."

Boy misunderstood his father's meaning. "He won't carry me away. I told him I can't go."

"Fine, that's fine," replied his father, shooting a glance at his wife. "You run along and play."

When the child had left, the parents concurred that maybe it was just a harmless phase he was going through, that it would soon pass, that school and friends and new interests would eventually wear down this present preoccupation with his grandfather's "ghost." But they also thought they had better keep a close eye on the situation, in the hope that it wouldn't get out of hand.

On the day before Thanksgiving, Boy slipped up the back stairs from the kitchen, having consumed his late afternoon milk and cookies. On the second floor he made a beeline for his parents' bedroom for what was now his customary visit with the ghost of Grandpa.

He was no longer nervous in the presence of the apparition, as he had been when the encounters first began. At that time, it had happened wholly unexpectedly. He had gone into the bedroom and sat in the small armchair by the three windows that looked out onto the catalpa tree, simply recalling in a listless, melancholy way those times when he had visited his grandfather there during the latter's final illness, wishing that he could still talk with the old man. In fact, as he had sat there, he had spoken to the empty bed as if his grandfather were in it, keenly feeling the absence as he did so, but uttering into the empty space between chair and bed just how much he wanted his Grandpa to be there. He had shut his eyes momentarily, because the tears were welling and, when he reopened them, he saw in the semi-darkness of the approaching evening a shadowy form taking shape on the bed. There was no mistaking whose form it was. The figure on the bed gradually became more fixed, more "in-focus"—as if it were a photographic image emerging in a tray in a darkroom. It seemed to be propped up on the pillows in just the way his grandfather had lain, and then undeniably before his eyes the features of the figure became recognizably those of the old man. The voice of the apparition had at first sounded strange to Boy— thin and piping, almost falsetto. But it also seemed to adjust its tones down into the bass voice that he remembered so well, the voice of his grandfather before his tracheotomy.

The conversations that ensued over the following days, as Boy repeated his visitations, weren't always entirely coherent. Boy could see there was some strain on the part of his grandfather's spirit to recall certain specifics of their past. For example, he seemed to have scanty recollection of the details of his rescue of Boy on the day of his birth—details that Boy had to fill in for him. Nor did he seem to remember picking blackberries and honeysuckle blossoms with Boy. Little things like that had slipped his ghostly memory.

"Death makes you forget so many things," was the explanation provided by the spirit.

Boy, for his part, was more than happy to remind him of the forgotten things. It was enough that his grandfather was back and, even in this insubstantial form, it was his greatest wish fulfilled.

And the form came and went. Sometimes it would appear for only a brief period, at other times it might remain for an hour or longer. Boy did most of the talking, as it seemed to require much exertion for the spirit to speak more than a few short sentences at a time. Boy naturally wanted to know where the spirit went when he departed from these visitations. And it was this curiosity that had triggered the most fulsome response from the ghost.

He told the boy that it was a wondrous world to which he returned each day. A world of rosy gardens and lush green valleys, where trees of every sort towered into the clouds, where pure water flowed from snowcapped peaks and formed wide azure lakes, where wild animals roamed without fear, and birds sang, and silvery flying fish skimmed the sea-green waves.

"I can take you there," he had said more than once. "I could show it to you and get you back by dinnertime."

And, as the days passed, he coaxed the child more and more to come with him to see the realm of the spirits, where night was no more and death a mere illusion.

"You needn't be afraid. I've always told you I'll protect you."

And so, on that Wednesday before Thanksgiving, after having long said to the spirit that he couldn't leave his father and mother, and the spirit responding that he would be brought home before they even knew he was away, he had resolved to go with his grandfather and see that magnificent land beyond the veil of death. The visions that had been described to him were becoming too enticing to dismiss, and he trusted Grandpa like no one else in the whole world, so where was the difficulty in his slipping off with him for a little while—just as he had done so often with the old man during life, whether to visit Tommy at one of the gas stations or to pick blackberries in the woods? When he entered the bedroom, the apparition was already there, seated upright on the foot of the bed and smiling benignly.

"So, you have come," he said softly to the boy. "I am so pleased. You were always a brave young man. You'll see wondrous things, astounding things. Trust me. And you'll never be afraid of death again once you've seen them. Here, put your hand in mine." And he stretched out a ghostly hand to the child.

His grandfather's smile filled him with peace and a feeling of perfect safety. The boy reached out his own small hand, eager for the adventure now. The shade moved further toward him on the bed as if he would stand up, and he took hold of the child's extended hand. Boy's back was to the three windows and the catalpa tree outside as the spirit took hold of him. Boy could hear behind him the windows unlatching of their own accord and sliding up in their casements.

But something, he realized all at once, was wrong—terribly wrong.

His "grandfather's" hand was rough and leathery in its texture—like how he imagined a monkey's paw might feel. The old man's nails dug into the flesh of his hand and the grip was so tight that

Boy's fingers were nearly crushed by it, and now it was impossible for him to free himself from the horrible grasp.

Then something else happened, in fact several things happened in rapid succession. First, he saw that the eyes of the spirit that gripped his hand darted past him and were fixed on something behind Boy. The expression on the spirit's face grew into one of pure, unadulterated rage, and as he shifted his eyes back toward Boy, he saw such malevolence in them that he nearly froze. But Boy forced himself, against his paralyzing terror, to turn around to see what was behind him—to catch a glimpse of whatever it was that had so infuriated the spirit.

There, in the dim light of the dark afternoon, he saw the shadowy form of his grandfather standing, and behind him other shadowy forms, and behind them the great "winged head" of the catalpa, which looked in the semidarkness exactly like a conscious, watching, grim countenance. His grandfather said nothing but stood staring silently and intensely at his facsimile on the bed, who instantly let go of the child's hand. Boy, as if released from a state of suspended animation, leapt away from the bed, trembling.

Looking back at his would-be kidnapper, he watched the figure on the bed begin to shiver and shake and dwindle in size, turning grayer and paler, his hair sprouting black and long all about his hunched shoulders, his eyes glaring yellow, his mouth emitting incomprehensible curses in slavering squeaks, his body only partially covered with what looked like animal skins. Then he suddenly vaporized before Boy, disappearing with a hiss like steam on a hot stove. Boy looked over in the direction where he had seen the assembly of ghosts, but they were no longer there—not even that of his grandfather. And the windows now were closed and latched, and the catalpa looked once more like a tree and not a winged face.

At the precise moment that he realized he was standing in the room alone, the door opened and in walked his mother. She looked first at Boy, then at the crumpled covers of her bed.

"What's going on here?" she demanded. "What have you been up to? What was all that thumping we heard downstairs?"

Boy knew that the thumping had been his doing, as he had leapt

43

clear of the "pukwudgie" his grandfather had warned him against so long ago.

"It was just... I was just..." he began.

But his mother wasn't listening. She was staring at an object lying amid the bedclothes, one that shone dully in the dim light. She picked it up and Boy instantly recognized what it was.

It was Grandpa's lost straight razor. And it was open, the blade out.

"Haven't I warned you many, many times," scolded his mother, "never to play with sharp objects like this?"

She snapped it up from the bed, folded the blade into the handle, and dropped it into her apron pocket.

"Don't you realize you could hurt yourself horribly?"

# From All Ill Dreams

"WHEN ALL THOSE ancient Jewish and Christian writers referred to 'evil spirits,' they weren't necessarily talking about 'fallen angels,' you know. As they saw it, 'evil spirits' could just as well be the ghosts of the malevolent dead."

It was an early February evening in 1983, and I was visiting Father Thomas Benson at "the Hermitage," the small, brown-shingled chaplain's cottage. He was an octogenarian when I knew him in the nineteen-eighties. He would pass away before the end of that decade. I was fifty years his junior, just starting out as a newly ordained Episcopal priest, and he, for his part, was serving as chaplain for the "Sisters of All Souls," an order of Anglican nuns not far from the parish where I was assigned as curate. The convent, with its eighty-eight acres, was an island of monastic peace, set apart and buffered from the bustling outside world by the surrounding barrier of Patapsco State Park.

Father Benson wasn't only a priest; he was also a doctor, a man of medicine, a psychiatrist with degrees from Johns Hopkins and renowned in the field. For decades he had exercised a chaplaincy at Spring Grove Psychiatric Hospital, and during that time, before his wife of forty-odd years had died, he had also been the rector of the same parish where I was currently assigned. These days he resided in this pleasant little home on the convent grounds. And for me, he was a mentor and guide.

On this singular winter evening, after sharing a simple supper, we had become involved in a discussion about, of all things, demonic possession. I confess, I had expected him, as a man of medical science, to be dubious about the literal existence of "evil spirits" or "demons," confident that he would likely—as I tended to do—relegate them to a variety of illnesses that the ancients could only explain by means of myth and traditional belief. Jesus, I supposed, must have been an astounding healer of sorts, curing persons

45

afflicted with various diseases and mental distress, but I interpreted references in the New Testament to "evil spirits" as nothing more than imaginary personifications of mental and bodily maladies. I had been surprised to discover that Father Benson assumed no such thing.

"Some of the phenomena deemed to be the work of 'evil spirits' were, no doubt, epilepsy or mental illness," he told me. "But others, I now believe, were not. Like you, I used to doubt that 'evil spirits' exist, but my experiences over the years have profoundly shaken my old physicalist presuppositions. You see, I've had a fair share of personal encounters with things that defy easy explanation. I'm a man of science, but some things..."

He paused for a moment, looking off into the shadows in the corner of the room. Then he looked back in my direction and casually made his observation that "evil spirits" had been thought by the ancients to be, at least in some circumstances, spirits of the dead. It was a view I had never heard expressed before, even during my time at seminary. It intrigued me.

"There's one case especially that has never ceased to haunt me," he went on. "It lingers with me still. It involved three people—a man and his two wives. That is to say, it involved his first wife, who died, and his second wife, who was a patient of mine at Spring Grove. The man had also died by the time his second wife came into my care.

"Now, here's the thing: I say the *second* wife was in my care, but I'm not certain that that's the right way to put it. I had before me, without question, the physical shell of the woman, but I can't say for a fact that I didn't have the *first* wife on my hands at the same time and occupying the same physical shell. To add to the strangeness of the case, the man who had been married to both women had died terribly with his mind torn to shreds. And his mental disintegration—and the accounts indicate this very strongly—were intimately tangled up with his marriages. Spring Grove still has the case files. And I had copies of them made for my own records."

I was a bit confused by all this. "Are you suggesting," I said, ruminating on his words and trying to make sense of them as they related to our larger discussion, "that the 'spirit' of the first wife, after she died, somehow continued to disturb this man and his second wife...?"

"I'm suggesting something you'll find even more alarming," said Father Benson. "It's a complicated story, but bear with me. It touches on the subject of possession we've been discussing, or at least the possibility of it. The man and his second wife both underwent therapy with two separate analysts. Spring Grove procured all their case notes. As the result of circumstances at home between her—the second wife—and her husband, she reached an emotional breaking point which brought her to the hospital and to me. I've kept all the paperwork on all three individuals—hundreds of pages—upstairs in my office. It's one of the few sets of files I've held on to over the past twenty years. If nothing else, assuming we keep an open mind about it, it's a case that forces us to entertain the possibility that one person's psyche can be possessed, against his or her will, by another person's—after the other person's death."

I began to understand, somewhat foggily, what it was he was telling me.

"Can you give me the whole story?" I asked. "Because now you've got my curiosity sparked."

"I can do better than that," Father Benson replied. "I can show you the notes themselves while I tell you about the case. I think you'll find it fascinating, at least."

So it was that he put before me that evening the copious notes and transcripts he had kept preserved since the early sixties and, as he did, he told me the story of—as I have called them here—John Harvey and his two wives, Elaine and Irene. When Father Benson died a few years later, I was able to obtain possession of his papers; and now that sixty years have passed since the events described in those files occurred, I believe they can be related without hurting any living soul. All three of the persons involved in the story are now deceased. I think their story is worth recounting, even if only for the sake of reinforcing Father Benson's belief that there are happenings in this world for which science offers no satisfying explanation.

When John Harvey married Elaine in 1954, he had already seen some warning signs—"red flags," we might say. But being young, in his mid-twenties, he had also dismissed them. He was in love, after all, and she was charming and vivacious most of the time, a shining light in his life. She doted on him, and the few things he found in her words and actions to upset him he allowed himself to believe were only minor character flaws. Besides, he told himself, who hasn't got character flaws? He stuffed them away in the broom closet of his mind.

Among these intentionally "forgotten" forewarnings of difficulties ahead, which he only brought back into the light for examination after it was too late, there had been the incident of the engagement ring. He had been working hard at the funeral home, just starting out in his chosen profession. His income was nothing fabulous and he had to be careful with every dollar he earned. But Elaine, unrealistic about the modest level of his income, had acquired a wish for a particular style of engagement ring—a ruby surrounded by diamonds—which was uncomfortably pricey for John's meager budget. She had pointed it out to him in an outdated jewelry catalogue that she had kept for years in anticipation of the big moment, telling him it was *the* ring she had always imagined on her finger. The ruby, she explained, signified the passion of true love and the surrounding diamonds represented guardian angels.

John wanted to please her, whatever the expense to himself, so he went in search for a ring that matched her specifications. He visited a slew of jewelry stores, but without success until, at long last, he found a shop that sold a ring that appeared to him to be close enough in style to the picture she had shown him. He bought it, had the box wrapped elegantly, and intended to give it to her on Christmas Eve, the day on which she had requested they become formally engaged. However, as soon as she learned from him that he had already bought the ring, nearly a month before Christmas, she insisted that she be allowed to inspect it. She wanted to be sure he had purchased precisely the right one.

Reluctantly, he took her up to his apartment, pulled out the ring in its wrapped box, unwrapped it delicately, and let her view it. At which point, she burst into tears, flung the box and the ring into a nearby armchair, and began to shout angrily that he had stupidly, callously purchased the wrong ring. It wouldn't do. He had obtusely gotten the wrong one, she informed him, and should have known it. If he had just bothered to pay any attention to her at all— the failure to do so being, as she expostulated, a failure of love— and had really studied the picture she'd showed him, like a truly loving man would have done, he wouldn't have dashed her hopes to pieces like this. Perhaps, she told him, he'd even done it on purpose—though why he would do something so petty she couldn't begin to fathom.

John Harvey was beside himself, both irritated and wounded, and demanded to know what exactly was wrong with the ring— after all, it had a ruby and diamonds.

"The ring I showed you," she said furiously, "had a ruby all surrounded by diamonds. I told you what that meant to me—love surrounded by angels! This one has a ruby, but the diamonds are on either side of it, not all around it."

Her anger passed as quickly as it had flared up, however, and Elaine soon cooled down and gushingly forgave him. At first, she wanted him to exchange the ring, but John made it clear that this was the only one he could find that looked anything like the one she wanted. After more tears (she reassured him that she wasn't angry anymore, just sad) she relented, saying it was a lovely ring after all. He had rewrapped it and on Christmas Eve they went through the pretense, in front of their gathered family members, of his "surprising" her with the engagement ring. She told everybody present that it was precisely the ring she "had always dreamed about."

There were other premarital clashes. These were provoked by what she alleged were his inadequacies in consideration, his lack of true affection, and his wandering eye. The last item on that list would become the most frequent charge, although John assured his analyst that he had always been conscientious to a fault in that regard. During their first year of marriage, nonetheless, Elaine repeatedly brought up the subject of "other women" with John. It soon became evident to him that she perceived other women—and frequently his male friendships, as well—as a threat to her relationship with him. She would, for instance, make acerbic and improper remarks about the married secretary who worked with him at the funeral home, sometimes in unexpectedly coarse terms, always implying that the woman clearly had sexual designs on John.

There was another episode that occurred early in their marriage, not seven full months after the wedding, that presaged worse to come. John and Elaine had found a new, larger apartment for themselves. One summer day, John came home only to have Elaine meet him with flashing eyes and wild accusations of infidelity. She held out her hand to reveal an earring she had discovered between the tiles in the bathroom. She knew it wasn't *her* earring. "So, just who the hell's is it?" she wanted to know. "One of your girlfriends'?"

With patience, he managed to calm her down, reminding her that there was no way he could have brought a girl home without her knowing it, that he worked all day, that the thought had never once entered his mind. She had to agree on the spot that that was true, but for months afterward she returned repeatedly to her suspicions that he had been womanizing behind her back.

As time went on, she developed a knack for bringing up the subject just as he was trying to turn in for the night. This became such an anticipated part of their nights together that he started to regard it as intentional on her part—that she took some sort of perverse delight in tormenting him in this fashion. As a result, his ability to do his job well during the day was soon deteriorating from lack of sufficient rest at night. He took to dosing himself with sleeping pills, sometimes washing them down with whiskey.

Most alarming of all, she would often repeat over and over to him in a hissing whisper, right beside him in the same bed and right in his ear in the darkness, as the pills and the alcohol were taking effect on his exhausted brain, "I hope you die, I want you to die..."

Over the next two years, she developed animosities toward every one of his colleagues' wives, and repeatedly found excuses to argue with them at job-related social functions. Her behavior, in private and socially, degenerated. It reached the point where he couldn't be sure she wouldn't cause a scene in a restaurant or at a store while shopping or at a dinner engagement. She seemed to have an abnormal sense for the inappropriate and erratic wherever they were, and

50

# From All Ill Dreams

John found himself apologizing almost habitually to all sorts of people when she was out of earshot. She could smilingly belittle people to their faces or fly into angry confrontations with friends and strangers without provocation. She would frequently become melodramatic or histrionic on occasions, especially when she had been drinking. More than once, with great embarrassment, he had had to drag her away from some gathering simply for propriety's sake. And always, before an audience, she would "jokingly" discuss what she considered John Harvey's many shortcomings, including his sexual ones. In more private settings, she either professed to adore John as "the most wonderful man in the world" or else loathed him as "the worst husband on earth." Either he was to be set high on a pedestal or to have his effigy cast into the gutter. Sometimes it was both within the space of five minutes.

At some stage she commenced threatening suicide on a recurring basis. The reason she gave, which she asserted loudly and groundlessly, was that her husband was secretly being unfaithful to her with all sorts and ages of women. On two or three occasions she dramatically locked herself in the bathroom and pretended to be killing herself, complete with sound effects. After breaking down the bathroom door the first time this occurred to "save her life," he realized what a fool he had been. He found her sitting on the edge of the tub, a contemptuous look on her face. All she did was walk past him into the bedroom, slamming its door behind her.

He never tried to "save her life" again, permitting her histrionics to simmer down in their own good time.

She would, on other occasions, proclaim her undying love to him, using a peculiar turn of phrase that gave him the jitters every time she used it: "I'm going to get you, get you, get you and eat you all up."

His breaking point came when she began to make indecent comments about the female corpses he tended to at the funeral home. She accused him of secretly having necrophiliac urges. She elaborated the charge with revoltingly graphic details, revealing an imagination on her part that left him psychologically shattered. The pictures she painted made his flesh crawl. The inevitable result was that he transferred his revulsion to her physical person, avoiding direct contact with her as much as he could. He had no doubt whatsoever that she took a twisted delight in watching him squirm.

Finally, John could stand it no longer and took his troubles to an analyst. The sessions continued for some weeks and John laid out honestly what he was enduring. The analyst understood John's situation. Elaine's mental illness was one with which he was familiar—he had encountered it before—but, unfortunately, he could offer little hope for a cure.

"The 'down' side," his analyst told him during one of their sessions, "is that her condition is virtually untreatable. I can try to talk to her if she'll come in. But usually, people like Elaine won't come in, and if they do, they won't believe they have a problem. Everyone else has problems, but never them. I have yet to meet anyone with your wife's condition that I could get close enough to treat."

John agreed that that would likely prove to be the case with Elaine and that there was little chance she would agree to see an analyst. However, he'd give it a go, he told the doctor. To his surprise, when he worked up the energy to propose the idea to her, Elaine agreed to it. As she put it, if it would help John deal with his problems, she was willing to oblige.

So, she went. Once. She emerged from the session in a rage, demanding to know what John had told his therapist about her. She verbally cudgeled John in the car on the way home.

"He's a goddamn fraud," she snarled. "But they're all goddamn frauds. It's obvious you told him I'm crazy—thanks for telling lies about me. I know you really want a divorce. You want to throw me over for one of your girlfriends. I always knew you'd betray me. Typical of you, using a shrink to get what you want."

When John saw his analyst again, the latter told him flatly, "You can't go on living in proximity with her. She's not able to love like other people do. The nearer someone gets to her, the more likely they are to get irreparably cracked by her. Her notion of love is *possession*, pure and simple. As far as she's concerned, you *belong* to her. I'm not telling you how to go about getting free of the situation. I don't know what your conscience will allow. But there's one thing I'll tell you straight. People like Elaine should never be in a relationship. I know that sounds harsh, but it's true. She'll ruin your mental health at the very least. For your peace and possibly your physical safety—I'm not exaggerating when I say, 'physical safety'—you need to extricate yourself."

Feeling all the mixed emotions such advice is bound to elicit, John ultimately made the decision to divorce Elaine. Overall, he was a quiet, diffident, rather unimaginative man. Perhaps it was his retiring nature that provoked some deep-rooted hostility in Elaine. One gets the sense, reading through the transcripts of John's statements to his analyst, that she wanted to stir up something in him that seemed deficient in her eyes. She often attacked him, for instance, because she claimed he lacked "manliness." She was, it seems, the more aggressive sexually, so much so that she accused him frequently of "incapacity." At any rate, reticent and pacific as he was, he firmly resolved to divorce her. A simple separation wouldn't be enough. He felt that his sanity was beginning to hang in the balance. He needed to sever the cords as brusquely as possible and start over. He was only thirty-two, he told himself, with lots of life still ahead of him.

So, one evening, after some understandable foot-dragging and two vodka martinis, he worked up the nerve to announce his resolution to an unsuspecting Elaine. There was disbelief, tears, fury—in short, a scene. Plates and pans were flung in his face, suicide was threatened yet again, and John, both relieved and unwavering, simply walked out and found himself a hotel room for the night.

Elaine took sleeping pills. When John returned to the house the following morning, he found her in bed. She was dead.

Looking at the photograph of John Harvey attached to the case notes, I see a clean-cut, dark-haired, nicely dressed, square-jawed man in his thirties. His height was recorded as six-two, he weighed two hundred and six pounds, and his eyes were hazel. At the time of his first wife's death, he was pulling in what was considered a fine salary and the couple had graduated to a brand-new split-level home in the suburbs. He had, in other words, what it took to attract a young woman's notice, and he had attracted Irene's even before Elaine's death. Truth be told, as his marriage was disintegrating,

Irene had also attracted John's. They had met at the barbershop where she worked part-time as a manicurist. They began slipping off together to share lunch at a local diner two or three times a week. Despite whatever risk that that immaculate impropriety might have appeared to invite in the eyes of anyone paying attention to it, their friendship was a chaste one. That changed, of course, almost as soon as John became a single man again. It took less than a year for them to become engaged and to marry.

Irene was the opposite in many ways of Elaine. She was as quiet and shy as John, never raised her voice, didn't drink or smoke, enjoyed playing bridge and watching soap operas in the afternoons, and she read romance novels and magazines about movie stars. At first, she wasn't sure she wanted to live in the same house where Elaine had ended her life, but John sold the old bed and purchased a new one, had the home's interior redecorated, and got rid of every item that might conceivably remind them of Elaine's existence. Even photograph albums with pictures from the former marriage were purged or pitched. Irene was satisfied with the result. Like her husband, whose vocation kept him in constant touch with the dead, she didn't suffer from squeamishness or believe in ghosts. So long as the physical reminders of bad memories were blotted out, the past was a closed book in Irene's consciousness.

John, on the other hand, after the initial happiness of a new life with a beautiful young wife gave way to the day-to-day realities of making a living, started to have a nagging suspicion that things weren't so easily left behind as all that. As he told it to his analyst later, his misgivings really took off when he had a chance meeting with a middle-aged woman at the funeral home. The occasion was an open casket viewing, and throughout it he couldn't help noticing that she kept looking over at him with what seemed to him to be a worried expression on her face. As the viewing drew to a close, he decided to ask her if everything was all right.

She told him, with no appearance of embarrassment, that she was a medium and sensitive to the presence of spirits. She showed him some newspaper clippings that she carried in her purse. They were articles about her. One was an interview with her from *The Baltimore Sun*, the rest were anecdotes about how she had helped the Baltimore City and Howard County police find the remains of three murdered persons. I will refer to her here as "Mrs. Crawford" instead of giving her real name. Police officers who were interviewed in the articles confessed that they had initially been skeptical about Mrs. Crawford's psychic abilities, but that without her assistance they might never have recovered the remains they were hoping to find. She had made believers of some of the toughest, most pragmatic men on the force.

After she had told John Harvey all this, she asked him pointedly, "Do you ever have the sense that someone you can't see is standing close by you, watching you? Even following you, maybe? Someone—how do I say this carefully? I don't want to alarm you—someone who might have something against you?"

John hadn't told anyone that lately he had felt precisely something of the sort, especially when he was alone. At odd moments, while working on a corpse, he had caught some movement out of the corner of his eye, as if somebody were standing between him and the wall, casting a shadow he could never quite see directly or creating a hazy distortion of the light. And then there were his nightmares, which plagued him two or three nights each week, in which Elaine's anger-distorted face would rise up before him and he would hear those words she had used as a sickly endearment—"I'm going to get you, get you, get you and eat you all up." Her voice was so sharp and clear in those dreams that they invariably woke him with a jolt. They didn't seem to come from his own head, but from outside.

"Why do you ask?" John asked Mrs. Crawford.

"I can see a spirit quite close to you," said Mrs. Crawford, glancing beyond him as she spoke. "Very close to you—and watching your every move. She's a 'she' and she follows you. She's an unhappy, I think bitter presence. And, dear me, she's powerful, too; I'd say she's not to be trifled with. Resentful is how I'd describe her. Possibly prone to be violent." The woman stopped and stood staring past John. Then she continued, "She doesn't mean you any good, young man. Do you know who she might be?"

John simply nodded his head. "I think I know her," he whispered.

Mrs. Crawford looked concerned for him and patted his hand. They were standing in the foyer outside the viewing room, off to the side away from the people who were beginning to file out. Suddenly, with a small yelp, Mrs. Crawford withdrew her hand quickly from his, as if she had just received an electric shock.

"She doesn't like it when I touch you," she said. "She knows that I know she's here and she's very annoyed about that. She pushed my hand off yours just now—it felt like static."

"Can you help me?" John asked, suddenly feeling desperate.

"If she were amenable, I might be able to converse with her. I get the impression she wouldn't be at all willing, though." Mrs. Crawford looked into John's eyes sadly. "I'm not an exorcist," she explained, "and I fear that's what's called for here. Do you belong to a church?"

John shook his head.

"I believe it's my first wife," he said, and as he said it, he felt a wave of guilt and shame wash over him. He knew his face was red and flushed.

Mrs. Crawford backed away, but it wasn't John she was backing away from, he realized, but from what she evidently saw behind him. Something had unexpectedly seemed to horrify her. John glanced behind him, saw nothing, and turned back toward Mrs. Crawford, who was shrinking against the lobby wall, her eyes still fixed over John's shoulder.

"She says you killed her." Mrs. Crawford whispered.

"That's not true," protested John.

"That may be," said Mrs. Crawford, her face ashen. "But she blames you for whatever happened. Look, I have to go—my husband's waving me over. But for God's sake, get some help. Find a priest or someone who performs exorcisms."

And before John could respond, she hastened away.

John Harvey didn't search out a priest or an exorcist, but the notes from this period show that he sought help from a psychotherapist—a different one than before—instead. Unfortunately, the files are missing pages, and those notes we have don't contain the same ampleness of detail as the earlier ones. The information in my possession falls short of giving us anything like a full picture. However, it seems obvious to me from what I do have that his encounter with Mrs. Crawford had shaken him profoundly. More than that, his nightmares of Elaine became nightly occurrences, and he felt as if she were also dogging his daily movements. He knew his feelings were illogical, neurotic, paranoid, delusional… but he couldn't dismiss the sense of oppression. And that sense kept growing.

He found himself talking irritably to "her" under his breath when he believed he wasn't being overheard. But Irene overheard and she quickly became apprehensive about his mental state. She pressed him, and he finally told her about Mrs. Crawford and what he was going through. Neither he nor Irene were religious persons, so the idea of going to a priest for help struck them as a throwback to "Dark Ages" superstition. This was the twentieth century, after all, and they were sophisticated modern-day suburbanites. His analyst, for his part, dismissed John's fears as the re-emergence of suppressed guilt feelings and unresolved trauma resulting from Elaine's suicide. He prescribed pills to help relieve his anxiety. He recommended diversions—golf, bowling, swimming, light entertainment, relaxing music, that sort of thing. He encouraged romantic outings with Irene. Normal all-American suburban life, in other words, with an emphasis on "normal."

"And, for heaven's sake, keep away from people claiming to be mediums," he added. "That way lies madness."

Over the next six months, John stopped seeing his analyst while Irene, on the other hand, began going to one. The cause for her seeking help was the ever more erratic nature of John's behavior. His words and actions were starting to unnerve her. She had, as mentioned, already noticed his tendency to "converse" in audible whispers to Elaine, often behind a locked bathroom door, as if the latter were alive and responding to him. He seemed to think that he couldn't be heard, but the walls were thin, and the door wasn't soundproof. More than once she overheard him repeat, almost in a state of childish hysteria, "No, you're *not* going to eat me up! You're *not* going to eat me up!" She didn't know what those exclamations might mean, but they horrified her.

As the months dragged on, John seemed almost to have become two persons in one body. At times he was the mild-mannered, quiet man she knew and loved, but at other times he would turn off, become aloof and sour in temper, then sarcastic and belittling. In those moods, he would take to calling her "the replacement." Sometimes, inexplicably, he would suddenly become angry with her, and on those occasions, he would refer to her as "the whore." When he raised his voice to her, which he did more and more, it could rise to almost a falsetto. He sounded "screechy," she told the therapist, as if he were mimicking a woman's voice. The loud whispering in the locked bathroom continued and, in time, it was no longer a whisper, but full-throated and unrestrained shouting. She would still hear his blood-chilling cries of "You're *not* going to eat me up!"—a protestation that had evolved into a desperate bellow. He would throw things around in the bathroom, whatever he could grab hold of—soap, shampoo, toothpaste, toothbrushes, pills. He would slam these items savagely against the mirror. Once he tore down the shower curtain with its rings and yanked a towel rack—screws and all—from the wall, leaving a gaping hole in the plaster.

In time, these displays of temper were daily occurrences. Irene was seeing her therapist twice a week now, frantic and on the point of leaving her husband. The downside of that "plan" was the fact that she had no money of her own. Her husband made all the money, and it was in a joint bank account. Her therapist asked if John was violent toward her, but she denied it at first. Possibly, at the time she was asked, he hadn't been. That changed, however, and when the therapist asked her for a second time, she confessed that he had started slapping her—but only when he was drinking. He was fine when he was sober, she said.

"What makes him fly off the handle at you?" asked the therapist. "What pulls his trigger—anything you can think of?"

"I don't know," said Irene. "Sometimes it's when I'm trying to calm him down, trying to hold his hand or something affectionate like that. It's also when he... you know, when he calls me 'the replacement' and"—here the analyst mentions in his notes that her voice dropped to a whisper—"when he calls me 'the whore.'"

"And then he strikes you?"

"Just with the palm of his hand," she replied. "And only if he's had a few drinks."

"Does he drink a lot?"

"More than he used to. It's every night… so he can sleep, he says."

But then came the critical night when Irene, clothed only in her nightgown and bathrobe, fled their bed and home in terror, and drove straight to her parents' house across town. As she put it later, she had "lost John for good." That wasn't, she told her analyst, a metaphor for the breaking of their relationship or the fracturing of their marriage. She meant quite literally that she had *lost* John. He just *wasn't there* anymore. His mind, his consciousness, couldn't be reached. His body was there, but he was absent—and something else had taken his place.

What had propelled her out of bed was the sound of John's voice crooning into her ear, his lips barely brushing it. It had jolted her from a sound sleep. She remembered the time on the face of the glow-in-the-dark alarm clock as her eyes snapped open—3:10 in the morning. She had been facing away from John, toward the night table. John's voice came out in a vicious-sounding susurration, his breath hot on the side of her face.

"I hope you die," he was saying over and over, his head positioned just above hers. "I want you to die…"

With a sudden burst of energy, she flung herself around to face him. "John! What the hell are you doing?" She saw his eyes in the darkness, white-rimmed and glaring at her like an enraged creature. They seemed to glow from within.

"John?" shot back John's voice purringly. "*John?* He doesn't live here anymore, honey. He's been eaten up. It's only me now."

At that, Irene switched on the light on her night table, jumped out of bed, grabbed her robe and the car keys, and rapidly made her getaway. John, she said, had made no effort to stop her. He remained right where he was, reclining in the bed; and Irene recalled that, as he watched her scramble to escape, the whole scene merely seemed to amuse him.

The following day, Irene's father and her two brothers went over to the house to collect clothes and a few other items of hers and to confront John if he was at home. Irene was still much too shaken to go along with them. Indeed, she was frightened enough of John now to worry about her father and brothers' safety. The men had taken her housekey and, when there was no response to their repeated knocking and ringing the front doorbell, they let themselves in. Inside all was quiet, except for the buzzing sound of the alarm clock coming from the bedroom. They assumed that John had left for work.

It was Irene's oldest brother who found John sprawled and contorted on the bed, his eyes wide open and upturned in their sockets, one leg outstretched and nearly touching the floor, an idiotic grin on his face. He was stone-cold to the touch, ashen, and rigid. In that same room and not far from the very spot where his corpse now lay, Elaine had also died a few short years earlier. It was determined a day later that the cause of John's death had been a massive stroke.

The church bell rang on the hill, signaling that Compline, the final monastic service of the day, was soon to begin in the convent chapel. It was eight-thirty.

"Shall we?" asked Father Benson. "I can finish the story after we return."

We made our way up to the chapel in the darkness. Inside, the lights were low and the candles on the altar were being lit by one of the sisters. The walls were whitewashed in the Cistercian style, the choir stalls and rood screen were of polished dark wood, and the high-arched plain glass windows looked out into the black night beyond. Once the service had gotten underway, the chanting of the nuns generated a soothing otherworldly atmosphere. Here, I thought, is peace. Although I had felt discomfited by Father Benson's unfinished account, Compline provided a respite. And certainly, the invariable texts of the office seemed to counterbalance the somber mood of the narrative.

"Brethren: Be sober, be vigilant, because your adversary the devil, as a roaring lion, walketh about, seeking whom he may devour," the opening exhortation had pronounced. "Thou shalt not be afraid for any terror by night, nor for the arrow that flieth by day; for the pestilence that walketh in darkness, nor for the sickness that destroyeth in the noon-day... For he shall give his angels charge over thee, to keep thee in all thy ways," the text of the ninety-first Psalm had assured us. And the second verse of the hymn *Te lucis ante terminum* plead for protection from every spectral evil:

*From all ill dreams defend our eyes,*
*From nightly fears and fantasies:*
*Tread under foot our ghostly foe,*
*That no pollution we may know…*

And finally, the Reverend Mother prayed in a monotone for the community's spiritual peace: "Visit, we beseech thee, O Lord, this habitation, and drive far from it all snares of the enemy: let thy holy angels dwell herein to preserve us in peace…"

The same sister who had lit the candles on the altar now extinguished them and then went to the rear of the chapel and rang the bell to signify the completion of the monastic day. With Compline concluded, Father Benson and I put our copies of *The Monastic Diurnal* back into the book rack, exited the chapel, and made our way back down the hill to the Hermitage.

"When I first met Irene," Father Benson continued his account there, after pouring us each a scotch, "it was at Spring Grove, and she was in a bad way. She had been committed by her family after a series of inexplicably violent episodes. This was only two or three months after John's death, mind you.

"The episodes had started almost immediately after his funeral. She had exhibited, at first, paranoid behavior, claiming she was being watched constantly and that someone was dogging her every movement. When her family members—her parents and her brothers and their spouses—objected that she was safe, that no one was following her, she accused them of not understanding her. She was staying at her parents' home now, emotionally unable to return to the home she had shared with John.

"Soon, her sleep became disturbed. She started reliving in her nightmares that last night with John, and she would awake screaming. When her mother or father tried to calm her down, she was beyond reason or comfort. These ugly scenes soon became full-blown nightly hysterics. She would lock herself in the bathroom—

just as John had done—and could be heard shouting as if someone was in there with her.

"Obviously, this couldn't go on. Something had to be done. They brought her to her former psychoanalyst, and he talked her into entering Spring Grove for ongoing treatment of her anxiety—although it wasn't easy for him to convince her to do it. She was becoming paranoid, distrusting everyone's motives. Somehow, though, he managed to persuade her—and that's when I entered the story, as you can see from the notes.

"By the time I met her, just three days after her arrival at the hospital, she was in a state of gloom and abject melancholy—on the verge of despair, actually. She'd stand staring for hours out her window. Anybody entering her room might get a stony glance, if she paid them any notice at all. She met us, it seemed, with sheer resentment. Well, it turns out she was being too heavily sedated, and that accounted for her icy immobility. Once I got the dosage reduced, she started talking.

"And this is where the story becomes exceedingly disturbing. What she told me didn't make sense to me at first. That is to say, it didn't make sense until I reviewed the notes her therapist had taken previously, which in turn led me to John's story and then, through that, to Elaine's. As I say, it's disturbing because... well, because Irene imagined herself to be Elaine. At least, sometimes she seemed convinced that she was John's first wife. She was at the same time, I could see, trying to hold on to her sense of self, but that seemed to her—and, frankly, to us as well—to be slipping away. She was losing her sense of self. And then she began to speak to me with Elaine's voice. Not literally, of course, but as if she were Elaine and no longer Irene at all."

I felt a cold chill quiver down my spine. "What did she say?" I asked.

"Here, you can see it's in the notes," Father Benson said. "Here—and here—and here." And he began to read the words that Irene had spoken to him in their sessions:

"'I'm not Irene... Irene's a whore, a substitute...'

"'I ate John's soul—ate it up. Ate it up, ate it up...'

"'I'm Elaine, not Irene. There is no Irene now. It's just me now...'

62

"'You can't force me to leave here. She took my husband and substituted herself, the whore, and now I'm substituting her with me. I win. *Win, win, win. Elaine wins…*'

"And it goes on like this, page after page," said Father Benson. "I'll confess, listening to that day after day scared the hell out of me. How does one deal with something like that? And it got worse and worse. Frankly, no modern medical treatment worked. None at all. No medicine of any kind, no talk therapy, no antidepressants, nothing."

There was a stretch of silence as we smoked and drank together and stared at the fire in the small fireplace, the psychiatric notes spread out on a low coffee table before us. Finally, I couldn't continue in my state of suspense.

"So, what became of her?" I asked. "What happened to Irene?"

"You saw her this evening," replied Father Benson, with a wave of his hand. "It all came round right in the end."

"Saw her?" I said, surprised. "When? Where?"

"In the chapel, at Compline," said the old priest. "The sister who lit the candles before the office and who rung the bell."

"That was Irene?"

"That was Irene," he said. "She's been here for the last seventeen years."

"But how…?" I began.

"There are older methods than that which psychiatry provides," said Father Benson. "Which brings me back to our topic of possession. What worked in the end was exorcism. That hoary, nearly universal act of commanding an intrusive spirit to depart. It took effort and it wasn't easy on anyone involved, but… Well, it's all there in the notes. Incidentally, she prays daily for both John and Elaine, she tells me."

I looked at the old man. He appeared relaxed and ruminative.

"You know," he said. "All we are, each one of us, is an aggregate of characteristics and qualities—if those are the best words—that we get from our heredity, birth, time, place, our genes, our education, and so on. Who knows what conditions made Elaine what Elaine became, poor thing, or John or Irene—or you or me, for that matter? Irene you now know about. She's safe and doing fine. John and

Elaine we can leave to God. Deeper than the aggregation of all our circumstantial qualities there exists a vital, salvageable essence. John is at peace, I believe, and Elaine, I feel certain, is healed or will be. There's a great Syrian saint who once said we should even pray for the demons. Everyone's deepest core is eternal and, as I said, we can leave it to God. Nothing can ever 'eat that up.'

"Irene believes that and so do I."

# The Debunker

PROFESSIONALLY, he called himself the "Astounding Runcible." He had always liked Edward Lear's nonsense word "runcible," so he borrowed it and made it his magician's moniker. His given name, once upon a time, had been Archibald—"Archie"—Spill, but he felt that that exuded all the charm and mystery of a ketchup stain on a sweatshirt. What he wanted was something whimsical, fairy-tale-like, suggestive of wizardry, and—being fond of "The Owl and the Pussycat"—he eventually struck on "Runcible" for a stage name. He changed his first name, too. It was now "Jules," which he adopted in honor of Jules Verne, his favorite novelist. "Astounding" came a little later, after he had already earned his stripes as a brilliant magician and an accomplished escape artist. Harry Houdini had been an idol of his in his teen years, and so he had followed in the great man's footsteps and perfected the arts of illusion and escape. Some said he had even surpassed the master.

Be that as it may, his chosen career made him a wealthy and celebrated man. When television was still in its infancy, he took his talents there, appearing first on children's programs and then, in later years, on night-time variety shows. For the first few decades of his growing fame, he never once let on publicly that he didn't really believe in the paranormal. He had learned to perform supposed feats of ESP that left his audiences amazed, but he knew very well that his apparent achievements in telepathy were clever, well-honed trickery. However, behind the scenes, he was more than merely skeptical about everything preternatural, over the years he had grown bitterly reactionary against it. He cheerfully affirmed as a matter of intelligence the most dogmatic brand of philosophical materialism.

By the late nineteen-fifties, he—just like his hero, Houdini before him—got a name for himself as a relentless exposer of fraudulent mediums, an outspoken disavower of extrasensory perception, and an investigator of alleged hauntings, which he sought out solely for the purpose of proving them bogus. He now began unveiling publicly the hidden mechanisms used by mediums to impress gullible minds. He also demonstrated to his audiences how he was able to manufacture his own "ESP" tricks. By the age of sixty, he had dispensed with his magician persona altogether and no longer practiced the art of escape, arthritis and a heart condition making such performances impossible for him anyway. Instead of magic shows, he now appeared on television to unmask prominent psychics, or to be followed around by television crews in this or that allegedly ghost-ridden location, matter-of-factly tossing off what seemed to be perfectly plausible natural explanations for whatever things were said to be going bump in the night there.

He retained his stage name, however. He was still Jules Runcible—the "Astounding Runcible"—and he dressed, however self-contradictorily, the part of a latter-day wizard. He sported a floppy wide-brimmed black hat with a peacock feather stuck in its band. His hair was wavy and snow-white and fell below his collar. His flowing, snowy beard was carefully groomed, and his moustache was waxed like Dali's. He dressed all in black—black suit, black shirt, black cravat tie (although, at Christmastime, which he still celebrated, this latter was replaced with a festive red one). He donned a black cape with scarlet lining, and he carried a knotted black cane with a silver death's head on the handle. Most strikingly, his height, or lack thereof, somehow increased the mystique he affected—he stood at an elvish four-foot-ten. It was, surprisingly perhaps, his very shortness of stature that seemed to tower largely wherever he appeared in public, as if the shadow he cast was a gigantic silent companion. There was no question but that the Astounding Runcible possessed charisma.

His home was an old brownstone mansion in Buffalo, New York, the city of his birth. It was there, one Sunday morning in early autumn, that his personal secretary and companion, who went by the name Alfonso Castiglioni (although his given name was Barry Rizzo), pushed an open newspaper in front of Runcible at the breakfast table and placed his index finger firmly down on an article.

# The Debunker

"Your next TV debunking," he said. "It's perfect. I mean, after the French girl, it's time you switched back to spooks and poltergeists."

The "French girl" Alfonso referred to had been a sixteen-year-old girl from the south of France who had a reputation for psychically healing sick people in her village and its surroundings. An article describing her remarkable gift and its apparent effectiveness had reached the Astounding Runcible the previous year, and he had arranged for the girl and her parents to fly to New York so that he could examine her supposed extrasensory perception. According to reports, she was able to diagnose a malady accurately simply by touching the afflicted person. Medical doctors who investigated her were amazed at her abilities and even more amazed by the cures they witnessed. Runcible, however, having separated the nervous young woman from her home and context and resituating her in an alien, sterile laboratory setting, in front of bright lights, television cameras, and a collection of unsympathetic strangers, pronounced her to be a clever fake before a watching world. In that unforgiving context, she had been unable to diagnose accurately a single patient brought to her. All her efforts had failed. Runcible took the credit for exposing yet another charlatan. She had flown back to France, crestfallen, deflated, and—for a short time—nearly suicidal. But, in time, she had returned to her practice in France, her diagnoses and healings once again drawing attention, much to the disgust of Runcible. But she was sixteen and in France and he had exposed her in America, and that was enough for him to claim yet another victory for science over superstition, at least on his side of the Atlantic.

Now, however, he and Alfonso were in search of something different to keep the debunking ball in play. It would be best to offer their viewers variety. Another psychic wouldn't do, but a haunting certainly would. They hadn't debunked one of those in a couple of years now. So, Alfonso's discovery that morning came as a godsend—not that Jules Runcible believed in godsends. The title of the article that Alfonso was eagerly jabbing with a slender finger was entitled: "Most Haunted Home in Maryland?" There was a photograph of the home in question—a stately neo-gothic pile with a tower attached that was as "haunted-house"-looking as it could possibly be. It was picture-perfect, in fact, and the home's very name—Hazelhurst Manor—gave the place that extra attention-getting *something* for which Runcible was always keeping an eye out.

"Well, fancy that," said Runcible, "and in the Buffalo paper, too. Must be one hell of a haunting to make the news all the way up here."

"Not really," replied Alfonso. "It's just filler. Typical haunted house lore—stuff you've given 'the treatment' to before. Gotta put something on page D-7, you know. But still, look at that place. You can't get a more photogenic estate than that for atmosphere. Makes Borley Rectory look shabby."

Runcible picked up the paper and read the article. For the next few moments silence prevailed. He read that Hazelhurst Manor had been built on eight acres of land in 1857 by a businessman named Frederick Todd Thorpe, whose wealth had been made from dealing in iron. He had amassed a fortune during the Civil War. The grand home, twenty rooms in all, along with its carriage house, cottage for guests, and three-story smokehouse, overlooked the village of Ellicott City and the Patapsco River far below. Thorpe had bestowed upon the house his wife's maiden name. As the decades passed, Hazelhurst Manor was the setting for a succession of family tragedies. The Thorpes lost several children. A daughter died in childbirth. Mrs. Thorpe, rumor had it, had taken her own life. And in 1898, learning that his only son had been killed in the charge up San Juan Hill, Mr. Thorpe had climbed the tower stairs, inexplicably opened one of the windows on the top floor, and then hanged himself from one of the rafters there.

The house had been bought and sold twice between Thorpe's suicide and the nineteen-twenties. The McGinnis family were the owners when, in 1923, the Christmas tree in the living room caught fire. The flames spread, destroying much of the home and the tower. The McGinnises restored it, however, and in doing so added a medieval-looking crenelated balustrade to the roof of the tower.

And then the hauntings began—as if, so the McGinnis family had said, the late Mr. Thorpe were aggrieved at the alterations. The newspaper account that Jules Runcible was reading gave no details of the hauntings in the nineteen-twenties, merely stating that a priest had been brought in and the disturbances had ceased.

But, in 1959, the hauntings had resumed. Cigar smoke could be smelled and—so the housemaid claimed—seen in the downstairs library, although no member of the current family occupying the home smoked. The family living there now was named Lilburn. On more than one occasion, reported by both the family and other eye-witnesses, dinners were disturbed by the sudden inexplicable swinging of the heavy chandelier. Without any draft in the room, as family and guests dined, it would start to swing gently at first and then gather speed, soon swaying wildly overhead until, all at once, its momentum would die down. Other unusual sounds and sights were experienced. The apparition of a man in the library, another of a little girl in a downstairs atrium (which, incidentally, had been photographed; the paper included the photograph, and one could make out the blurred shape of a small girl peering from behind a large potted plant).

But one haunting in particular was said to occur nightly and had been heard and seen by everyone in the house, but by Mr. Lilburn most frequently of all. Every night, just a few minutes past midnight, the sound of footsteps could be heard ascending the tower stairs. Mr. Lilburn, who didn't turn in until well after midnight, could attest to its punctual nocturnal recurrence. And every morning the tower window was discovered to be open. Mr. Lilburn had shut and latched the stubborn window again and again, but every time it would be found open the next day. He had even tied the window down twice, and both times the rope had been unknotted and laid on the floor beneath the open window. The article ended with Lilburn saying he might do what the McGinnis family had done and call in a priest.

"I sure hope he doesn't do *that*," snorted Runcible, biting down on a slice of toast.

"Do what?" asked Alfonso.

"Call in a priest," replied the Astounding One. "Do that and sometimes you get unfortunate results. If it's a prank, and the prankster's smart, he or she'll often knock off the shenanigans. It's better than keeping up appearances indefinitely and eventually getting caught. The chandelier thing sounds bogus as hell. Could've been some electrical anomaly, though. And the ghost photo here—

well, hell, that could just be some trick of the light. It looks like a little girl, but it's possible it's just shadows playing tricks on the eyes. Lots of things look like other things. And the 'cigar smoke'—could just be some odor wafting in from the chimney or something."

Alfonso laughed and clapped his hands. "Good, good," he said. "I see your mind's working. Is it time to play Sherlock and get the game afoot?"

"The tower, though," went on Runcible. "Now, that's really got 'prank' written all over it. Somebody in that family's playing a joke on the others. I wouldn't even be surprised if the *paterfamilias* himself isn't responsible. I see here that the two children are too young to be suspected—four and five."

"So, do I make inquiries? Arrange for you to pay a visit?"

"Oh, absolutely," replied Runcible. "The story's already made the papers, so it's just begging for me to step in. I bet the family wouldn't mind the publicity, either. Sounds like they kind of court it. Even if it's a prank, all the prankster has to do is not pull the prank while I'm there. Then it's still a mystery and people like mysteries. I'll give my opinion, that it's mice or popping floorboards or something like that, and the family can say whatever they want to say. Everybody'll be happy, and it'll be money in the bank, and I never object to that."

"Consider it done," said Alfonso, handing Runcible a glass of orange juice and two blue pills. "Now, take your pills like a good boy. We don't want that ticker of yours giving you a fit again today."

Runcible did as he was told and took his heart medication. As he did, he could feel the stirring of that constant, self-restrained sense of panic, which always rose up in his breast whenever the slightest suggestion of his own mortality was brought up—as indeed it had been often enough in recent months by his physician and those who cared about him most. It always made him think of his father for some reason, dying in that unkempt and awful place… He pushed these feelings back down through the force of his will, casting the upsetting thoughts from his mind.

Alfonso Castiglioni got to work the very next day in his usual efficient way. Before the week was out, everything had been arranged for a visit to Hazelhurst Manor by Runcible, his personal secretary, and a four-man film crew from CBS. Raymond Lilburn seemed comfortable with the idea of having someone as famous as Runcible investigate his home. Alfonso in turn explained to him how Runcible went about his investigations.

First, he told Lilburn, it was Runcible's custom to spend three or four days on site. On the first day, the television crew would film interviews with the family members.

"Please," said Alfonso, "make sure you and your wife have something prepared beforehand to say, detailing the goings-on as thoroughly as you can. We'd very much like to have you give us a guided walk-through in the home as you recount your experiences. If it's all right, we'd like to ask the children a few questions, too—nothing too demanding or scary for them, of course."

After this, the family would move to a fine hotel in Baltimore, all expenses covered by the network. The house, in other words, would be left by its everyday occupants so that Runcible and his crew could investigate on two successive nights on their own. Since the tower seemed to be at the center of the hauntings—with its nightly footsteps and the self-opening window—it would probably get the most scrutiny from Runcible personally. He might opt, as he had in the past in other allegedly haunted locales, to remain alone there—although, added Alfonso, "he has a heart condition and maybe someone else might be asked to fill in for him," if the way up into the tower proved to be too much. The second day would be a time for rest until late afternoon. By then, Runcible would probably have formulated some possible explanations for whatever he had experienced, assuming he had experienced anything at all. The second night would be a duplication of the first, just to make certain everything had been covered adequately. The family would return to the house on the third day and there would be a summary interview with Runcible on location, with the family given their opportunity to respond to his assessment. If there were anything that might require a fourth day for the investigation, they would be prepared to extend the visit. Otherwise, they would call the investigation complete and the network, with Runcible's oversight, would edit the film for airing nationwide sometime after New Year's Day.

All this met with Raymond and Blanche Lilburn's approval, and the investigation was scheduled for the second full week in December.

🐦

Runcible and his team arrived at Hazelhurst Manor at half past eight in the morning on the eleventh of December, a Tuesday that year. What astounded Raymond Lilburn most about the Astounding Runcible was how short he was. He had seen him on the air from time to time on television, but due to the artifice of the medium he hadn't really paid attention to it before. Now that the great man stood before him in his full sartorial splendor, Lilburn couldn't help recalling some of Arthur Rackham's illustrations of fairy tales.

The senior Lilburns were not yet forty and their children, Ray Junior and Cindy, were five and four respectively. A more pleasant all-American family, Runcible discovered soon enough, would have been hard to find. To Runcible, such ingenuousness suggested gullibility on the part of all except, perhaps, the possible prankster among them. Raymond Lilburn came from one of the first families in town. It was literally his fortune to be one of the co-owners of the enormous flour mills that had, in one form or another, been an established feature on the banks of the Patapsco for two centuries, known locally as the "Doughnut Factory." He had always wanted to own Hazelhurst Manor, so when it had come up for sale, he had purchased it. "It was a bargain," he was pleased to tell Runcible.

What impressed Runcible most about the grand home was how ideal it was as the setting for "a haunted house debunking," as he phrased it, although he was careful not to call it that in front of the Lilburns. Great and gray, decorated with enough neo-gothic gingerbread that he thought it could be used by Universal or Hammer as the set for a monster movie, he fell immediately in love with its unusual—some might say "spooky"—ambience. It made him think of Charles Addams' cartoons in *The New Yorker*. To the rear of the house stood the infamous tower, with its balustraded roof, and its top room in which Frederick Todd Thorpe had hanged himself, and where now the nightly footsteps on the stairs could allegedly be heard and where the window refused to stay shut.

# The Debunker

He had plans for that upper room.

As they introduced themselves in the foyer, Runcible was flanked on his right by Alfonso, dressed conservatively under his long black overcoat in a dark blue suit, white shirt, and maroon tie, and on his left by a tall man in gray tweeds who held an unlit pipe in his hand. The latter introduced himself as "Chet Banks, the man from the network." It was the job of "the man from the network" to conduct the interviews. Remaining outdoors for the time being, despite the wind and falling snow, were three film technicians in winter coats, eagerly awaiting the signal to collect their stuff and get inside. They didn't have long to wait. After the amiable reception in the foyer, they were waved inside.

"Would you gentlemen like some coffee?" asked Blanche Lilburn. "It's cold out there."

Runcible and Alfonso declined, the others said yes, and then preliminary details for the sleeping arrangements were briefly presented. Runcible and Alfonso would have the guest cottage on the grounds and Chet Banks would take the upstairs guestroom. It had already been decided that the three technicians would stay—as they had the previous night—at the hotel on Main Street.

"Before we film the walk-through," said Runcible, "could I have a quick look around with one of you—just to get my bearings?"

"Of course," said Raymond Lilburn. "Follow me." He showed Runcible where to stow his coat, cape, and large black hat, and then led him into the living room adjacent to the foyer. It was a spacious room, with a large fireplace, nine feet from floor to ceiling.

"Off in that direction," Lilburn informed Runcible, "is the library. That's where Ray—my son—tells me he sees 'a sad man' sometimes."

Something inside Runcible was strangely affected by the words "a sad man," moving him at some obscure, subliminal level. It was an unusual and unexpected reaction, evoking latent emotions he hadn't felt in years. He didn't like sentimentality, and he adamantly shoved the unwanted sensation to the rear of his mind.

"But first, let's go through here into the dining room," continued Lilburn. He conducted his guest through a large entranceway, set between two open wooden sliding doors. "This is the dining room,"

73

announced Lilburn, "and"—he laid heavy emphasis on the words—
*"that's the chandelier."*

This room, like the living room, was enormous. It was furnished
with a massive eighteenth-century marble-topped sideboard and
three glass-cased corner-cupboards full of chinaware. At the center
of the room stood a table of dark wood, long enough to accommodate at least sixteen diners comfortably in the splendid chairs placed
about it. Suspended over it was a magnificent chandelier of exquis-
itely cut glass.

"That's the chandelier that swings on its own initiative?" asked
Runcible.

"Only three times in my experience," said Lilburn. "My wife witnessed it, too—and our dinner guests. I could ask some of them to
come by if you would like to interview them."

"Please do," said Runcible. "Maybe we could do that on Thurs-
day. Check with Chet about it."

"What could make that happen?" asked Lilburn, not looking at
Runcible but at the chandelier. "The swinging, I mean. What could
make something so big suddenly start moving like that?"

Runcible had no idea, really, but he also had no intention of saying as much. "Oh, maybe something electromagnetic," he said.
"There's usually some perfectly rational explanation for odd occurrences."

"Not a poltergeist?" asked Lilburn, glancing down into Runcible's
face.

The little man laughed. "Certainly not," he said.

"Why not?" Lilburn asked.

"Because poltergeists don't exist," replied Runcible, as if this pro-
nouncement settled the matter.

Lilburn said nothing in reply, but it was evident to Runcible that
he wasn't terribly impressed by the latter's casual dismissal of poltergeists. All Lilburn said was, "Well, let's look over the rest of the
downstairs, shall we? Then I'll show you the tower."

Lilburn led Runcible back to the large, well-stocked library, then
once again through the dining room into the kitchen. The door that
led into the tower was just outside the kitchen and opposite the
door to the dining room, in a back hallway. A third entrance led

into an atrium, one wall of which—as Runcible could see from the hall—was a series of high windows.

"We grow plants in there," said Lilburn, waving a hand toward the atrium. "It's a sort of mini-arboretum, really, if not a jungle. Cindy says another little girl plays with her in there sometimes. You saw the photograph?"

Runcible nodded. "In the newspaper article," he said.

"We had a dog," said Lilburn, "who died just this past year, named Isabel. Isabel wouldn't go into the atrium to save her life. Absolutely refused. If we picked her up and carried her toward it, she'd bolt out as soon as we set her down."

"Maybe some high-pitched electronic noise is in there," remarked Runcible, "on a frequency you can't hear, but that a dog can. Happens sometimes. And, of course, little children have their imaginary friends."

"Hmm," hmm'd Lilburn. "Here's the door leading into the tower. We'll go up to the top. It's just three flights. Then on the way back down we'll go through the door above that leads onto the second floor in the house. You up to it?"

"Lay on, Macduff," said Runcible.

Before they stepped over the threshold into the tower, though, a voice interrupted them from behind. Alfonso had caught up with them, and he was saying, "Wait, wait, wait."

"My secretary," said Runcible to Lilburn as if in confidence. "He's always watching out for me. What is it, Alfie?"

"Your heart," said the secretary. "Did I hear you say *three* flights, Mr. Lilburn?"

"I did," replied Lilburn, "but it's not a strenuous climb."

"You know what Dr. Hibbert told you about climbing stairs," Alfonso chided Runcible.

"I took my pills," said Runcible. "I'll be fine. I'll take it slow. You coming? This is the infamous tower, you know."

Alfonso looked displeased, but he followed the other two into the ground floor of the tower and up the stairs. At the top of the first flight there was an open entrance that led into the upstairs hallway. "Our bedroom is right next to this entrance," said Lilburn. "That's how I can hear the footsteps on the stairs each night so easily. My

75

head is only a few feet away, really. The staircase is just on the other side of the wall from me. You can hear everything."

Before taking the next flight up, they stopped and looked around the tower room in which they now stood. It was a comfortable sitting room, with two overstuffed chairs, a rocker, side tables, and lamps.

"Do all the rooms in the tower have that sort of radiator?" asked Runcible, pointing with his stick at an old-fashioned steam radiator directly under the window. Just as he said this, a rattling, gurgling noise erupted from the contraption.

"Yes," said Lilburn. "And I know what you're thinking, but that's not the sound I hear each night."

Runcible didn't answer but started up the next flight of steps ahead of them. The room above was less comfortably furnished, and it seemed to be a storage place for toys. There was an electric train set spread out on the floor. Boxed board games were stacked on a few old bookshelves. A few battered stuffed animals lay about. Toy soldiers were scattered here and there, some of them cast in lead and painted to look like World War I doughboys, and there were Lincoln Logs in an old cardboard box.

"A lot of these were mine," explained Lilburn. "Never had the heart to dispose of them. My children like to play with them now."

"Don't let them put those lead soldiers in their mouths," remarked Runcible.

He noted the steam radiator under the window on this floor, as well. And as he did, the same clanking and sputtering noises they had heard below could be heard as the steam in the pipes ascended. Without a word, he led the way up the steps to the top floor.

When he reached it, he was out of breath and his heart was pounding. Alfonso came up behind him and laid a hand on his shoulder.

"Take it easy, old boy," he cautioned Runcible.

Lilburn joined them.

The top floor was relatively empty, except for a table, a standing lamp, and an old rocking chair, painted robin's egg blue, with a natty cushion on the seat. The room was icy cold. The reason for this was immediately evident—the window was wide open, and the wind was blowing through it, carrying in snowflakes which settled and quickly melted on the hot radiator directly beneath it.

Lilburn rushed over to the window, slammed it shut and latched it.

"See?" was all he said.

Runcible shot a knowing glance up at Alfonso behind Lilburn's back, rolling his eyes as if to say, "Staged."

Lilburn turned around, then he pointed upwards, directing the others' attention to a particular rafter overhead. It was one of four such rafters that spanned the ceiling of the room. "If my information is correct," he said, "that's the one Frederick Todd Thorpe used to hang himself."

"I'll be on stakeout up here tonight," said Runcible. "Seated right under that beam, then. We'll see if we can figure out what's going on up here—the footsteps and the window that opens by itself—without resorting to any supernatural hypotheses. Then, perhaps, you can sleep better at night."

Lilburn then led them below, taking them through the second floor past the bedrooms, and finally down to the first floor by way of the main staircase. The technicians had set up their equipment in the library for filming, and Chet Banks, clipboard in hand, was looking over his notes in preparation for the interviews. Blanche Lilburn and the two children were seated on a sofa in one corner of the room, having already been coached by Banks as to what was expected from them.

Everything that morning and early afternoon went smoothly. Banks put the four Lilburns at their ease and conducted the interviews without a hitch. When it came time for the film team to follow Blanche and Raymond through the house and up into the tower, Alfonso remained below with the children and kept them amused with magic tricks around the kitchen table. By four-thirty in the afternoon, with only a short pause for lunch, the succession of interviews was concluded, and the family was ready to depart for two nights away in Baltimore, expenses covered by the network. It was still blustery outside, and the snow was coming down, but it was only light flurries. The weather didn't threaten to hinder the family's short trip to Baltimore.

77

"Do some holiday shopping," said Runcible cheerily, reminding Lilburn of a diminutive Monty Woolley. "Nothing like being in the big city between Thanksgiving and Christmas. The lights, the decorations—the kids'll love it. Take in a movie or a play. Enjoy yourselves. We'll take care of things here. I promise we won't break a thing. And when you get back, we should have some answers for you about your 'ghost' problem." The way he said "ghost" implied that it should be in quotes.

After the family had driven off, Runcible turned to Alfonso and said, "Now, dear boy, we can get down to business."

The plan for the evening was this. The three audio and visual technicians would leave their equipment at the house and head back to their hotel for the evening. "But be on call, if we should need you," Chet Banks told them before they left. The remaining trio would stake out what Runcible designated the three "hot spots" in the house. Banks would remain in the library, Alfonso would take the dining room and check on the atrium now and then, and Runcible would station himself in the top room of the tower. They would stay in contact with walkie-talkies.

After a supper of sandwiches and soft drinks (nothing alcoholic on stakeouts, Runcible was strict to insist), the men idled away the time playing poker until eleven.

"Well, gentlemen," Runcible announced at that hour, "I think we should man our stations. Remember, same rules as always. Got your walkie-talkies and flashlights? No chattering on them unless you've got something worth everyone's time. And keep lights off except for the flashlights. Any questions?"

"Shall I help you up the tower stairs?" Alfonso asked Runcible.

"Alfie, you're very sweet," replied the latter, "but no. I'll take it slow." And the three went their separate ways.

By the light of his flashlight, Runcible entered the tower and began his ascent of its stairway. Arriving at the first sitting room, he stopped to catch his breath. The loud clanking of the radiator could be heard under the window, and he flashed his light over in its direction. The window caught the reflection, and at the sight his heart skipped a beat. The wind suddenly gusted outside and rattled the windowpanes. He felt a chill go through him.

"Stop that," he said to himself, annoyed at his racing heart and foolish trepidation. It was an old fear returned, one he hadn't felt since his childhood until that same morning, when Lilburn had said the evocative words "a sad man." But he refused to allow such feelings admittance—after all, he was the master skeptic. His reputation hung on his ability to debunk irrational fears, and anything deemed uncanny by more credulous minds. A fleeting humiliating memory of a small boy curled into a fetal ball under the bedclothes, terrified and trembling, flared up in his mind.

"Stop that," he said to himself again. "Go away."

He resumed the ascent.

At the second floor, he paused to rest again. He swept the light over the floor. The old toys and electric train looked strangely lonely and abandoned to him, and an unaccountable feeling of despondency began to weigh upon his mind. How like the toys of his own boyhood, he mused. The lead soldiers awakened sharp recollections in particular. His father had been a veteran of the Spanish-American War and he remembered that wonderful, long-ago Christmas when he had been given a similar set of toy soldiers—stalwart painted soldiers that looked to him like little effigies of his father and filled him with a sense of pride. That had been before the bad time, before his father's war experiences, delayed and festering, began to take their toll on his father's peace of mind. Runcible winced, remembering how his sense of pride had become one of shame instead. His father had sunk into a morbid state of melancholia, unable to do his job. He had begun to drink heavily and have blackouts; when he was awake, he either sat passively or sometimes wept. Runcible felt a lump rise in his throat at the memory of it.

"What a lousy life," he whispered to himself, the beam of his light falling steadily on the motionless toy soldiers. "What a gloomy goddamn saturnine hellish life."

His father had ended his days in an asylum. When Runcible had visited him there, he seemed sane enough, composed, and pitifully solicitous of him. Runcible—a teenager—had received this attention awkwardly, even coolly. His father had died when Runcible was sixteen.

And then *it* happened. His father's ghost, he had been sure at the time, had come to his bedroom at night, hoping to visit him one last time, hoping to receive from his son some sign of affection. He hadn't actually seen his father's ghost, but he had felt its closeness, he had heard the footsteps, he had heard it speak to him in a whisper close to his ear—audibly, imploringly, clearly, indisputably *his* voice. Or so it had seemed to him at the time, there in the dark, in the middle of the night. But, instead of greeting that sad man, that despairing man, Runcible in his dread had pulled the covers over his head and begged God—he had believed in God then—to keep the ghost away from him.

"I was irrational," said Runcible, justifying himself to himself, looking morosely at the toy soldiers as he whispered the words. "I was just a scared dumb kid."

But he remembered, guiltily now, begging God that he should never see a ghost or anything else of that sort ever in his life. It had become his nightly prayer. And then a miracle had occurred—the miracle of unbelief. Sometime before he was nineteen, he realized he had stopped praying altogether and that he no longer believed in God; he no longer believed in spirits or the paranormal or anything that couldn't be elucidated by sound reasoning, clean cold cogitation, the rigors of science. At this thought, he now shook himself defiantly to clear his head.

"Buck up, you old idiot," he said harshly to himself, and proceeded up the next flight of stairs.

Now he stood on the top floor. He cast the beam of his flashlight around and saw that everything was as it had been earlier in the day. No open window, though, and he smiled at the memory of Lilburn's play-acting that morning—as if the fellow hadn't opened it himself earlier. He chuckled at that.

"He certainly must have a low opinion of my brain," Runcible muttered. Then he held down the PTT button on his walkie-talkie.

"Just letting you know I'm up here on the top floor," reported Runcible to Alfonso.

"How's your heart?" came the reply.

The Debunker

"Don't be silly, dear boy," said Runcible. "I feel just fine. Can't wait to sit down now and twiddle my thumbs. Over and out."

Runcible made his way over to the old rocker and seated himself at an angle from which he could observe both the staircase and the tightly latched window. The wind was still gusting outdoors, but the sky was now partly clear, and the light of the full moon was bright enough to illuminate the room with a pale glow. Runcible settled in for a long vigil, as he had done so often before, not expecting anything more than a few hours of reflection and possibly some easily explained noise to investigate. But if he thought his own mind would leave him in peace, he was sadly mistaken. Once again, gloomy memories came over him.

A sad man, a despairing man, that had been his father... those were the words that had occurred to him moments before on the floor below. What was it the little boy—Ray Junior—said he had seen in the library? A "sad man," Lilburn had recounted. No doubt, he had intended for Runcible to think of Frederick Todd Thorpe. Thorpe, who years before had come up these very same steps, into this very same upper room, to hang himself from that very same beam overhead—and Runcible cast a glance into the shadows above him. Thorpe had been a "despairing man," too. It would take a despairing man to hang himself, a man depressed and inwardly suffering, confused, not thinking straight.

"But I think straight," Runcible muttered. "Thank God for that."

Then the irony of that last utterance hit him, and he chuckled again. But as quickly as that laugh had passed his lips, his heart sank again into melancholy meditations. If he hadn't known better, he would have said that the tower itself was filled with an abiding presence of despair, that there was *something* in the very atmosphere, something heavy and morbid, influencing his sensibilities. So much rubbish, he told himself. The feelings were inside him, not outside—and to think otherwise was delusional, insufferable nonsense. No, he was just having a bad evening.

And then he found himself recalling that poor French girl, whose gift of healing he had so devastatingly debunked last year. She had been one of the many he had "exposed" as frauds, one of that class of practical illiterates who believed in what they were doing, in

81

whom there had been no discernible desire to deceive, but whose very existence in the age of science he found distasteful. "Genetic throwbacks who should never have been born," he had once called them in vexation during an interview.

But now he remembered vividly how shy the French girl had been, how young, how unsure of herself, how pitifully vulnerable to criticism, how unused to the cold laboratory surroundings in which Runcible had insisted that she "perform" (as he had called it). He remembered, with a pang of something like regret, her growing anxiety in that context and the satisfaction he had felt at her failures, watching with a smugness that was unexpectedly disturbing to him now, in this dark gloomy tower room, how her "powers" had miscarried again and again under his intensive scrutiny. He remembered her tears, her excuses for failing the tests, the whole doleful, wretched episode. But now something in him wasn't pleased with what he had done. He recoiled with an atypical sense of revulsion as he remembered not the girl, whose dignity he had tried to destroy, but his own arrogant callousness.

"God, what a bastard," he muttered. And whom he meant by that was himself, the Astounding Runcible, the former Archie Spill, the boy who used to cringe like a craven coward under his bedclothes until sometimes his bladder forced him out in a mad dash to the bathroom, afraid of ghosts and the undead, pleading with God Almighty to spare him even a glimpse of the paranormal. The boy who couldn't even face the "sad man," his dead longsuffering father, who had come to him tenderly only to say farewell one last time because he loved his son...

"Rubbish," he grumbled. "It never happened. He never came. It was all in my head. Damned demeaning rubbish."

The vigil had begun to seem like an interminable exercise in mental agony for Runcible. The atmosphere of the room had become, he felt, intolerably oppressive as the long minutes stretched on and on and on. The moonlight cast a spectral pallor over everything and that, too, depressed him. He was caught in a swirl of gloomy reveries, one memory flowing out of and into another, and all of them unflattering to himself. He sat physically motionless, but his mind was in a turmoil. His own phony moniker—"Jules Runcible," the "Astounding Runcible"—suddenly annoyed him. It was as fake as the whole persona he had adopted. A magician who didn't practice magic, a charlatan who wore pathetically outlandish clothes and a silly hat and a ridiculous cape to garner attention, who had built his career on fooling people but now went about attacking those he in turn deemed to be fooling people. A little man with a big waxed moustache and a pointed beard like the Mayor of the Emerald City, with a reputation for pissing on others' reputations, those people he loathed irrationally for being irrational, those people he proclaimed to be "fakes" when he damned well knew he really, really hadn't investigated them fairly, people like that little French girl…

Suddenly he wished he could go back, start over, not do this anymore.

"This place is getting to me," he moaned out loud.

And then a thought occurred to him, one that troubled him more profoundly than any other that had preceded it. Maybe these unbearable feelings of dissatisfaction with himself, this new or previously unrealized self-hatred, this sense of bitter despair—maybe *this* was a kind of *haunting*. And as this bizarre new idea forced itself into his consciousness, his ears heard something. *Something on the stairs.* Something creaking, moving, as if ascending step by step from below.

He got up from the rocker and went over to the head of the stairs, listening, his senses on full alert. He didn't dare press the PTT button on his walkie-talkie for fear of interrupting his concentration on the approaching sounds—and they *were* approaching. Step by slow, ponderous step, he could hear what really sounded to him like someone ascending the staircase. A part of him wanted to descend to investigate, but he couldn't make himself budge from where he stood. He couldn't move, because like scared little Archie Spill under the bedclothes, he was filled with something he hadn't felt for years—the blood-freezing, muscle-juddering penetration of terror.

Suddenly he felt something in the air at the top of the stairs, some motion, a fluttering, a tingling in his body like static. Something seemed to move past him toward the window. He jumped backwards, turning to face in that direction. And now, to his immense horror, he watched as the clasp at the top of the window turned slowly on its screw, seemingly of its own accord, until it was unlatched...

And then the window slid up and open as if moved by invisible hands.

A pain shot through Runcible's chest at the sight of it, and he grasped the front of his shirt tightly in his fist. As he did so, he heard something above him, a sort of strangulated groan coming from the rafter overhead. Although he was in pain and nearly doubled over, he managed to look up. The moonlight revealed a man's face suspended in the air directly above his, itself moonlike in its paleness, with eyes staring down directly into his. The vision was momentary, and then the face faded and dissolved into the surrounding shadows.

Another stabbing pain shot through Runcible's breast, his arms ached, and his legs buckled beneath him. He rolled himself into a fetal ball, heaving himself against the radiator directly under the window, where he came to a stop, and there he huddled until blackness overtook him.

The Astounding Runcible's will left everything to his friend and secretary, Alfonso Castiglioni. Alfonso's grief had been inconsolable for some weeks after the Hazelhurst Manor affair. It was he who had ventured into the tower's upper room before dawn, only to discover Runcible's body, still curled up under the open window. The snow had returned, and a dusting of it, having blown in, had added an extra pallor to his friend's corpse. The investigation, of course, had come abruptly to an end, but not before Alfonso issued a statement to the press explaining what had occurred and some resolutions of his own in the wake of events.

He intended, he said, to carry on Jules Runcible's important fight against superstition and credulity. All extraordinary claims regarding the paranormal should be examined scientifically, as Runcible had always stringently maintained, and he would seek to further those ends. There was nothing allegedly "supernatural," Alfonso declared, that couldn't be explained by the sound principles of rationalism and empirical research. Nothing immaterial existed, he said, and a healthy mind was a dedicated materialist mind. Jules Runcible had died, he went on, of a weak heart. Apparently, he hadn't been feeling well in that upper room and, by endeavoring to open the window for some fresh air, he had put too much strain on himself.

"Lastly, I blame myself for not having been more insistent with him," Alfonso told the press. "I should have been with him or been the one that night to investigate the tower. As it is, we found *no evidence whatsoever* of a haunting at Hazelhurst Manor. *None whatsoever.* In that sense, at least, the Astounding Runcible succeeded one last time."

The Lilburns, on the other hand, continued for years afterward to claim that strange happenings occurred routinely at the grand old home. But following the investigation one new feature had been added to the alleged hauntings. The footsteps that could be heard on the tower steps most evenings had now acquired an echo. It was as if there were now two persons ascending the stairway, one directly on the heels of the other.

# The Conjuring Song

"IF YOU WANT to hear that song, you got to come tonight."

Shell Dorsey was on the other end of the phone. For the past four weeks I had been imploring him for the opportunity, hoping he would relent and permit me to hear—and record—what he had repeatedly assured me was not for the ears of those outside his family.

"But I thought..." I began.

"I know," he interrupted me. "I know what I told you, but I've been giving it some thought, and it don't matter now. It'll be the last time that song will ever get sung. After I've done it, that'll be the end of it."

"But, why?" I asked. "Why now? What's changed your mind?"

"They're going after my daughter now," replied Shell simply. "Those same two cops who went after me. I could take it when it was just me. But not Violet. You remember what I said I'd do if they tried that, and I'm going to do it. They say they're going to 'get' her one night—going to 'have' her. You understand my meaning."

I did understand, and it made me feel sick inside just to hear him say it. And I knew now why he had changed his mind, why he would sing the song one last time. But it put me in an ethical jam. My quandary was this: would it make me an accessory to murder if I showed up that night with my recorder to capture the song on tape? If what Shell had said to me earlier about it was to be believed, would I be involving myself in the deaths of two men—two policemen, at that? Worse still, would I be complicit somehow in Shell's own death, a man I had come to think of as my friend?

I have to tell you that I didn't know what to believe about any of it. It all sounded so ridiculous—a "conjuring song," a cursed hat, the conjuring up of the dead... How had I gotten myself into this? Well, in fact, I knew damned well how I had. Very simply, I wanted to hear that "forbidden" song for myself and have it placed in an archive for safe keeping, and I knew I had better say yes to Shell's unanticipated offer and take my chances. There wouldn't be any second opportunity.

"I'll be over tonight," I assured him. "I promise. Wait for me."

I need to back up and explain the background to these events as succinctly as I can, before I try to put into words what constitutes the most harrowing experience of my life.

I'm old now, but I was young once. And when I was young, I was part of a new generation of researchers during the most electrifying era in American ethnomusicology. Those who shared this enthusiasm were serious about getting out into the field, inspired as we were by such trailblazers as John Lomax and his son, Alan. Our self-appointed mission in life was to seek out *authentic* "folk" and "race" music, as it was then called, get it on tape, catalogue it, and save it for posterity. The times were changing so fast that we felt we hadn't much time left to catch hold of the caboose end of a disappearing tradition, to interview the few remaining folks who could still sing the old stuff. What passed for "folk music" on the radio was mostly ersatz concoctions for college kids—pleasant, harmonic, sweet, socially conscious, but a million miles away from the grit and sweat and rawness of the genuine article. This was our last chance, the final roundup, a rescue operation, a labor of love (God knows, it didn't pay anything)—to track down the really good stuff, the honest-to-God stuff, the weird and timeworn stuff before the last lingering black folks and white folks who knew it took it to their graves with them. In retrospect, I believe we did the job about as well as anybody could have done in those hectic times.

But this isn't a memoir of all our herculean labors way back when. Rather, it's about a single occurrence forever driven into my memory like a hard iron spike. Of all my many experiences, it was by far the most disquieting. It gave me the creeps then and it gives me the creeps now. It's not that I didn't encounter a lot of other exceptionally offbeat people in my journeying days—you couldn't help but bump into them, say, in rural West Virginia or down in the Tennessee mountains or out around El Paso or just about anywhere else in the remote wooded backwaters and dusty ranges and rustic boondocks of crazy America. I could write a big fat book or three describing the many eccentrics and sometimes downright scary individuals I struck up acquaintances with in downtown hangouts and crumbling cabins and railroad yards and prisons and the like during my travels—all of them like characters in the songs they sung (or, frequently enough, even worse). And many of those songs and tunes we recorded revolved around uncanny themes or told blood-soaked tales of murder, revenge, and rapine. Those were recurring ingredients in a high percentage of them, and America has never had a shortage of violent accounts rendered hauntingly beautiful in song. But none of my other encounters with strange characters and their music were ever as chilling as this stand-alone brush with the nightmarish.

It all started with a tip I received from a colleague who knew I had developed a particular interest in the Stagger Lee ballads. "Stagger Lee" or "Stagolee" or "Stackalee" or "Stack O'Lee" (and other variants) was a real, historical figure. His given name was Lee Shelton, and he had been a pimp of some notoriety out in St. Louis. John and Alan Lomax claimed he'd taken his nickname from the *Stack Lee*, a riverboat out of Memphis, which was in point of fact a floating bordello. Shelton belonged to a wild bunch who referred to themselves as "macks"—i.e., pimps who dressed fancy and strutted their stuff around the city's tenderloin district. He was the "captain" of a society of black men called the "Four Hundred Club," and he also owned a dive called the Modern Horseshoe Club. Employed as a carriage driver, he was in an enviable position to direct white gentleman travelers, as they came out of Canal Street's Southern Railroad Station, either to his own club or to his bevy of working girls or else to other bordellos and joints with which he was associated. Standing at just five-foot-seven and having a crossed left eye, Lee's ability to impress others was a matter of his forceful character and not his appearance. But impress others he did.

The story goes (and I take what follows from the authentic eyewitness accounts) that on the night of Christmas, 1895, Lee Shelton strode into the Bill Curtis Saloon, another infamous joint, dressed to the nines—black coat, crimson vest, yellow shirt, gray striped pants, gold rings on his fingers, carrying a gold-headed ebony cane, and wearing dove-gray spats over a pair of St. Louis flats—shoes

88

with low heels and long, pointed, upturned toes that were decorated with mirrors for catching the light. Topping off all this resplendence, he was sporting an immaculate white highroller Stetson hat with an image of his favorite girl, Lillie, embroidered on the hatband. In the saloon, he ran into an acquaintance, a levee hand named Billy Lyons. At first, the accounts tell us, the two men got on fine, laughing and joking together. But after a few drinks, their discussion turned to the volatile subject of politics, and their friendly chitchat degenerated into an argument.

The physical conflict began when the two men started batting at each other's hats. Shelton, having finally had a bellyful of the hat-smacking foolishness, snatched Lyons's derby right off his head and smashed it out of shape. Lyons, not to be outdone, grabbed Shelton's white Stetson and refused to give it back until Shelton gave him "six bits" to cover the cost of his own damaged hat. Shelton retorted that he had no intention of paying for Lyons's derby, and—just to make it clear he meant what he said—he pulled out a .44 Smith and Wesson and said he'd blow out Lyons's brains if he didn't hand over the Stetson forthwith. He then reinforced the threat by clobbering Lyons over the head with his pistol. But Lyons still wouldn't let go of the hat and instead pulled a knife.

"You cockeyed son of a bitch," Lyons said to Shelton, "I'm gonna *make* you kill me." Which wasn't the smartest thing for Lyons to do, given his circumstances.

Lee Shelton coolly stepped back, took aim, and shot Billy Lyons dead. Then he sauntered over to the still quivering body, bent down, detached his hat from the corpse's fingers, brushed it off and, putting it on his head, said before exiting the saloon, "I told you to give me my hat."

And that's the story. "Stack" Lee Shelton was subsequently arrested, convicted in 1897, paroled in 1909, but arrested again in 1911 for robbery and assault. He died in prison in 1912. Already before his death, in fact as early as his 1897 conviction, songs were being sung about him.

Now, I was intrigued with the evolving musical tradition surrounding that murder in a red-light district, committed by a shadowy, vaguely remembered figure who had been in his grave for half a century. "That bad man Stagger Lee," as the ballad referred to him, had developed over time into something of a hero or antihero, larger than life, defiant of the law, a law unto himself. Not just black folks sung about him, but white folks did, too. There was something attractive about the myth of the man, even though the real story was sordid and Stagger Lee a criminal. But that's part of the enduring, inexplicable mystery of folk music.

So it was that I got a tip from another ethnomusicologist who knew of my interest in the ballad. He had discovered, in that word-of-mouth way that tips got passed around in our work, that living just a few miles north of where I was then residing, in a town on the Patapsco River, Ellicott City, was a grandson of Lee Shelton. The grandson's name, in fact, was Shelton Dorsey. His mother had come east from St. Louis around the turn of the century and had married a Maryland man. According to my colleague's information, she had been the daughter of "Stack" Lee Shelton by one of his girls, a French-speaking Creole originally come up from Louisiana. It seemed, too, that Shelton Dorsey was a singer of old songs, not just the Stagger Lee ballad, but of a lot more besides, and that he sang and accompanied himself on the guitar at one of the local dives in Ellicott City. My colleague suggested I go up there and look for him. Whetting my appetite further, he added that the story he'd received had it that Shelton Dorsey knew a version of the Stagger Lee song that nobody else knew and—this was the real kicker—he also had in his possession the very same white highroller Stetson that had led to the shooting of Billy Lyons.

"Man, you got to be putting me on," I remember saying over the phone to my colleague. "If that's on the up and up, I'd give anything to see it. But it sounds too good to be true."

"You never know," said my friend. "It could just be a lot of bunk, but if I were you, man, I'd go check it out. You're right there in the D.C. area. The guy's almost in your backyard. I'd go there myself and cut you out of the picture, except I'm down here in Atlanta right now and, besides, I'm not a sneaky bastard. I think you should go for it."

I really didn't need too much urging. Go for it I did. Over at the campus library I got my hands on a phone directory for Howard

County, Maryland and looked up the name "Dorsey, Shelton" and, finding it, gave the house a call. A girl picked up the phone, and when I said I was looking for Shelton Dorsey, I heard her say to someone at the other end of the line, "It's for you, Daddy. Some man."

"Ask who's calling and what he wants," I heard a husky man's voice say in the background.

And the girl came back on and said, "Who's this? What do you want?"

I explained who I was and why I was calling.

The girl said to the man, "You better talk to him, Daddy. Says he's a effnomusic-something and wants to record your songs." I heard some muffled sounds over the line, and then the husky man's voice came on and we talked.

Shelton Dorsey, who preferred to be called "Shell," seemed somewhat reluctant at first to have me come up to his house and record him. He said that maybe I should drop in at the joint where he played some Friday or Saturday night and hear him do his gig first and then decide if I still thought recording him was worth my while.

"I ain't no recording artist," he said. "I just play songs in a bar for a few extra bucks on weekends to entertain folks who come in for drinks. My real job's over at the flour mills."

I told him I wasn't looking for recording artists but for people just like him, who knew some genuine folk and race music and didn't mind putting it on tape for posterity, and that, sure, I'd come up to the bar first and hear him if that's what he wanted. We went on talking for quite a while on the phone after that and, as we did, he relaxed and opened up a little. In fact, he changed his mind entirely about my coming to the bar where he played—he said the patrons there were mainly "colored folks" and that I might not be comfortable there. I told him that that didn't make any difference to me, but he insisted I come to his home instead, after all. I didn't question the about-face and asked him whereabouts in the town he lived. His house was outside of town, he told me, on a wooded lane called New Cut Road. When I asked whether my coming there with my reel-to-reel and other equipment might disrupt his family's routine, he told me his wife had died some years before of pneumonia and that only he and his eighteen-year-old daughter, Violet, lived there now. We ended agreeably and that's when he told me to call him "Shell" and that I'd be welcome. We set the time for a week from Sunday, and that was that. I said nothing about Stagger Lee or Shell's alleged relationship to him during that call, figuring it might better be brought up after we'd spent some time together and he'd gotten comfortable with me. After all, his grandfather had been a murderer and I didn't have any way of knowing there and then how my nosing around about him might be taken by Dorsey at our first encounter.

When the warm early October Sunday of our appointed meeting came around, having my map open on the passenger seat and my recording equipment in the backseat of my VW Beetle, I headed north to meet Shell Dorsey. It took me little over an hour to get up there and to find the house, but I was there by one-thirty. New Cut Road was one of those back lanes along which the poorer black families resided. It was surrounded by woods on both sides and the houses along it were, with few exceptions, in rundown condition. Dogs lay in the shade of trees and under bushes or were running loose in the dirt yards. Chickens strutted here and there by the road, and in front of one house I saw a young pig trotting about behind wire fencing. And children, mostly barefoot, were at play, and their laughter and shouts were the only cheerful sound I heard on the street.

I found the house with little difficulty and parked on the side of the road nearest to it. I retrieved my large tape recorder from the backseat, leaving behind my battery-operated portable recorder that I sometimes found useful as a backup. As I headed toward the house, I noted that it had been recently repainted in a dark shade of green and was skirted on three sides by a white picket fence. The backyard, as I would see later, was naturally bordered on the edge of a running creek. All in all, the home was markedly in better condition than those of the surrounding neighbors.

I unlatched the gate of the picket fence and made my way to the front door, which swung open as soon as I approached it. Before me stood a young woman in a print dress.

92

"I'm Violet," she introduced herself. "My dad's in the living room. He's not feeling too good today, though. He had a bad night."

"I'm sorry to hear that," I said. "I can come back some other time…"

"No, sir," she said. "He said bring you on in. He's waiting on you in the sitting room."

I stepped inside and Violet shut the door behind me. The interior was tidy, and it smelled as if bacon had been fried there recently.

"We just ate," Violet said, taking my hat and putting it on a chair by the door. "If you're hungry, though…"

"No, no," I replied. "I ate lunch before coming. I'm just fine, thanks."

"Then, let me take you in to see Daddy," she said.

She escorted me to their small sitting room and then slipped away, leaving me there alone with her father. The furniture was old and worn, but looked comfortable, and the drapes were open letting in the sunlight that percolated through yellowing autumn leaves outside. Seated on the sofa in the room was a large man, not fat but muscular and obviously over six feet in height when standing, wearing a checked shirt and gray slacks. The reason for his "bad night" was evident at first glance—his head was bandaged, and his left eye was puffy and bruised.

"Sorry I don't get up," he said in a deep voice. "But I get dizzy if I do. Doctor says that'll pass. I'm Shell Dorsey," and he extended his hand over the coffee table in front of him. I shook it, and he said, "Put your stuff anywhere and take a load off your feet. Want something to drink?"

"Sure," I said. "What's on offer?"

"Whiskey?" he asked.

"Certainly," I replied, sitting down in an armchair at an angle where the sunlight lit up his damaged features.

"Got some here," he said. He pulled out a bottle of Jack Daniel's from somewhere beside him on the sofa. He unscrewed the cap, took a swig, and passed the bottle over to me. I guessed this was some kind of test. Would I drink from a bottle after a black man had drunk from it? Without hesitation I received the bottle and took a drink and gave it back to him. It seemed to me he was pleased by

93

that, although he didn't say anything to indicate it and he didn't smile.

"An accident?" I asked, gesturing toward his bandaged head.

"An accident," he snorted. "Yeah, the sort of accident cops give you for being a negro after dark outside a bar."

This set me back on my heels. Just beneath the hospitality he'd shown me, Shell Dorsey was simmering. He was also challenging me again, I felt, by saying what he said. It was another test, weighing my character, seeing if I was the sort of white man he could trust and not some candy-assed Caucasian collegiate full of nice egalitarian rhetoric but without substance. To accentuate the nature of the trial he was putting me through, he took a long swig from the bottle and passed it over to me again. I took a similarly long swig and passed it back.

"Goddamn cops," I said. "What'd they do?"

"Watch your language," said Shell with a frown. "We don't talk that way in this house. There's a young lady in the other room and we're God-fearing people. But, yeah, the cops..." He took a drink from the bottle. "Look, they ain't all bad news. I know some decent ones. There's even a negro cop in town now. But the two I tangled with last night got it in for me. These same two boys been giving me trouble for years. What they done to me this time was hit me upside the head with a nightstick."

"But why?" I persisted.

"Who can say?" said Shell, his eyes wide with mock astonishment. "You're the white man here. You tell me why they do it. Maybe it's 'cause I dress pretty sharp when I'm entertaining nights. Some white folks hate a smart-looking negro man. Makes them feel cheap. Or maybe it's 'cause I keep my home looking too decent to suit them. Or maybe it's just 'cause I'm a negro man standing outside a colored bar for a smoke before going back in and playing some more. Same thing happened to Miles Davis a couple years ago. You know who Miles Davis is?"

"Of course," I said.

"You like him on the horn?"

"Yes, sir, I really do," I said, truthfully.

"You're a smart white man," he said. "Anyway, it's also probably

94

'cause my daddy was a jailbird and them two cops—Watts and Powers is their names—know it. They know my daddy was a con. Him being that puts a bad taste in their self-righteous mouths. Like father, like son, they told me. They always try to start something when they see me round. Another shot of whiskey before we begin?"

I took another pull from the proffered bottle, then asked him where I could plug in my recorder.

"There, under the window," he replied. "Hand me my guitar while you're over there," he added, pointing toward a corner of the room where the instrument was propped against the wall. "I got to tune her up some."

I handed it to him, got the recorder plugged in, tested the mic, and we began.

The rest of the afternoon was sheer delight, utter transport. He played song after song and filled up a good three hours of tape. I heard stuff I'd never heard anybody play before, and when he played, he played as if in a trance. We'd talk between songs, and he'd explain what this or that one meant, where it came from, what it pertained to, who had sung it before him, and so on. His repertoire was varied—spirituals, railroad songs, chain-gang chants, love ballads, murder ballads, ghost ballads, and just plain strumming and picking, which he did like a master. His music seemed haunted by a sepia-tinted past just beyond our sight, by voices of the dead ventriloquizing through his husky vocals, and, like I said, he sometimes seemed to go into a trance like a medium contacting the other side while he sung, and there was occasionally, too, a physical strain so great inside him that outwardly his swollen face broke into streaming sweat and the muscles on his thick throat went taut. I was in seventh heaven. Here was the real thing, the living tradition, the stuff people like me wanted to preserve forever, although all things are impermanent, and nothing lasts forever. And that fact—impermanence—somehow made this ecstatic and melancholy endeavor of preservation all the more needful and precious.

And in this way, we spent the afternoon, which imperceptibly darkened into evening. Violet brought us some homemade stew and a couple bottles of beer, which the three of us consumed right there in the living room. And then, finally, after finishing our meal and with Violet washing up in the kitchen, I worked up the nerve to ask Shell about his grandfather and the Stagger Lee ballad, which he hadn't sung or even mentioned once throughout the long hours we'd spent in each other's company.

"I was wondering how long it'd take you to ask about that," he replied. "I figured you would've heard. Yes, it's true, I'm the grandson of 'that bad man, Stagger Lee.' My mama was his daughter, you see, and my grandma was a Creole girl he'd known in the biblical way."

"I heard you have his hat," I said.

"You heard right," he replied. "I guess some blabbermouth round here spilled them beans."

"I guess so," I said. "And I also heard you know another version of the Stagger Lee ballad no one else does."

"You sure heard a lot," he said, eyeing me with something like suspicion. "But that last thing ain't true. I don't know no *other version* of the song. Who'd you hear that hogwash from?"

"A colleague of mine," I answered, feeling a bit let down. "I guess he got his information wrong."

"Sure did," said Shell. "But I didn't say I don't know *another song* that's got Stagger Lee in it. People round here know I know that *other* song. But it's a whole 'nother song, and it's a different kind of song—one I never sung to nobody and wouldn't sing with nobody round unless I trusted them enough to satisfy me. But it's best just to leave that song alone if there ain't no call for it."

Violet brought in some apple pie and coffee and sat down. Shell leaned forward and poured some whiskey into his and my mugs with the coffee, then picked up his guitar. Seeing him do that, I had the presence of mind to switch on the recorder. I'm glad I did, because he sang a version of the familiar Stagger Lee ballad, the one I knew best, but with this single unfamiliar addition:

> *Stagger Lee went up to heaven,*
> *And he met Saint Peter there;*
> *Pete say, "Turn round, go down t'other way, we won't*
> *Take no gamblers here!"*

# The Conjuring Song

*Stagger Lee went down t'other way,*
*Told the devil, "Git down off your shelf—*
*My name's Stagger Lee, I'm takin' over down here,*
*Gonna run this place myself!"*

"It's all lies," said Shell, setting down the guitar. "Stagger Lee wasn't no gambler like in the song. They didn't fight over no card game, like the song says. And Billy Lyons—that fella my grandpa shot—wasn't no nice family man neither. You know the true story, don't you?"

I told him I did.

"Well, the only true thing in that song is that they fought over the Stetson hat—Violet, go on upstairs and bring us down that hat..."

"Yes, sir," said Violet. "If it's still there."

"Still there?" I ventured to say, a little anxious that I might not get to see it, after all.

"Oh, it's in the house, wherever it is, and it can't have gone far," said Violet in reply, smiling. "It just has this habit of *moving around*, if you know what I mean."

I didn't know what she meant, but I let that pass.

"Go and find it, honey" ordered Shell. "I think it's still up in my closet. I saw it there yesterday. This man come up here all this way to see it."

Violet left and I heard her going up the steps.

"I didn't just come up here just to see the hat," I said, "I came for the music and..."

"I know that," interrupted Shell. "But I also know you'd like to see that hat, too. It has a habit of moving round, like my daughter said. On its own, I mean. It's a spooky, skittery thing, that old hat. Got some kind of Creole magic in it. That part about Stagger Lee's meeting with the devil in the song might not be *exactly* as it happened, but it's got a drop or two of truthfulness in it. You can be certain of that. Stagger Lee ain't too far away. He can be conjured back if he's called up by someone who's got hold of that hat and knows what to do to bring him up. And believe me, he's got a bellyful of hell all packed inside him, busting to get out. That's why I won't sing you

97

that other song—that *conjuring song*. It conjures up old Stagger Lee, and it's only used for special reasons, when he's needed."

I was perplexed by this, not knowing how to respond to such an unexpected flood of bizarre information. I realized that the whiskey was having its effect on Shell and had loosened his tongue, which didn't stop him from lurching forward and draining the remainder of the bottle of Jack Daniel's into our two coffee mugs.

"I don't… I don't know what a conjuring song is," I confessed.

"Just what it sounds like," retorted Shell. "It's a *song* that *conjures*. My grandma was a Creole, like I told you. You know what that means—it means she knew all about strange things and dark things… Ghosts, spirits, spooks, the walking dead. That's what I'm talking about."

I heard Violet's footsteps coming down from the second story.

"My grandma got hold of Stagger Lee's hat after he died," went on Shell, "and she made a conjuring song for it. Just for our family. She used that song a few times herself, but I don't know nothing about that. I know she was feared on account of whatever she done, or whatever people thought she done, and nobody dared rile her up after she got that reputation. She taught that conjuring song to my mama and my mama taught it to me. My mama used it once, too, back in 1938—and once is all you can use it for. That was when my daddy got put in jail for robbing a white man on the streetcar, which he never even done. It was a respectable white man's boy that done that. I have that on good authority." He tapped the side of his nose knowingly. "But my daddy was a black man, and nobody was going to take my daddy's word over that white boy's."

Violet came in and stood there by the arm of my chair, and she had in her hands a battered navy-blue hatbox.

"The judge at my daddy's trial was a crooked white man, and he knew that other white man whose boy done the robbery, and either for money or else to save that white boy's father's face, or maybe for both reasons, he sentenced my daddy, knowing full well he wasn't the one. I never saw my daddy again. He did hard labor and died in prison.

"But I'll tell you something else. He didn't die before that judge died. And that judge's dying was something terrible, too. It's on record. You can look it up. Someone came into that judge's house one night, with his old lady upstairs in bed, and shot him right through the head. He was downstairs at his desk, the papers said, with his office door locked. The window was locked, too, from the inside. But the top of his head was blown off—and he didn't have no gun of his own there. See what I'm getting at? And here's another thing. They never found no bullet—not in the wall and not in his chair. Not in that room at all, though his brains had been blown out all over the place in there. It stumped everyone in town who it could be that done the killing. Excepting my mama, that is. She knew what happened and who done it and why there wasn't no bullet found. And then she died that very same month."

He drained his mug. "You know why?" he asked—rhetorically, I knew.

"I have no idea," I said in a hushed voice.

"You see," went on Shell, "there's a *stipulation*—that's the word—in the conjuring 'contract,' if 'contract' ain't too fancy a word for it. That *stipulation* is that the one who done the conjuring will die a month after the job's done. That's the agreement that was made with Stagger Lee. A person can use that conjuring song, but only *one time* and then never again. The *stipulation* is a life for a life. It's a tough bargain. But some crimes can't be let go of. Something's got to be done. There's got to be an 'avenger of blood,' like the Bible says, when innocent 'blood crieth from the ground.'"

Shell paused and looked up at Violet. "Show him that hat, honey," he said.

Violet placed the hatbox on the floor beside the coffee table on which were set our empty mugs and pie plates. She made a space in the middle of the table, pushing the creamer and sugar bowl off to one side, and then carefully took the lid off the hatbox and withdrew from it *The Hat*. She set it on the table—a once-white, now-yellowed highroller Stetson hat, on the band of which could be discerned an embroidered image, faint but visible, of a smiling dark girl. On the hat I could see small spots, reddish-brown in color, like dried blood. I could feel a tingle run up my spine and the hair on the nape of my neck stand on end as I looked at it. This was—it couldn't be any other—Stagger Lee's very own hat, the one over

99

which he had gunned down Billy Lyons in the Bill Curtis Saloon in St. Louis in 1895. It took my breath away. I reached out to touch it, but Shell extended a cautioning hand and placed it on mine.

"Careful with that," he said. "It ain't no ordinary hat. My grandma filled it with powerful magic."

I withdrew my hand. "That's okay," I said. "It's enough merely to look at it."

A thought occurred to me just then, and looking up into Shell's bruised and battered face, I asked what I probably would never have dreamed to ask him if I hadn't been drinking with him all afternoon.

"Have you thought of using the conjuring song yourself? I mean, like your mother with the judge, with these two cops who've been leaning on you...?"

"No," he said. "Watts and Powers ain't worth my own life for theirs. They ain't worth my spit, really. I mean, if someone was ever really to hurt someone I love or something like that—Violet, for instance—well, then, that'd be a different story. I'd use it then, without feeling bad 'bout it neither. But for this? No, sir, not for this."

I felt relieved by that answer. I can't say I bought what he'd told me about the hat and its magic, but I was relieved, nonetheless.

"Look here," said Shell. "It's late and I ain't going in to work tomorrow or Tuesday—the boss told me to take care of my head and come back on Wednesday. Point is, I'll be here in the morning. It's late and we're woozy from all that whiskey, and there ain't no need for you to go driving back to Washington tonight unless you want to. So, why don't you stay the night? We don't have no guest room, but if you don't mind this sofa you can sleep on it. I'm going to let Violet help me up the stairs to my bed and she'll come back down with some blankets and a pillow for you."

I took him up on the offer, feeling, as he said, quite "woozy" myself from the whiskey. And I had a lot of thoughts to process. I didn't know what to make of all his talk about magic, conjuring, and ghostly retribution, but I saw that both he and Violet took it very seriously indeed. I tended to be a skeptic, but I had to admit his story spooked me. Spooked or not, however, I was too tired to drive back to D.C. So, I slept on that sofa that night and the hat was on the coffee table, not six full feet from where I lay. Before I nodded off, though, I swear I could sense something like vibrations emitting from it and I thought I could discern in the darkness a still darker shadow surrounding it. But I brushed the notion aside and, exhausted, sank into a deep sleep.

When I awoke the next morning, the hat was no longer on the table. It was in the armchair where I had sat the evening before. Shell and his daughter, when they greeted me later in the morning and I asked about it, denied having moved it during the night.

When I returned to D.C., I went over the tapes of Shell's songs and was delighted by how well they had turned out. Colleagues were likewise impressed and there was the suggestion that maybe he should become better known, record more music, go on a circuit, and so on. I called Shell about a week after our taping and put some of these ideas before him to consider, which he said he would do and get back to me. So it was that I visited him three more times over the course of the following four weeks, each time recording previously unheard songs and occasionally re-recording ones he had already put on tape but wasn't happy with how they had come out the first time. And, I like to think, we became friends over that short period. In time we were openly sharing things of a personal nature with one another.

One thing in particular must be mentioned here, because it had everything to do with what was about to happen. His love for his daughter, his only child, eighteen-year-old Violet, was profoundly moving to behold. He doted on her. He hated the fact that she worked late nights on the weekends, cleaning pots and pans in the kitchen at the Ellicott Inn—"a joint for white trash," he called it—to earn extra money to support the household. He knew that Watts and Powers hung out there after hours when they came off duty. He fretted about that because he knew that they knew that Violet was his daughter.

And during those four weeks, I must admit with some shame in retrospect, I pestered him to let me hear that conjuring song. Call it immature of me, which I know it was, but I couldn't let it go. He accepted my persistence with good grace, but he remained adamant that he wouldn't expose me to it. I suggested that maybe he could sing it without the hat around.

"Maybe I could," he said. "But I just ain't going to risk it."

And then, as I've already recounted, I got his surprising phone call. He was finally going to let me record it, after all, and with the hat present. In other words, it was going to be the real thing, an attempted *conjuring*. That thought scared me, I confess, but how could I pass up the chance to see and hear it and to get it all on tape?

Watts and Powers had gone and done the only thing that could ever have moved Shell to compromise his principles about using that song: they had threatened his daughter. He had nowhere, real-istically speaking, to turn; he certainly didn't and couldn't trust the police. In Shell's position, there was no recourse left open to him but to prevent, at any cost, the unthinkable, even if it meant risking his own life. That was the *stipulation*, he had told me. A black man in a white man's world had no reason to trust that world to protect him or his. "They say they're going to 'get' her one night—going to 'have' her," he had told me, and it made my blood run cold. I knew he had no natural way to stop them from doing whatever they pleased. They'd get away with it, sure as hell. He knew that. So, reluctantly, he would use the hat. I had no doubt he'd do it, whether I was there or not.

"You know the shed back of my place?" he asked.

"Yes," I replied. "Down by the creek."

"Violet works tonight," he said. "She won't be 'round to stop me. Meet me at the shed at ten o'clock. There ain't no electricity in it, though. Just an oil lamp. If you want to record that song, you'll need that recorder you got with the batteries."

That night I drove out to Shell's place, my heart pounding and my head filled with anxious thoughts. I pulled up in front of the house shortly before ten o'clock. The streetlamps along New Cut Road gave out only a muted gold-tinged light in the misty darkness. A fog had set in, and the air was clammy. I got out of the car, walked around it to the other side, and gathered up the small recorder from the floor on the passenger's side. I also retrieved a slim "pencil" flashlight from the glove compartment, which I routinely kept there. No outside light was on over the front door or anywhere else on the property, and as I made my way past the white picket fence into his yard I switched on the flashlight.

No dogs appeared to be outdoors at this hour. No humans either. It was deathly quiet, except for the eerie hoot of an owl from somewhere out in the murky woods and the crunch of fallen leaves beneath my shoes.

I made my way around to the back of the house, which bordered on the small running creek, and saw there the wooden shed where we had agreed to meet. It was more of a garage than a shed in its design, large enough to house two automobiles or a tractor—but Shell kept nothing of the sort in it. It had slat-walled sides with windows, and its two wide doors, which opened out like barn doors, stood open now. They faced the back door of the house. I shone the flashlight into the shed and saw tools and tires and other paraphernalia there, but no Shell. In the center, though, there was a sort of table fashioned from two broad planks laid across two stout barrels. I had been in there once before with Shell, on a sunny Sunday afternoon, and at that time there had been no such makeshift table. The table, I guessed, had been put there specifically for tonight's event.

All at once, the light beside the back door of the house came on and I saw Shell come down the back steps and across the yard toward me. He was carrying something in a sack—something that I saw was moving jerkily—and he was wearing the Stetson hat of Stagger Lee on his head.

"You there?" he said in his booming voice.

"Yes, I'm here," I replied.

He came up to where I was standing, and together we went inside the shed. He handed me a pack of matches and gestured to an oil lamp that hung directly above the plank table.

"Light the lamp," he ordered.

I took down the lamp, fumbled with it in the light cast by my slim flashlight, which I had clamped between my teeth, but finally got it lit and rehung on its hook in the rafter. Shell plunked the sack down on the table. There were scrabbling noises coming from it, and it was jerking and shaking. He took off the Stetson and placed it on the table crown down. Then he picked up a metal basin from under the table, about twelve inches in diameter, and set it in front of the hat.

"You go on over there and sit down," he said, pointing.

I looked in the direction he indicated and saw an old wooden straight-back kitchen chair standing in the shadows outside the circle of the oil lamp's flickering amber light.

"And turn off that flashlight," he commanded, which I immediately did.

"You can see and record from there," he went on. "But you're not to say a word and not to react to whatever you see happening over here. If I do this right, you'll see plenty, and it'll probably scare you plenty. It should, but you'll be okay. You just work that recorder of yours and don't do nothing else. *Do not move.*"

He turned his attention to the sack, opened it, and now I saw what was making the scrabbling noise and jerking movements. It was a live rooster which Shell pulled out of the bag by its legs, desperately flailing and struggling to escape. I say it was a "live" rooster, but it wasn't alive for long. Shell held the rooster over the twelve-inch basin and before I could take in what had happened, he had drawn out a wicked-looking knife and severed the bird's head. Then he set about draining the blood into the basin.

When he had done that, he set the carcass aside and, with the same knife he cut open the palm of his left hand. I flinched at the sight, but at the same time I pushed down the "record" and "play" buttons on the small tape recorder and pointed the microphone in the direction of the action.

Shell made a fist with the cut hand, squeezing his own lifeblood into the basin along with the rooster's. When this procedure had been completed, he took out of his pants pocket what looked like a sprig clipped from some plant. He dipped it into the mixed blood and sprinkled it onto the hat of Stagger Lee. As he did so, he began murmuring in what sounded like French. I couldn't make out the words.

The song, or rather the chant, was rhythmic, his voice was low and barely audible, and once or twice I'm certain I heard the name "Lee Shelton" invoked. Or, at least, it struck me as an invocation, because Shell leaned directly over the hat's inner lining whenever he pronounced it, as if he were peering into a pool. The rhythm of his chanting picked up pace and his voice grew louder and more intense.

Again, he sprinkled the blood, and as he did it a third time, I noticed something like a shadow or a dark, smoky cloud forming around the brim of the upside-down Stetson. Shell's chanting stopped at once, and he stepped back from the table and watched as the shadow lengthened and appeared to become denser. The substance became a strange combination of the cloudy and the gelatinous. More appalling still, I heard a sound like a low animal snarl that seemed to come from the form taking shape. Terror seemed to grip me by the scalp and the hand with which I was holding the mic started to tremble furiously. My whole body was rigid and as immobile as I could make it, but I was sweating profusely.

I remained motionless, watching as Shell began, it seemed, to converse with the dark form wavering and glowing darkly before him under the light of the lamp. I thought I distinctly heard the names "Watts" and "Powers" spoken, and then a sibilant voice could be heard speaking, evidently in reply to Shell—a voice that resonated with malice. At that precise instant I dropped the mic and instantly lurched forward to retrieve it.

When I came back up, mic in hand, what I saw was this: the solid form of a man stood on the other side of the table from Shell. He looked like no living man, though, but rather a desiccated corpse, clothed in garments perhaps once fine but now moldy and rotten— a once-crimson vest, now faded and stained, a soiled black coat, a tattered yellow ruffled shirt. He stepped around the table and jangled toward the open doors of the shed. I could see the flash of tarnished mirrors on mud-caked pointed-toed shoes. The mirrors were making the jangling noise. The clammy air in the shed now reeked with a scent like rotting meat and mildew combined. The creature's lower jaw hung open, and when he spoke—because he did speak to Shell in that sibilant whisper I had heard already—his mouth didn't move. The voice merely came up from inside him and through the gaping mouth as if through a trumpet. I could make out nothing that the revenant said, but Shell handed him the hat and, as he did, he said quite clearly:

"When you've done what you're going to do, take this hat back with you to the grave. You're free. We ain't never calling you up here no more. This is the last time for you. You can rest now. Ain't going to disturb you again."

The revenant said nothing. He placed the hat on his moldering head with creaking, shuddering arms and went out into the misty night. I heard the jangling of the mirrors on his shoes as he went, and the crunching they made in the leaves outside. The sounds receded and then were heard no more. He was gone.

Shell placed both his hands on the table to steady himself and, as he did, he let out a deep sigh. He looked drained.

For some time, I couldn't move for the horror that filled my mind, but somehow, after what seemed hours but could only have been moments, I shook the paralysis off and forced myself to get up from the chair.

Shell said, "Violet is free now. Free of both things."

"*Both* things?" I whispered.

"Free of them two who would've hurt her," he replied, standing erect now and facing me. "And free of the temptation to use that conjuring song herself someday. I want her free of that evil thing. It ain't clean, ain't right."

"But you just used it," I protested.

"Yeah, I did," he said. "And I ain't regretting it neither. But I'd regret it if she ever did. You've seen the last of Stagger Lee and that hat. He'll be taking it back to his grave now."

We put out the lamp and walked together to the house. I stayed over that night, still shaken but weary, and before I finally succumbed to sleep, I heard Violet return home around two in the morning and head upstairs.

I knew then that Shell had been right.

Four weeks after these events, I received the news that Shell Dorsey had died suddenly. The medical cause was an aneurysm of the brain. I attended the funeral and, while there, I met the man Violet was soon to marry. Later still, Violet formally granted permission for me to produce an album of recordings of her father's music.

Given how much of it I had recorded, it led to two subsequent albums. I made sure contractually that Violet received a large percentage of all the sales. I have remained in touch with her ever since, and today she is the mother of five children and the grandmother of thirteen.

Just two days after the grim events that occurred in the shed, while Shell still lived, I read in the newspaper about two mysterious murders in the Ellicott City area. Both had occurred in the early hours of the morning. They involved two victims, both of whom had been off-duty police officers, one named Watts and the other Powers. Both incidents had taken place in their individual homes, situated miles apart from one another. The two murders had been committed within the same timeframe. In both cases, no signs of break-in were discovered. The men had been killed in the same fashion—a single bullet to the head. And yet, no bullets were recovered, either from their bodies or from anywhere in their homes. The newspaper compared the killings to a similar murder, that of a judge, that had occurred back in 1938. Beyond that, the police were clueless.

The tape of the conjuring song remains in my possession, under lock and key. For reasons I can't understand myself, I've held on to the cursed thing. But I have never listened to it, and I never will. Before I die, I intend to destroy it.

# Henry

H E REMEMBERED. He always remembered. The scene had made itself indelible.

A summer afternoon more than forty years ago, the two of them strolling southwards hand in hand between the railroad tracks and the river. Very much in love.

They pause and look up at the brown-shingled cottage. It looks like a miniature castle set high on the summit of the wooded hill. Their free hands shade their eyes against the dazzling sunlight, refracted by the house's enormous arched window.

"The first thing I'll do when we move in there," Frank Bayliss had said to Jenny, "is take off those damn silly shingles, so the place can shine again like it used to."

"If you did that," Jenny had replied, brushing from her eyes a straying strand of shimmering blonde hair, "it would resemble Sir Launcelot's castle—you know the one I mean—what's its name?—in the Arthurian stories… 'Joyous Gard,' wasn't it?"

"Yes. That's what it was called. Joyous Gard."

"It would look like Joyous Gard. A bit shrunken in size, I suppose, but nevertheless…"

They had been well aware of the absurdity of their conversation at the time. It would never happen, they knew, but they enjoyed the romantic game notwithstanding.

Yes, he remembered that afternoon in June of 1921 with an unusual clarity. He remembered that conversation word for word. He remembered how beautiful Jenny had looked as she gazed up at the old house. That day replayed itself in his mind countless times throughout the subsequent years, even sometimes in his dreams. And Jenny's loveliness had never diminished in his eyes, even after the gold of her hair had gradually changed to silvery gray and wrinkles had creased her once-firm flesh.

"It would be joyous to live there," she had said. "You would come

108

home in the evening, after a long day of doing whatever you'd been doing, and I'd be there to greet you at the front door. Then I'd show you around to look at whatever I'd been busy doing that day."

He had liked the sound of that.

But more than four decades separated that lazy summer day from the present. In the intervening years, he and Jenny had been remarkably happy together. They were wedded a year after that summer stroll. The only profound disappointment they had known in all their years of marriage had been her inability to bear children. But they had been philosophical about it. Every marriage has some sorrow to bear, after all. Why should theirs be an exception? A far lesser disappointment, but disappointing nonetheless, had been Bayliss's transfer to upstate New York in 1948. Overall, however, they had spent their years contentedly together. They had never quarreled—unless the occasional disagreement or fleeting irritation could be counted. In that, as in many other ways, they had been blessed as few other couples have.

Then it all changed, much too rapidly, much too terribly...

That long-ago conversation between the tracks and the rolling Patapsco hadn't been the first time that Frank Bayliss and Jenny had joked about someday occupying the Gothic revival "castle" on the heights, with its crenelated roof and church-like windows. The strange old place was on full display up there, visible to anyone heading across the bridge into town from the east. In earlier times, when passenger trains still travelled the route, the place had been pointed out to sightseeing travelers. Around the turn of the century, though, one of its less imaginative owners had covered the house's original bright stucco and granite exterior with dingy brown shingles, and its attractiveness had consequently diminished. It was this unfortunate, lackluster addition that Bayliss disliked so much and rarely failed to mention when discussing the place. The couple had never really believed they would ever live in that house. It was a wistful and hopeless amusement they shared. And as it had happened, the couple had lived out their entire married life in other homes.

But then, in 1963—to Bayliss's utter amazement—he found himself in a position to purchase the property for a song. And he did. He bought it.

He knew the place must be worth much more than what he eventually agreed to pay; but agree to pay he did. When it first came to his attention that Castello di Torcrescenza—as the home had been grandly named by its first occupant, a Frenchman with the odd Mesopotamian-sounding name of "Marduk"—was up for sale, he doubted it would be affordable even for someone of his relatively substantial means. Still, he told himself, nothing ventured, nothing gained. So, having made all the necessary arrangements beforehand, he set out on a Monday in early March to tour the property. It had been archly named after the Castello di Torcrescenza in the ancient city of Rome. It overlooked, after all, another city, this one in Maryland, that—like Rome—had been built on seven hills: "the ancient village of Ellicott City," as H. L. Mencken had once referred to it. It was a lovely, single-story chateau, constructed in the early 1830s, on a spot whimsically named Tarpeian Rock—christened by the same bygone wits, no doubt, who had also dubbed the stream flowing through the middle of the town the Tiber.

Bayliss and Jenny had grown up as neighbors on one of those seven hills, south of town. After Bayliss's transfer to Rochester, he and Jenny had had every intention of returning to their hometown, once he retired, to live out the remainder of their earthly days there. As it turned out, though, it was Jenny who came home first, and only after she had no remainder of earthly days left. She died of lung cancer in 1961, one year before Bayliss was due to retire. She was buried in the town's Catholic cemetery. Bayliss's one great wish was to live as near to that bit of land where he would eventually lie down beside her. With no offspring, he claimed for himself no binding ties to anywhere or anyone else; and since he had no expectation of going anywhere beyond this earthly realm, he wanted to be planted in the town where he—they—had bloomed. It was then that the surprising opportunity had presented itself to him: he could purchase Castello di Torcrescenza and occupy his and Jenny's long-ago dream home. It felt to him as though this was the work of Fortune, even though his reason habitually eschewed signs and wonders, and to buy the property would be the fulfillment of a sort of crazy promise he had made to Jenny. It was surely pure sentiment to feel this way, he realized, but he had little else to look forward to in life.

110

# Henry

Unlike Jenny who had retained a sincere, dignified, and quiet faith throughout her life, Bayliss was a nominal Catholic. When she was alive, he had attended Mass to please her, and he never once gainsaid her faith during all their years together. But Bayliss had no personal belief in an existence beyond the grave, and any concept he might have entertained once of a benevolent God had been eroded in the wake of Jenny's sufferings. He accepted the inevitable fact of his own death, and yet he also deeply feared it. He didn't fear hell for the simple fact that he didn't believe in it. But the thought of absolute oblivion—of his own ultimate nothingness—truly terrified him. He told himself that this "existential angst" was ridiculous; after all, once he no longer existed, he would no longer care that he no longer existed. But he couldn't persuade his gut with such syllogisms, no matter how reasonable they sounded. And although he believed that Jenny, once dead, no longer existed in any form, he had no desire to share that same nonexistence.

Sometimes his equivocation, indeed his cowardice, shamed him. He felt it showed contemptible disloyalty on his part. But he was honest enough to acknowledge this unwelcome truth about himself. There was no escaping death, he knew, so he had little choice but to accept his moral flaccidity and get on as stoically as he could by honoring Jenny's memory instead. Anyone who knew him on a casual basis would never have suspected that this fearful, craven side of him even existed. Those few friends who knew him well might detect an occasional wandering in his thoughts, a momentary distraction, an expression of fleeting sadness, as if he were mourning his loss—entirely natural, they might surmise, given how greatly he and Jenny had been in love. But no one could have guessed the morbidity of his true feelings.

And so it was that he remembered. And that remembering was both a source of consolation and of humiliation.

He had, of course, assumed he would be up against some stiff competition in the purchase of Castello di Torcrescenza. He couldn't have been more wrong in that assumption. He was astonished to discover that he was, in fact, the only prospective buyer. Others had looked over the property with the thought of buying, but they had all said pretty much the same curious thing about it to the realtors after their tours: there was *something* about the place that unsettled them. They all expressed that they were taken with its architectural beauty, its location, the wooded surroundings, and especially the great room with its two-story-high arched window that looked out over the racing river and valley below. They all declared how marvelous was the impressive rose garden on the west side of the house, with its elaborate maze and cast-iron gates. But in the end, even with these alluring features, not one of them opted to buy. The price had dropped twice by the time Bayliss had come down from Rochester, looked it over, and—amazingly!—signed the papers. Whatever the *something* that had decided the rest against purchasing it may have been, Bayliss felt no such misgivings. He felt no qualms himself and he didn't care about the qualms of others. He felt only gratification with his good luck.

Before returning to Rochester to settle things there, Bayliss paid a visit to the current owner. He had memories of her and her husband, still in their prime when he and Jenny were in their twenties and coveting their home. Now she was a widow in her late seventies, no longer able to walk on her own, tended to by nurses and other sundry helpers, and got about mostly in a wheelchair that looked older than herself. Her imposing name—which matched her equally imposing demeanor—was Madeline-Louisa Champayne Snowden Clark. Although Bayliss remembered her, he had never spoken with her until now; but she was "old Ellicott City" and so was he, even if he had lived away for so long, and he knew the proprieties, the prejudices, and the right words to use in such interchanges. And his family connections helped. The two instantly established a rapport.

Like Bayliss and his wife, Mrs. Clark and her late husband had had no children. "The castle," as she chose to call it, had become too much for her to handle now, even with the hired assistance of Dora, her housekeeper, the rotating nurses, her two occasional groundskeepers—a pair of brothers named Bill and Bob, and a burly fifty-something fellow called Corky who was handyman, electrician, plumber, and errand-runner rolled into one. Bayliss would get to know all of them in time, except for the nurses. Mrs. Clark had reluctantly decided, after much persuasion from her relations, to take up residence at a nearby elite home for the aged and to sell the home. No one else in the family wanted the residence, and with no one to whom she might bequeath it, she had given in to the pressure and put it up for sale.

"I'm glad it's going to be in the hands of someone of old local stock," she confided to Bayliss after they had already chatted for an hour or so, seated before the high window, the late morning sunlight flooding into the great room. "If you'll permit me, I'll come by and visit you after you've moved in."

"You'd always be more than welcome," Bayliss assured her.

"Don't make too many changes," she said. "When I see it again, I do want to recognize it."

Bayliss told her he would maintain the home with the greatest integrity.

Then Mrs. Clark leaned forward in her wheelchair, and looking intently into his eyes, said solemnly, "There are a few things you really should know about this dear old place. A few little secrets, shall we call them. I'm probably the only one who would even dare to bring them up to you. Others around town know some of the stories, but I doubt they'd bring them up to you. And the realtors were probably too afraid of scaring off a potential buyer, I dare say, to tell you anything about them if you didn't ask first."

Bayliss's curiosity was piqued.

"Oh? Why would that be?"

"It's a bit sensitive, perhaps," Mrs. Clark went on. "And in the cold light of day, some things just seem too silly to most modern people."

"Well, the realtors certainly never hinted about anything here of a sensitive nature or anything likely to 'scare me off,'" said Bayliss.

"Well, as I say, they wouldn't have." Mrs. Clark drew herself up in her Edwardian-era chariot; the downturned corners of her mouth and uplifted nose communicated scorn. "They're 'old Ellicott City' themselves, but they're as worthless as tits on a boar hog if you want any real information about real estate."

Bayliss grinned at the crude analogy she used; he hadn't heard it since he had left the region. His mother had used it frequently.

113

Mrs. Clark went on. "Every old residence of worth has a 'biography,' as I'm sure you know. Any house of significant age has a history—and sometimes a secret history, too. This one does. But it's nothing to worry about, really. I don't want to sound dramatic when I talk about these things. There are just a few small details you should know about when the time comes."

"You don't have a resident ghost lurking about the house, do you?" Bayliss said this with a smile.

She merely smiled back—rather enigmatically, he thought. He wasn't sure whether it was a "no" smile or a "yes" smile. More disconcertingly, she winked at him and tapped an index finger against the side of her nose, as if she assumed they were both engaged in some intrigue.

"Well, we'll have ourselves a good discussion once you're all moved in," she said. "But I want to put just two words in your ear right now, while I have you here. You should take them to heart."

As they were conversing, Bayliss was glancing through the great arched window. Its panes were of plain glass, with a marvelous view of the river, woods, and beyond. But what caught his attention at that instant was a white cat walking along the edge of the ridge. From where they sat, he could also see the very spot where he and Jenny had long ago made their imaginary "plans" to occupy this very home.

The cat paused and batted at a passing insect.

"Yes?" he said. "What two words are they?"

"If you find that he's hanging about the property, you mustn't let Henry come indoors," Mrs. Clark said. "He's very bad, very disruptive, and if he gets inside, he's bound to make another horrific mess. We had one hell of a time getting him out the time he did get in—pardon my language. Lucky for me, Father McManus—the priest over at St. Paul's—came by and he said a Mass and that did the trick."

Bayliss noticed that she had also been watching the cat's antics through the window.

"Got him out, did he?"

"With a great deal of effort, he did," said Mrs. Clark. "He's a good priest. He knows his business."

Bayliss wasn't sure how a priest's expertise, much less a Mass, was related to the apprehension of a cat that had gotten indoors, but he let the curious remark go without making any comment.

"I take it that Henry doesn't belong to the household here, then."

"Good Lord, no," replied Mrs. Clark. "He used to show up here from time to time, but outside around the garden mostly. He's a thoroughgoing scoundrel—a monster, really, if that's not too strong a word for him. He just comes and goes—you never know when he'll pop up. He might disappear for a while, then show up again just when you thought he'd gone for good. Heaven knows why he lingers around this place and the maze. Ed—that was my late husband's name—Ed was the one who named him 'Henry.' He named him after 'Henri,' which was the first name of the man who had this place built back in the eighteen-thirties."

"Monsieur Marduk," said Bayliss. "The mysterious Frenchman."

"Yes. Mister Marduk—such an odd name, even for a foreigner," sniffed Mrs. Clark. She lowered her voice to a confidential whisper and added, "Some say he wasn't really French at all, you know."

"Not French?"

"Not French. Something that starts with an 'A'—Armenian, maybe...? Abyssinian? Assyrian? Albanian? Andalusian? Definitely not Argentinian or Australian or Austrian..."

She was staring somewhat trancelike at the cat cavorting on the ridge, absorbed for the moment in the subject of nationalities beginning with the letter "A."

"Ah, I have it," she said, her eyes brightening. "Algerian."

"Algerian," repeated Bayliss. "I might have guessed Assyrian— *ancient* Assyrian, what with that name."

"But as for Henry," she continued in her usual tone of voice, oblivious to Bayliss's last remark, "luckily enough for us he disappeared after Father McManus's Mass. Ed said it was an omen, a portent. He was as hardheaded as a man can be, my Ed—you remember, he owned the hardware store downtown, right across from the old train station. He was no-nonsense, tough as leather. Like Corky, our handyman, who used to work for him. Anyway, my point is that Ed was a practical man. But he had a superstitious streak a mile wide. He always said the hardware store was haunted, you know, and I see no reason now to doubt he was right, although I used to laugh at him for saying so back then. After Henry got in here and made such a terrific mess, I stopped laughing at his superstitions. Ed said Henry was an omen. And wouldn't you know it? He died only a few months later. Anyway, Father McManus shooed Henry off, thank God. But that doesn't mean he's gone for good. He seems to have a habit of showing up again after a lengthy hiatus. So, be on your guard."

But Bayliss could plainly see the cat, alive and frisky, just outside the window. He was sure Mrs. Clark could, too. If he had gone anywhere, it certainly wasn't "for good"—there he was, gamboling on the lawn to his little heart's content. Perhaps, Bayliss thought, Mrs. Clark wasn't "all there," that she was a bit addled. Maybe this was an indication why her relations had urged her to live at the sanitorium. He politely said nothing to betray his concern, however.

"Well, I'll certainly try to keep him out, if he's as naughty as all that," he said.

"Don't just *try* to keep him out. Whatever you do, if you learn he's anywhere about on the grounds, don't let him get inside *at all*. Otherwise, you'll regret it as sure as God made little green apples."

She was quite energized and insistent, gripping the armrests of her wheelchair tightly as she spoke.

"It's one of the two things you should absolutely be most careful about here. That and keeping that door in the basement sealed."

"The door in the basement?" he asked. "What door in the basement?"

She relaxed her grip on the chair, sighed, and sat back, half closing her eyes. "The door in the basement downstairs. The one that's all sealed up."

"I don't recall a door in the basement," said Bayliss. "The realtors didn't point out anything like that to me."

She harrumphed.

"Typical," she said. "Well, it's not very noticeable, I'll admit. Maybe they forgot to show it to you. It's in the corner on the east side, right next to the furnace, out of the light. You'll see it if you look for it. But you won't be able to open it. It's been sealed shut and painted over. You'll just see an outline—it looks like part of the wall now, but it's visible—and you'll see some words carved on it, if you look hard. Anyway, there's an old tunnel on the other side of that door that's been there ever since the house was built. After Monsieur Marduk's time, it was used for the Underground Railroad. It supposedly leads out to a path that goes straight down to the river. I never checked any of that out and neither did my husband. We never had the nerve to—I told you that Ed was superstitious. He just had the door painted over to match the wall. Anyway, you'd be wise to keep that door sealed up like we did. There are reasons, but we can talk more about it when you've moved in."

"More ghosts?" said Bayliss.

"Could be, could be," she said.

She suddenly looked exhausted. She waved her hand, as if to indicate it was time for Bayliss to take his leave. "That's enough for now. I'm feeling terribly weary and need a lie-down."

Outside the window, the cat had vanished.

Bayliss said his goodbyes, promised to let her know once he had moved in, and left. Further discussion about either the door in the basement or about "Henry" would have to wait.

As he drove away, he reflected, a little guiltily, that he had been only partially attentive to what Mrs. Clark had to tell him. He had been distracted by his own thoughts. During their conversation, he had resolved to do two things, both prompted by what he regarded as promises made to Jenny long ago. He would have the brown shingles stripped off the house as soon as he could, and he would rechristen the property "Joyous Gard."

Five months had passed before Bayliss was able to establish himself fully at "Joyous Gard." Between March and August, Madeline-Louisa Champayne Snowden Clark had made her own drawn-out transition to her new accommodations. In the process, she had bestowed centuries-old antiques and heirlooms to sundry members of her family, excluding those, of course, to whom she was no longer on speaking terms. Details surrounding the suitable distribution of property had to be handled delicately and diplomatically, and that had taken time and patience and, in fact, it had involved more than a little family intrigue and strife. Nonetheless, the allocation of valuables was finalized, hurt feelings were meliorated as best they could be, and Mrs. Clark left the home vacant for Frank Bayliss's arrival. His movers unloaded his possessions in early July, and by early August he had—with the help of Corky, the handyman, and Dora, the housekeeper, both of whom he had arranged to employ—unpacked and put in place every item he had brought. He could finally relax in his new home.

In all that time, despite her expressed wish in March, Mrs. Clark did not come to pay a visit, and he didn't think to pay her a visit either. The matters of "Henry" and the basement door had been pushed to the back of his mind, concentrated as he was on the move and its immediate aftermath. He had, of course, been to the basement many times during the period of settling in and he had noted the sealed door near the furnace. Its appearance was not prepossessing or even interesting. It looked like nothing more than an oblong outline in the wall, a bit rounded at the top. There was no discernible lock or handle. Just the outline, painted over with white paint. The surface was flush with the wall, but he could see that a cross had been carved on it, and below the cross an odd, squarish arrangement of carved letters in Latin. These had also been painted over, but not obscured. The thing was a peculiarity, but he had lived in old houses before and knew they often contained curiosities. Bayliss gave it no more thought.

Bill and Bob, the two brothers who did the gardening, came by every Tuesday and Friday to tend to the maze, hedges, and flowerbeds. Corky was around most days, at least for an hour or two, tinkering with things. Dora was there faithfully, Monday through Friday, from nine in the morning until she considered her daily work done. The routines at Joyous Gard quickly fell into a natural rhythm. Outside the home, Bayliss made successful efforts to reconnect with old friends and relations, and very soon he was acclimated to the slow and easy pace of Ellicott City life. He became a daily presence around town, an old thin respectable-looking man with white hair, who used a cane, wore an old-fashioned fedora in rain or shine, dressed in tweed in the cold months and seersucker in the warm, and was never seen without a tie.

118

Henry

But Bayliss, for all his sociability, didn't contact Mrs. Clark, and in November, just three days after the assassination in Dallas, news reached him that he couldn't visit her even if he wished to do so. Madeline-Louisa Champayne Snowden Clark had taken a turn for the worse and had died in her sleep. Bayliss was saddened to hear of her passing and, being conscientious, he berated himself for not having gone to see her before she died.

He attended the funeral. It was there by the graveside, following the burial, just as a flurry of snow began to fall, that Father McManus came over to him and pressed into his palm an envelope. He glanced at it and saw that his name was scrawled on it in spidery letters, as if the writer's hand had been shaky.

"It's for you," the priest told him. "It was left on her bedside table. I thought I might see you here, so I brought it. You should have it."

Bayliss had become acquainted with the priest and liked him. He appreciated the fact that Father McManus never chided him for not attending Mass, though he knew Bayliss was nominally Catholic. They had first met when Jenny had been buried in the same grave-yard.

"Something about Henry, maybe," Bayliss said with half a smile.

"So, she told you about Henry, did she?" said Father McManus.

"Yes—and the Mass you said at the house for him, too," replied Bayliss. "A pretty strange story, if you don't mind my saying."

"Oh?" Father McManus shot back. "Why's that?"

"Well, I mean... a Mass for a cat," said Bayliss, openly smiling now. "That's a bit unusual, isn't it? Maybe for a dog—a dog's a man's best friend, after all. But—for a cat?"

The priest raised an eyebrow, genuinely surprised by the remark, it seemed. But he had no opportunity to say another word on the matter. An elderly couple had come over to speak with him, and he had no choice but to turn away from Bayliss.

Bayliss carelessly put the letter in the pocket of his overcoat and went home to Joyous Gard. And just as he had forgotten to visit Mrs. Clark while she was still alive, he now forgot the letter in his overcoat. It remained there unopened for another five months.

It was at night that Bayliss felt the loneliness most keenly.

It had been this way with him since Jenny's death. He had found ways to distract himself most evenings—occasional dinners with friends and relatives, the nightly news, a television program that might catch his interest, his record collection, novels. But it was the late nocturnal and early morning hours when the loneliness entered him like oil soaking into his bones. It was more irksome to him than his rheumatism. He couldn't sleep soundly because of it. It was wearing him down bit by interminable bit.

And then there were aspects of the old house that he hadn't thought through sufficiently when, optimistically, he had decided to buy it. It creaked and groaned and made other odd noises like old houses tend to do, but these were amplified in the vacuity of his solitude. The home's seclusion and its Gothic appearance—which delighted him during the daylight hours—contributed, in the loneliest hours of night, to a sense of dereliction, of an abysmal absence.

The absence of what—of *whom*?

He knew perfectly well: the absence of Jenny. She was *so* absent that she was a presence to him. She wasn't there, and so to make up for that fact he would talk to her as if she were, sometimes off and on for hours. He had put her portrait above the fireplace in the great room—the same room where the two-story-high arched window looked out over "that river of dark source," to borrow a phrase of Thomas Cole's that he had read somewhere—and on those nights of sleeplessness he would place lit votive lights before it. There he would sit and speak to her painted features. In those moments he could almost feel her palpability, although he knew the fleeting sense was only the product of his achingly tired and troubled brain. There was something residually Catholic about these actions of his; they were devotional in nature: flickering candles accompanied by prayer of sorts. Rationally, he knew his behavior was pointless and pathetic. He knew she was nowhere, gone. Entirely unreachable. But reason had little to do with it, especially in his sleep-deprived condition in this empty, dark house, all by himself. He spoke aloud to her, his reason suspended. He summoned her in his imagination, though he knew she no longer existed. Worse, still, he dreaded joining her in her nonexistence. Her perpetual oblivion was more than he could bear to contemplate for very long; the thought of his own eventual cancellation froze his spine. He honestly confessed all that to her, too, how he didn't want to die, didn't want to lose himself as he had lost her, and that he was profoundly remorseful that he didn't desire death, even if by it he might share her nonexistence—and could she ever forgive him such cowardly falseness to their bond?

His penitence gave him no solace.

In the daytime, when his mind was reasoning soundly again, he pushed such shameful irrationality out of his head. He visited Jenny's grave regularly, every few days leaving fresh flowers on it. In the warm months, the flowers came from his own garden. But there, too, he would speak to her, in more rational terms to be sure, and tell her the daily goings-on at Joyous Gard, tell her of his plans to strip off those brown shingles, tell her the news of the world—she had always been engaged with current events.

Once or twice, he stopped by Mrs. Clark's grave, as well, and left a flower or two on it. And it was while he stood by her grave one April afternoon that he suddenly remembered the letter in his overcoat that Father McManus had passed on to him—Mrs. Clark's last words to him. Cursing himself for his selfish neglect, he drove back to Joyous Gard, went without delay to the closet in the front hall, took out the coat, found the sealed letter there, and headed with it in hand to his small study adjacent to the great room. He sat down at his rolltop desk, hastily slit open the envelope with a letter opener, and took out six neatly folded lavender-hued pages, on the front and back of which was Mrs. Clark's thin, wobbly script in purple ink. It was difficult for him to make out her handwriting at first, but with some effort he eventually deciphered it. And what he read took him aback.

*My dear Mr. Bayliss*, the letter began,

*I very much regret that my poor health in recent months has kept me indoors. I had so hoped to visit you after your move, to see the old place under its new management, and to continue our talk begun last spring. I suppose you have been frightfully busy, getting things in order there, and hence could spare little of your valuable time to come and visit with an old, sick lady like myself. I hoped you might, but I fully understand why you couldn't.*

Bayliss bit his lip. His conscience was pricked by these words, just as he knew that she knew it would be. He read on.

*Be that as it may, I would be remiss not to lay out for you as best I can those few things about which you should be apprised concerning Castello di Torcrescenza's history, and also why I brought up in our conversation that sealed door downstairs in the basement and the matter of "Henry," our resident ghost.*

"Resident ghost"! All at once it dawned on Bayliss that "Henry" hadn't been a reference to the cat outside the window at all. That was why, it now hit him like a two-by-four, that his mention of the cat to Father McManus at the funeral had elicited such a look of mild surprise. Bayliss had simply assumed that the cat and "Henry" were one and the same. "Henry," then, was the name that Mrs. Clark's deceased husband had bestowed on... well, on what exactly?

*First, a tiny shred of history. I can only tell you what very little I know, and it really is quite meager. Ed, my late husband, and I never bothered to pursue it deeply, alas. But perhaps some records exist somewhere that might back up what I will relate. I must leave that sort of research in your hands.*

*As you know, the house was built by Monsieur Henri Marduk back in the early 1830s. I suspect that "Marduk" might have been a pseud-onym, although I can't guess why he would have adopted one. Even for an Algerian, that name is no doubt unusual. But at any rate, he was a mysterious figure and only lived in the house until he went missing in 1850 and was never heard from again. There are stories about him, though, rather unsavory ones. I don't know how true any of them might be, frankly. He was said to have abducted young women, both black and white, always poor and easily missed. It may all be hogwash. According to the tales, he did unspeakable things to them, so unspeak-able evidently that no one can tell you what any of those unspeakable things were. But it's said that he murdered them all and took their corpses down through the tunnel behind the basement door, which led to the river below, and disposed of them there. Some say the number of missing girls was around seven, others put it in the tens, and some say it was a hundred or more. I think it's probably balderdash, but perhaps there's a grain of truth in it, that there was murder involved and some girls went missing and the two were connected. I think that may be the case because, during his life, Marduk was increasingly loathed around here and, as I said, he just plain disappeared one day. There are tales about that, of course, that have to do with black magic and whatnot. I suspect the real story is less sensational than that. I'd be willing to bet he just skipped town (he had plenty of money), changed his name, and fled out west or back to Europe.*

*After that, his furniture and goods were sold off, as was Castello di Torcrescenza. Apparently, the rumors about its evil past had no effect on the sale. It was the Catholic Church that purchased it and used it for a while as a rectory. When St. Paul's built a new rectory in 1857, the house was purchased by a man named Burgess. He was involved in the Underground Railroad, and that tunnel in the basement was put to good use, it's said.*

*It was early in this century, however, sometime around 1905 I believe, that the ghost stories started up. Sounds in the basement were said to be heard by the occupants. Some said they even heard screams in the night, echoing from behind the tunnel door, the screams of young women who sounded as if they were in agony. Laughter was supposedly heard, too. The owner turned to the Church for help, and a priest performed a ritual of exorcism. I guess that it was then that the carvings were etched into the door, the cross and those Latin words. You must have noticed them. They look like this:*

*SATOR*
*AREPO*
*TENET*
*OPERA*
*ROTAS*

*I asked Father McManus about those words once. He looked them up and told me it was a very old sign. If you rearrange the letters, he showed me, they come out looking like this:*

```
           P
           A
           T
   A   E   O
           R
P A T E R N O S T E R
           O
   O   S   A
           T
           E
           R
```

*"Pater Noster" is "Our Father" in Latin. But you know that, of course. So, it's the invocation of a prayer, the Lord's Prayer to be exact. And the leftover "A" and "O" are "Alpha" and "Omega," and they refer to God. And the whole ingenious thing comes out in the form of a cross. So, it was a sign of protection, meant to ward off evil. Whoever engraved those words and the cross over it understood a thing or two, Father McManus told us. Ed and I kept that door sealed and covered it over with coats of whitewash. We weren't about to disturb anything on the other side of it. I told you Ed was superstitious, but I think he was right not to meddle with that door.*

*And we also had Henry to contend with. As I told you when you came to visit last March, my husband called him "Henry" after Henri Marduk, although neither of us truly believed it was the ghost of Henri Marduk. But I am getting ahead of myself; I must begin at the beginning, as the King of Hearts said to the White Rabbit. Going back in my mind, I can't quite recall when Henry first showed himself to us. It wasn't long after we moved in; of that, I'm sure. At most it was a year after that.*

*He seemed to frequent the garden, the maze in particular. That's where we would see him, catching only fleeting glimpses of him. He would run when he was spotted, or "glide" might be a better word for it. And he would leap and—how can I describe it?—"caper" seems like the best description to me. He would dash into the maze, and he could bound over the hedges, some of them higher than a man's head, just like Spring-heeled Jack.*

*How can I describe his appearance? He was cloaked like a monk, but it was more like a dark shadow or cloud that encased his figure than a cloak made of fabric. And his face; well, he had many faces. I can't put it into words, so I won't try. Even that might be too much of a description because we only saw him in glimpses as he dashed by, after all. Our gardeners saw him, too, and threatened to quit more than once. But then he disappeared for a long spell, and we didn't see him again for years. The gardeners calmed down and stayed on. Dora was never afraid of him, I believe. She's a strong type of woman, but then Henry was always seen outside when he was seen, and she was always indoors.*

*Until he got into the house, that is. Right before he did, we started seeing him again around the maze. It was wintertime, and Bill and Bob, the gardeners, weren't around for it, thankfully. We kept seeing him outside for days, flitting around and disappearing just when you thought you'd finally get a good look at him. That's when Ed started saying that Henry was some kind of portent. He thought it was a sign that something bad was going to happen. I tried to laugh it off, but as I told you, Ed died not many months after these occurrences.*

*Once we caught sight of Henry pressed up against the kitchen window, peering in. It was night and he was just a shadow, but his palms—I won't ever forget them—were flat against the panes, all white and long-fingered. He was there just for an instant. My husband ran outside, but he was gone before he could reach him. I think it was the protective instinct on Ed's part to go after him in the dark. Normally, Ed wasn't terribly courageous, but Henry shook him up a bit and Ed just reacted.*

*It was Christmastime when Henry managed to get inside. We had a twelve-foot Christmas tree erected in the great room and lots of trimming all round the house, evergreen branches and the like, and a large crèche on the mantel. He got inside, though, and we never did find out how; but it might have been when we were bringing in the greens. The first we knew he was inside it was late at night, after we had gone to bed. The house was dark, we didn't have pets, but we heard a scampering sound out in the great room. We thought it might be a burglar. Ed* grabbed a flashlight and the handgun and went into the room and there he was. No mistaking, it was Henry. Then he simply vanished, darting into the kitchen and disappearing. Scared us both, but somehow, we went back to sleep, albeit with all the lights turned on. The following night, however, we had much the same experience.

The third night was far worse than the previous two. It was as if a whirlwind came through the place. Trimming was thrown every which way—we came into the great room and stood gawking as things went flying about, including the crèche, which was smashed to pieces right before our eyes. We couldn't see Henry. He didn't manifest himself. But there was no doubt in our minds that it was his doing. Last of all, our twelve-foot-high Christmas tree was literally lifted off the ground and flung with great force against the fireplace. Thank goodness there had been no fire laid there earlier; if there had been live embers in the hearth, we might have lost the house that night. That's when we called Father McManus, who was good enough to come and say the rites and a Mass. After that, Henry disappeared. Things went back to normal. Until Ed's death, that is, and I remembered what he had said about it being a sign of something bad to come.

Anyway, although he's not been around for a long while, Henry may come back. Maybe he won't, but he did before. So, stay on the look-out. Be vigilant.

The letter was signed in formal style with her full name: Madeline-Louisa Champayne Snowden Clark.

Bayliss folded it slowly, returned it to its envelope, and sat back in his office chair, fingering his tie with his left hand, and tapping the top of the desk with the forefinger of his right, lost in thought. From where he sat, he could gaze out the window at the entrance to the maze. Bill and Bob were outside, at work among the rose bushes. The sun was shining. Birds sang. A soft, sweet April breeze was blowing in from the west. And although everything outside seemed at that moment to exude a paradisal peace and tranquility, the unsettling contents of the letter and the mental weariness induced by his nights of sleeplessness combined to leave him feeling drained and despondent. He was starting to regret what was looking more and more to him to have been a precipitous move. In earlier times, he might have considered the history and associations attached to the house entertaining, but he felt that his life had disintegrated gradually since Jenny's death. Her presence would, he had no doubt, have made Mrs. Clark's accounts seem lighter. Perhaps he might even have been amused by them. Jenny had had that way about her. She had effortlessly relieved his ills and comforted him. But she wasn't here; she no longer existed. And the romantic spell of Joyous Gard, which had enthralled him for so many years, had diminished so critically that it was now as nonexistent for him as she was.

🐦

Still, he had the dingy brown shingles removed and the home's exterior sanded and buffed and repainted a gentle shade of off-white over the summer. Now the cottage shone on the hill as it hadn't done in decades, like a miniature castle from a Gothic tale. This transformation did cheer him somewhat, but his nights of sleeplessness continued.

His physician urged him to use sleeping pills and he did. They helped and he slept better. Even so, their effect was limited. He still had long vigils before Jenny's portrait in the dead of night, he still spoke to her even as the sense of her absence weighed upon him, and he still experienced gripping moments of anxiety. He couldn't prevent himself from dwelling on the subject of death. It crept into his thoughts at every opportunity, through every channel, spoiling every joy, leaving him moody and disconsolate. He confided in his physician and asked him if he thought he should go to a therapist. His physician, who was older than he was by two years, didn't think highly of psychologists and psychiatrists. He told Bayliss that he didn't need a therapist—he just needed to relax more, maybe buy a puppy, maybe find a lady friend, and eat more protein-rich foods. He recommended the "Jack LaLanne Breakfast," along with moderate exercise—"Nothing too stressful. No jumping jacks..."

He also told Bayliss that his heart was beating irregularly.

"You're not getting any younger," he told him, as if that declaration were news and not a cliché. "Stop worrying yourself to death. People do, you know."

"Do what?" Bayliss asked.

"Worry themselves to death," said his doctor. "So, don't."

This had made Bayliss question whether the doctor wanted him to worry about worrying himself to death in addition to the worrying he was already doing. That had made the physician laugh.

"Just don't stress that ticker too much," he said, "and you'll be fine. You're still grieving your wife's death, that's all. And we old people get depressed easily enough as it is. Hang in there and you'll be over the worst of it before too long. Take my advice: do some stretching and eat a Jack LaLanne Breakfast each morning—that'll lift your spirits."

Bayliss did take the doctor's advice, including the egg and beef breakfast. But he didn't buy a puppy and he certainly didn't go looking for a lady friend. He was noticed by more than one widow in town who entertained fond hopes of finding a new companion in life, but he knew he wasn't ready to go down that road and probably never would be. Nevertheless, the physician's advice aside, Bayliss's inner world was as bleak as ever.

Mrs. Clark's letter still weighed on him. He read it more than once and he ventured to ask Dora about "the Henry incident." She confirmed the account but was unwilling to say what it was she thought had caused such destruction in the house. Yes, she told him, she had seen the mess after the event and, of course, it had fallen to her and Corky to get most of it cleaned up. She remembered that the priest had come over and said Mass. That was all. No speculation, just a tacit acknowledgement that Mr. and Mrs. Clark had experienced something that had scared them. She said that they had spoken to her about "Henry" and that Bill and Bob had claimed to see a ghost in the garden, but she had never seen any ghost.

Bayliss approached Corky, but Corky merely wrote off the whole Christmastime event as some sort of accident and said he didn't believe in "spooks." He didn't know what had made all the fuss in the house, but he wasn't about to start believing in spirits to explain it.

That left Father McManus, and all he said about it to Bayliss, when asked, was that Mrs. Clark's account fit the facts as he knew them, that he had indeed performed his duties, and that the prob-

Henry

lems had subsequently stopped. And that was all that Bayliss could get out of any of them in the way of confirmation.

🐦

Summer changed to fall. Leaves began to accumulate in the garden, and Bayliss asked Dora whether Bill and Bob planned to rake them up. He hadn't seen the two gardeners in days and the grounds were beginning to look unkempt.

To his surprise, she told him that the two brothers had quit for good.

"Why didn't someone inform me about it?" he asked.

"They only just told me yesterday," Dora replied. "I saw them downtown and I asked them why they hadn't been around, and they told me."

"Did they say why?"

Dora hesitated, looked off to the side as if embarrassed, then said, "Yes, they told me why. They said it was on account of that ghost in the garden. They said he was back, and they saw him, and they weren't going to be working here no more because of it."

That was all he could get out of her about the matter. That was on a Friday in late October. Dora wouldn't be at Joyous Gard during the weekend, leaving him to himself, and he was determined to track down replacements for Bill and Bob when Monday arrived.

Saturday morning dawned, gray and damp. Bayliss had been awake since three that morning, seated as usual in front of Jenny's portrait. Sometime around six, in his bathrobe, bleary-eyed, still exhausted, his head swimming, he made his way wearily into the kitchen to make coffee. He went to the large sink to fill the percolator with water. Above it the window looked out on the maze of high rosebushes. He turned on the faucet, glanced through the window, and stopped cold.

A hooded figure could be seen off to the right, near a wheelbarrow, a gray figure as dark as the leaden sky above the trees. He was enveloped in a robe that was almost cloudlike in its appearance, filmy, blurry, billowing. He moved with an odd jerkiness, as if he were busily engaged in some task that Bayliss couldn't make out. He was perhaps ten yards from where Bayliss stood at the sink. Then, all at once, the figure turned toward Bayliss and looked directly at him.

Bayliss couldn't make out his features, but he saw flashing eyes and a broad grin. Then the figure leaped wildly up and scrambled over the tall hedge of rosebushes and disappeared from view.

Bayliss dropped the percolator in the sink and headed for the backdoor that led into the garden. There was no doubt in his mind that he had just seen "Henry"—the phantom was real, "just like Spring-heeled Jack," and—before he fully comprehended what he was doing—he was outside giving chase. He ran to the corner of the garden where he had seen the apparition.

Nothing. No trace that anyone had been there just moments before.

"Hey!" shouted Bayliss. "Hey! Come back here and show your-self!"

Nothing. No response.

He tried again. "Hey! Where are you? Come on, come out of there! I saw you! What do you want?"

Nothing.

He stood there motionless, straining to hear. How long he stood and listened, he couldn't tell, but after a while he turned to head back indoors. He had taken only a few steps when, from an entirely different direction, he saw the same figure running toward him at great speed. Bayliss froze, then recovered himself, and leapt to one side as the thing in the cloak swept past him. As he did, the cloak flew wide and Bayliss saw what was beneath it.

Time seemed to slow down. The figure moved easily, flowingly, but against his fluid motion was juxtaposed an even more rapid succession of features. His face and body manifested a constant sequence of transformations: white, black, American Indian, Asian, old, young, male, female, brunette, blond, redheaded; bare-chested, shirt and tie, woman's blouse, leather jacket, tweed waistcoat... All in a ceaselessly revolving sequence, like images flashing on a screen. Only the mouth and eyes stayed the same, the mouth distended in soundless laughter. He ran past Bayliss, looking sharply into his eyes, flapping his arms as he went by, a mere few inches from him. Bayliss could only stand and stare, startled and horrified. The figure

130

ran once more in the direction of the maze and, with an incredible bound, disappeared over the wall of bushes.

This time Bayliss didn't give chase. Shaken, trembling, his heart racing crazily, he headed back into the kitchen and bolted the door behind him. He went over to a kitchen chair by the table and sat there staring at the floor for a long while. Eventually, he regathered his stricken wits and filled the percolator and made himself a strong pot of coffee. He felt numb of mind, almost concussed, but after draining the entire pot, followed by a quick shower and shave, he dressed and resolved to phone Father McManus as soon as the hour seemed appropriate. He waited until nine and rang the rectory.

No answer.

He remembered it was Saturday. Father McManus, he surmised, probably had early Mass, a wedding or a funeral to attend to, and no doubt a sermon to prepare for the morrow. Bayliss concluded that his phone call would be inconvenient. He would just have to bite the bullet and wait a bit longer. He could do that, he believed. He had never been an impatient or pushy man. He would wait until mid-afternoon tomorrow and try to reach the priest after he had celebrated the Sunday Mass and broken his fast afterward.

Bayliss put on an old moth-eaten jacket and a cap, grabbed his cane, and headed outside to inspect his garden. The day was dark, a chill was in the air, but it wasn't raining. Everything was quiet and undisturbed. He went over to the spot where he had first seen Henry. The wheelbarrow had a good half-inch of rainwater in it. He dumped it out, then headed through the open iron gate and into the maze. He had become well acquainted with its twists and turns, so he snaked his way between the barriers of bushes directly to the maze's center. A stone bench was there and a birdbath. A crow was splashing himself in the bath, but quickly flew off as Bayliss approached. Bayliss looked around. He swiped at the bushes with his cane. Nothing moved in them. He heard the cawing of the crow among the overshadowing limbs of the towering beech that grew on one side of the maze. Further off, in the nearby woods, he heard the eerie moaning of a mourning dove. The leaves and branches dripped. Otherwise, all was stillness.

Bayliss headed back to the house. He spent the remainder of the day as casually as he could manage, pushing the morning's experience far to the rear of his thoughts. It was best, he thought, if he got on with practical things as if it had all been a bad dream. He refused to allow Mrs. Clark's comments concerning Ed's talk of "omens" to fill his head, although he caught them trying to assert themselves when his cogitations wandered too far unchecked.

He decided he needed exercise. Ignoring his doctor's warnings about overexertion, he went outside and raked leaves for about an hour. Feeling taxed by that activity, and despite the fact that he was now sweating profusely, he went indoors and built a fire and tried to relax in front of it. He played LPs of Chopin and Beethoven on the Hi-Fi. He read. He tried at first to concentrate on an essay by Emerson, but found it wasn't distracting enough. Ed and his omens kept interfering with his concentration. He had better luck with *You Only Live Twice*. He ate a peanut butter and bacon sandwich for lunch; he had canned tomato soup and rolls at supper. He watched the news.

At last, daylight gave way to darkness outside, and Bayliss found himself seated before only glowing embers in the fireplace. A single standing lamp turned on low stood by his chair. He had lit a candle before the portrait of Jenny. He began to speak to her. He told her that Joyous Gard had belied its name, that joy was impossible for him in this place—what he had wished to be, in some delayed sense, their home—without her, that he missed her more than he could express, that he was infinitely lonely and now suddenly plagued by something more. He told her about Henry's appearance. He told her he had no idea what or who it was or why it was out there in the garden. He told her it scared him, but that he would call the priest tomorrow—just like she would have done, he said—and try to get it sorted out.

The darkness closed in around him. He heard the familiar noises of the house—sounds of wood expanding or contracting, the hissing and burbling of the radiators, the gurgling sound of waterpipes in the walls, the pattering of a soft rain on the great arched window off to his left.

And then, without warning, came the heavy thumping sound of something making repeated impact against the window from outside. Bayliss snapped around in alarm to see what had made the noise. He expected to see a branch blown by the wind, beating on the panes.

But instead, he saw something there that robbed him of breath—a sight that filled him with horror.

Pressed against the window was Henry. He seemed to grip the glass with one of his hands and with splayed knees; the hands were ghoulishly white and long-fingered and somewhat froglike. With the free hand he slapped the windowpane repeatedly, evidently for the purpose of getting Bayliss's attention. He stopped the beating once he saw that Bayliss was facing him. That the thing could cling to the window in that fashion seemed to Bayliss to defy gravity. And then there was its face, its nose pressed to the glass, that face that was a sequence of constantly rotating faces, his mouth wide and—so it appeared—soundlessly laughing.

Bayliss's whole body stiffened. He felt his heart palpitating wildly. Then, adrenaline pumping through him, he leapt up from the chair to confront the thing. Instantly, Henry dropped from the window. Something sticky seemed to remain behind on the glass.

An instant later, Bayliss heard a clattering noise emanate from the kitchen. Without a moment's hesitation, he dashed there and saw to his dismay that the window above the sink was wide open, and that Henry was not only inside but crouching on the counter. His mouth moved in laughter, and now Bayliss could hear it; but it sounded as if it was coming from an old radio speaker, tinny and scratchy, and it didn't match the moving mouth—as if he was looking at one of those films where image and sound aren't synced properly. Bayliss reached for a nearby spatula, though what he intended to do with it he had no idea.

Henry hopped from the countertop and dashed madly around the kitchen, opening drawers, flinging utensils every which way, overturning the chairs and table, opening the refrigerator and, in a blurring flash, emptying all the contents noisily on the floor. Bayliss couldn't keep track of him, he moved so rapidly. Cabinets flew open, dishes crashed down, pitchers shattered, and Henry scuttled sideways along the high walls like an enormous spider. Then with a wild flopping leap, he shot over Bayliss's head and dashed crazily into the great room. Bayliss stumbled after him with the spatula.

133

At this point, Bayliss had only one thought in his head: to save the portrait of Jenny. As the lamp by his chair went flying across the room, Bayliss sped directly to the hearth, his chest pounding unnaturally, and he snatched the painting from the wall. He held it tightly to his chest, clinging to it for dear life, and he collapsed into his armchair still gripping it. He felt as if his heart would burst. He struggled for his breath. Meanwhile Henry scampered around the room, the crackling radio-transmission laughter following just behind him, overturning furniture, snuffing out and hurling the candle that had been above the fireplace against the wall.

Bayliss watched the destruction through his steadily dimming vision.

Then Henry sprang into the hallway and flung open the door at the head of the stairway that led down into the basement. As Henry did this, before he could fully comprehend what he was doing, Bayliss found himself flying with great rapidity after Henry. The painting had been left behind, although he couldn't recall letting it go. But now he felt he had the strength of a dozen men—the strength and speed of Henry, in fact. And now he was hot on Henry's heels.

Henry looked back at him, still laughing. He seemed to relish the chase. Down the stairs he rushed, Bayliss bounding after him. Bayliss felt as if he were lightning, a bolt of sheer power. He skyrocketed after Henry; and now they were both in the basement.

To Bayliss's amazement, the engraved door in the wall stood wide open.

Henry paused there before it. Behind him was a glow of light. Bayliss could see that the doorway was, just as Mrs. Clark had said, the entranceway to a tunnel that appeared to extend far into the distance beyond. Henry gaped at Bayliss. He motioned as if he wanted Bayliss to follow him into the tunnel. Bayliss ran at him, and Henry fled into the tunnel. He turned some distance away and seemed to be dancing mockingly. Bayliss took hold of the door—what should have been an exceedingly heavy door, he realized as he pushed it—and slammed it shut. But the door was as light as if it had been a pillow stuffed with goose down.

Without a second thought, Bayliss turned and headed back up the steps, feeling unusually elated on account of what he had done.

# Henry

At the top of the stairs, he was met by Jenny. Not old Jenny, not dying Jenny, but young Jenny of the golden, sunlit hair. The Jenny who had once stood with him below the castle and dreamed with him of one day possessing it. It seemed perfectly natural to him that she should be there.

She held out her hand and he took it in his. She led him through the great room, where he saw himself still seated in the armchair and clasping the portrait tightly in his arms.

"Where are we going?" he asked, though he wasn't entirely sure he had spoken the words aloud but only thought them.

He heard her voice inside him as they left the house. Everything outside was bathed in summer sunshine.

"Joyous Gard."

The flowers, he saw, were all in bloom.

# When the Hurlyburly's Done

THROUGH THE LENS of nearly sixty years, I can view the scene still.

We have congregated in the spacious third-floor room reserved for such events, about seventy-five of us in all. The massive squarish, gray-stone edifice in which we are congregated had once been the elementary school, looming over the town below like some fortification of old. It had, in fact, been my elementary school when I was a boy; but now, with a more modern school on the other side of town, it had been converted into city offices on the two lower floors, and the top floor—this floor—had been renovated for community events and family gatherings. Our coming together is of the latter sort, an occasion of mourning by extended family and friends.

My Uncle Harry, my mother's eldest sibling has died, aged sixty-nine. A sudden heart attack took him while he was trimming a hedge along the street outside his home a few short blocks up the hill from where we are now. He was buried this very morning in St. John's Cemetery, under the canopy of the copper beeches there. I find this room dreary and oppressive, the result no doubt of the sad associations it presents to me. Only two years before we had gathered in it to mourn the simultaneous deaths of my mother and father. They had drowned together in a freak accident; their station wagon and camping trailer had jack-knifed as they avoided hitting a milk truck coming too rapidly around the bend from the other direction along one of the narrow roads above the Patapsco River. Both car and trailer had had to be fished out with considerable effort.

And now here we all are again on the renovated third floor of my old school, in a room just a bit too tight to accommodate seventy-five persons comfortably.

Despite this being an occasion of mourning, the room is noisy with loud voices and laughter. Sandwiches and beverages are served at a long table over at one end of it. The alcohol is freely flowing there and the surviving two brothers of my mother—Uncle Bill and Uncle Bob—are hobnobbing with others and drinking whiskey and yelling to be heard by one another over the surrounding noise.

Near them, but not joining in their conversation, is my cousin Edward—"Teddy"—fourteen years my senior, the only son of Uncle Harry. He's been drinking quite a lot and his square head and fat neck are flushed and so rubicund as to cause his crewcut of red hair to look like pale peach fuzz. His balance is unsteady; he must keep one hand on the table just to stand up straight—and he's been getting increasingly louder and his gestures more energetic as he appears to be educating a pretty young woman I don't recognize about some subject he—not she—regards as absorbing. She's probably some second cousin or the wife of a relative I don't really know. She looks restless, like she'd like to move along, which perhaps explains what seems to be Teddy's persistence on keeping her from doing precisely that. Teddy is one of those people who'll get hold of someone's ear and never let go; and he'll chase anything in a skirt, especially when he's tanked to the gills.

Betty, attractive and dark-haired and a cousin only one year older than I, the daughter of Uncle Bob and Aunt Fran, a lifelong playmate of mine, is watching him from where we stand side by side. She says to me, "God, he's such an ass."

I look at her and smile. She smiles back and takes a sip of her gin and tonic. I'm not drinking anything, but I don't feel like pressing my way through the packed assembly to go get something, and I don't have any desire to bump into Teddy either.

"You'd think he'd learned his lesson by now," says Betty. "Doris won't sleep with him anymore, you know. If I were she, I'd divorce the goddamn satyr."

I nod at this unsought piece of intelligence. Betty has, in fact, already divorced one husband. She delicately picks a piece of cigarette tobacco off her tongue.

"Anyway, he and Doris are on the outs, it seems," she adds.

Seven long cantilevered casement windows, each about four or five feet high, let in the outside light, what little there is of it today. All of them open out on hinges over the tarmacked court below where kids can often be spotted shooting hoops after school hours. It's one of those humid overcast Maryland summer days, not raining but threatening thunderstorms later in the afternoon, with persistent balmy gusts blowing the thick green foliage of the oaks and maples across the road so hard that they appear to sway at times like inebriated giants. As inebriated as Teddy over by the table boring the young woman appears to be, for that matter. Inside, the room is dimly lit and the cigarette smoke creates a pervasive haze. Something is wrong with the overhead lights and they're refusing to operate. But it's daylight outside, even without sunshine, so it's not a total bust.

I'm pondering a curiosity that's intrigued me for the last few minutes.

"Not to change the subject, but what's Aunt Katy doing on that chair?" I ask Betty.

I gesture toward the old woman. Aunt Katy is my great-aunt, but I barely know her. Betty smirks.

"I don't know. She's been standing there just exactly like that ever since we got in here," she answers. She waves her cigarette in Aunt Katy's direction, a bit dismissively, I think. "She was acting pretty odd at the funeral, too. Standing off to the side the whole time, not talking to anybody. Uncle Bill insisted she come—or I think she wouldn't have bothered. She's a total recluse these days."

Aunt Katy stands across from us and off to our left, opposite the table with the food and drinks at the other end of the room. She is somewhat wedged into the corner there and only a few inches from the furthermost casement window on that side. But that isn't all. She's also standing motionless on top of a chair and looking away from her family members who surround her perch on three sides. You might think more of those present would notice something so strange, but you'd be mistaken. It's as if she's invisible to them. She stands there upright and isolated and incommunicative and staring blankly at the white wall. No one, other than Betty and I, seems to take the slightest notice of her. Those nearest her are babbling away and laughing and smoking and nibbling and drinking in their little knots but paying no attention to the old woman at all, even when brushing past her. But I watch her, struck by the bizarre behavior.

# When the Hurlyburly's Done

She, for her part, reciprocates the attendees' inattention and just balances on the chair and gazes blankly into the nothingness in front of her. Her back is resolutely turned to us all and her arms are folded as if in mute defiance of something.

"She's always been a weird one, Peter," Betty says to me, as if that were all the explanation necessary. She takes a drag on her cigarette and exhales through her nose. "I mean 'weird' in the old sense, that is. Like Shakespeare's Weird Sisters—'By the pricking of my thumbs,' 'when the hurlyburly's done,' and all that. She used to scare the living daylights out of poor old Uncle Harry at times, you know."

I teach English Lit at this time in my life down in College Park and I say to Betty, rather foolishly, as if she had been trying to impress me (which she hadn't), "I still respect you, even when you don't make references to Shakespeare."

I'm still staring at Aunt Katy's immobile form. Outside, through the window beside her, the drunken giants sway ominously in the wind.

"You don't really mean 'weird' in the Shakespearian sense, do you? That's just silly."

"Well, that might be a stretch," Betty says. "But none of her nieces and nephews like her—or *liked* her, in your mother's case. And now Uncle Harry's, too. Always something crazy about her that kept them at arm's length. Something they didn't like to talk about. Don't ask me what it is. Just something *off* about her. Anyway..."

I recalled that, in fact, my mother had intensely disliked Aunt Katy and, on those rare occasions when they met, their interaction had been edgy. And they had argued in my hearing more than once about things that I, as a child, couldn't understand. My father had treated Aunt Katy kindly enough but made no bones about the fact that he thought her more than a little unusual. He had called her "the old witch," in fact, but only as a joke. At other times, he altered the phrase to "the old bitch."

Betty finishes off her G and T and says tipsily in a loud whisper, putting her mouth close to my ear, "You know, she and your mother had one hell of an argument the same morning as the accident."

I don't want to discuss that memory. I think it's time for me to make my exit. I'm suddenly remembering why family affairs are something I avoid whenever I can. I'm on the verge of saying to Betty, "Look, I've got to get back to Silver Spring," when it begins.

A sudden loud banging on the refreshments table alerts everyone that something is happening, and our attention is required. We all simmer down, swallow our conversations, and turn to look at Teddy, who's thumping on the table with one of his hammy hands and raising a glass in the air with the other. The young woman he was cornering earlier has since made her escape, probably with an irritated husband. Teddy has gotten everyone's attention now, except for Aunt Katy's, who remains steadfastly looking at the wall with her arms folded across her birdlike chest. Teddy stands red-faced and wobbling on his unsteady legs.

"A toast!" he bellows. "A toast! Everybody, raise your glass! I want... I want to propose a toast."

He's now looking directly at Aunt Katy's back. The people raise their glasses, unsure and looking at each other questioningly.

"What's all this about?" I mutter in Betty's direction.

"Who the hell knows?" she responds, but she halfheartedly raises her empty glass anyway.

Teddy now has the floor. "I want to propose a toast—a toast to my dear Aunt Katy," he says loudly.

All eyes now shift to the old woman they were ignoring for the past hour or so, standing on the chair with her back to them. I feel a chill run down my spine.

"To Aunt Katy, everyone! To Aunt Katy, who finds a wall much more likeable than her own family. Who can't be bothered with her family... who is so grand and—ha! ha!—*elevated* that she won't even look down at us or talk to us like a normal, sane human being would. Who shows up at a funeral just to ignore everybody, even the deceased."

Both Uncle Bob and Uncle Bill put their hands on Teddy's shoulders, trying to shut him up. No such luck.

"Look at her up there," Teddy persists, shaking off their hands. "What are you playing at, Auntie, you crazy old buzzard? Well, never mind. Who cares? I don't. Act like a loon if you want to, Aunt. Here's to Aunt Katy anyway, who really hated my father and cursed him out just one day before he died and upset him so much it killed him. Well, you got your way, didn't you—he's dead and buried. Another one down. So, cheers. Cheers, everybody! Cheers, you old bat!"

And Teddy drains his glass before the stunned assembly.

And then, as we look on, Aunt Katy stirs on her perch. Everyone has turned to look at her. And now she slowly turns herself about on the chair and faces Teddy. She unfolds her arms and looks him in the eye. Teddy steadies himself with one hand on the table's edge, his other arm still extended with the glass in it. There is nothing to read on her features. She just stares at Teddy for some moments, and he begins to look tense.

I feel Betty press against my side anxiously. No one says anything. We're all watching Aunt Katy wonderingly. The moments—just a few brief instants, actually—seem to stretch out interminably. And then her features relax and a sad smile—a faint one, but a smile nonetheless—appears there. She unfolds her clasped arms and sweepingly waves her right hand in a gesture as slow and graceful as a ballet movement, as if in a dream, her eyes fixed all the while on Teddy's. And then, before anyone can do a thing to prevent it, she unlatches the casement window next to her, swings it outwards, and steps through it.

The silence of that moment is broken by the thud of her body hitting the pavement below, immediately followed by a sudden gust of wind shaking the leafy giants into wild action, and then a scream that Teddy emits as his glass slips from his fingers and shatters on the floor. He collapses there after it in a faint.

Loud gasps, cries of horror and dismay, profanities mingle in the dense smoky air. Betty begins to sob. A few of us make a dash for the exit to go in search of a phone to call for an ambulance and the cops. And in minutes they arrive. We are all downstairs now, outdoors, except for Teddy who lies unconscious and forgotten for the moment on the third floor. Aunt Katy is taken up dead and, inside the old school, the police ask us questions and the whole affair takes hours before we are allowed to disperse. Teddy has been revived and sits, with head in hands, beside the refreshments table, unable to talk and blubbering like a baby. I drive Betty home.

141

I return the following week for Aunt Katy's funeral. Her ashes are interred in the same graveyard that has received generations of my family, including my mother and father and Uncle Harry and his predeceased wife, my Aunt Adelaide. In fact, her remains find repose beneath the very same overspreading copper beech that casts its shade over the other four graves. The attendees are few in number, only twelve not counting Mr. Rich, the officiating Episcopal priest. It's raining, but I know that that isn't the real reason for the sparseness of the gathering. Betty is there. Teddy is not. And I'm there only because my conscience won't allow me to be anywhere else.

Nonetheless, I can truthfully say I'm deeply marked by the tragedy. It haunts my thoughts and darkens my moods. A gloom saturates everything I do and it's impossible for me to focus on my work. To the point of obsession, I keep turning the tragedy over and over in my imagination and asking myself unanswerable questions about it. Had Aunt Katy really meant to do what she did? Had she intentionally committed suicide, or had she been so shaken in mind by Teddy's "toast" that her reaction was one of sheer muddled impulse? What had been her psychological state as she stood there motionless on the chair, refusing to be involved or interact with members of her family? And why had nobody, including me, had the good sense to intervene when it was—or should have been—obvious that she was emotionally disturbed? These thoughts have been nagging at me and disturbing my sleep throughout the past week.

The graveside service is over in fifteen minutes. We head down the path toward the line of parked cars and Betty catches up with me, slipping her arm through mine.

"Not so fast, buster," she says. "Do you have time for a bite?"

I wasn't yet married at the time, so there's no one for me to rush home to. I assure her I do. We drive separately to her split-level house in one of the new developments outside town, where she lives sans husband and without offspring, and there she prepares sandwiches and coffee. As we sit at her kitchen table by the sliding-glass door, looking out at the weeping willow in the backyard, she begins to tell me about her own past week.

She had gone with her parents, my Uncle Bob and Aunt Fran, to look through Aunt Katy's small cottage up on College Avenue and determine what needed to be apportioned, thrown away, and sold off. The property had years before been allotted to their care upon Aunt Katy's death. On the spot, Uncle Bob decided—against Betty's protestations—to have Aunt Katy's one companion, an old and shaky French Poodle named Jacques, put down.

"Poor thing," says Betty, looking shiny-eyed into space for a brief moment as she tells me this.

I ask her if there was anything out of the ordinary at the house, reminding her with a sad smile of her comment about Shakespeare's weird trio.

"No," she replies sheepishly. "Nothing. No bodies in the basement or in the upstairs bedroom à la Faulkner. Just ordinary books. *National Geographic* and *Life* on the coffee table. Even a TV in the living room, with an open *TV Guide* on top. Nothing... *occult*... nothing *weird* at all. I feel like such a damn fool. I hope she forgives me in heaven. But I did find out some details about her life from Dad that I'd never heard before, and it's very, very sad. Heart-breaking, really."

Betty takes a cigarette out of a silver cigarette case and puts it between her lips, and I snap open my lighter and light it for her.

"Do tell," I urge her.

Some of what she tells me I know from my mother, but other details are new to me. Aunt Katy had been born in 1885, an only child. Her father was a banker in town; her mother had been raised on a farm. They had lived above Ellicott City on College Avenue, in what was at that time considered "the country," on the very hill where the elementary school was built while Katy was in her teens. She had been, by all accounts, a homely girl and a lonely girl, with few friends, not popular with the boys. She lived in her own world, some said, and was painfully shy. She was a voracious reader, and she liked to sketch what she saw in nature. She frequented the woods near her home. Her two great desires had been to become an artist and a naturalist. She became, instead, a schoolteacher and taught in the elementary school that would one day be the site of her death. Her parents had died—first her father and then her mother—when she was in her thirties. It was during that same decade that an elderly man, twenty-odd years her senior, by the name of Morgan Burgess, proposed to her and she accepted. He also had lived up on College Avenue, not far from where she had grown up, and owned the small cottage that would later become hers alone, following Morgan's death in 1937. He had known her all her life, and she had been his second wife after the death of his first. After Morgan's death, another teacher in the same school had moved in and shared the cottage with Katy. This sort of domestic female companionship was not uncommon in those years, but in Aunt Katy's case it became the cause for whisperings and gossip. The arrangement didn't last, however. Her companion—a Miss Poole—suddenly took ill and died.

There had always been rumors about Aunt Katy. Her pupils tended to dislike her and, in fact, feared her. Her temper was well-known, and the children in her classroom could expect little mercy from her when they misbehaved. For that matter, adults feared her tongue-lashings, as well. Most of her relationships were either strained or came entirely to an end in acrimony. As her pupils grew older, they took revenge on her by pulling pranks on her at her cottage—overturning her trashcans, ringing her doorbell and running, egging her windows on Halloween, that sort of thing. They knew they could always get a rise out of her, and she lived up to her reputation more often than not. Where hurling curses and displaying fury were concerned, it was averred, she was unsurpassed in the region.

And the rumors went deeper and her reputation became more sinister. The deaths that had followed her throughout her life were taken stock of, particularly by those who indulged in embroidering the local lore. The more unsavory or uncanny, the better with such people. Even her own family spread tales about her, and the fear of her grew in the area. If anything good could be said to have come of her baleful reputation, at least it brought to a halt the pranks her former students played on her. Now they steered clear of her cottage.

According to the local legend, any time Aunt Katy had a falling out with anyone, that luckless person could expect to die soon thereafter. Whether the story should be credited or not, it was gossiped that she had had a ferocious dispute with her own parents and cursed them horribly in the presence of two or three others, and within two years' time both were dead. Likewise, it was said that her husband's death had occurred after the two of them had quarreled. And again, in the case of Miss Poole, the two had fallen out, Aunt Katy had sworn at her, and—as luck would have it—Miss Poole had died within the year. Two of her former pupils had also died young, both after being chased off her property for some pranks. Then there were my parents and now Uncle Harry. Others, too, but I forget now who they were.

Betty pauses and a brief period of silence ensues. I realize that we've been talking about Aunt Katy now for two solid hours.

"Sad, isn't it?" she finally says. "Shall I make us some more coffee?"

"Sad," I say. "Very sad. What a lonely, miserable life. I really should get on the road, but I'll take another cup, thanks."

As the coffee begins to perk on the stove, Betty says over her shoulder from where she stands, her back to me, "By the way, that thing she did before she went out the window..."

"You mean the chair?" I ask, not exactly sure what "thing" Betty is referring to. "Standing on the chair?"

"Yes," says Betty. She turns slowly around to look at me, and she's looking a little spooked. "Standing on the chair and looking at the wall, and not moving or talking to anybody."

"Yes?"

"Well," says Betty, "can you guess what her preferred punishment for misbehaved children was when she was a teacher right there in that same school, maybe even in that same schoolroom?"

I think I can guess, but I let Betty say it.

"She'd have them stand motionless on a chair at the back of the classroom and they'd have to face the wall until she gave them permission to come down."

Summer slips gradually into autumn and autumn transforms from vibrant golds and reds to gray, stripped limbs with a few clinging russet leaves and yellowed grass. I am deep into the semester, teaching my courses at the university and advising my students. In the evenings I work in my townhouse apartment in Silver Spring, correcting papers and preparing for upcoming lectures. I watch the evening news, put something on the record player to soothe my soul while I study or read, and on the weekends I might even be lucky enough to go out on a date. This is the routine night after night. But tonight I'm interrupted at around ten o'clock, and it's Betty on the other end.

She tells me—although she's already given me the news in a previous call—that Doris left Teddy about a month ago. I tell her yes, I know, and then comment on how worried she sounds now over the phone.

"I *am* worried about him," she admits. "But not just because Doris left him. God knows, I really can't stand too much of Teddy, but he *is* our cousin and I'm worried—really worried after talking with him on the phone tonight."

"Okay," I say. "What's going on that's got you so worked up?"

"He's not himself. You'd have to see him to know what I mean. He's not showing up for work, for one thing. It's lucky for him he works for Dad at the department store. If he worked for anybody else, he'd probably have been fired by now. And he's drinking heavily and barely eating."

"Losing Doris hit him hard," I venture.

"No doubt," says Betty. "But that's not everything. He's also talking about Aunt Katy. A hell of a lot. Obsessively, even."

"That hit him hard, too," I reply. "I know he blames himself for her death. And maybe he should take some of the blame on himself. What he did was outrageous."

"No, you don't understand," Betty says. "It's not just what happened at Uncle Harry's funeral that's made him such an emotional wreck. He told me tonight..." Her voice drops down to a near whisper. "He told me that Aunt Katy is there now, at his house, *with him.*"

"Hmm," I hmm back. "He's been drinking, no doubt. That must be it. He's distraught. He's feeling guilty. His wife just walked out on him. He's not eating like he should and he's sitting around in his empty house all by himself. If he's going nuts, there's a cause for it."

Betty comes to the point. "Could you come up here and talk to him? He respects you. He'll listen to you. You're a relaxed, balanced guy and you're his cousin. Maybe you can give him some moral support or a few tips or something."

"Can't you?" I counter. "I'm really busy here, with a pile of papers to grade and all that…"

"No," she says emphatically. "I can't. I'm a woman and Teddy doesn't respect women. And then there's the unpleasant fact that, first cousins or not, he's a goddamn masher and I don't want him trying to put the mash on me. I'm terribly worried about him, but not enough to put myself in that situation."

I have to admit that that's true. He's the type who might all too easily forget about "the laws of consanguinity," and I care about Betty too much to put her in the unenviable position of planting him a kick in the beanbag.

"Okay," I say. "I'll come up Saturday and pay him a visit."

Betty thanks me and we hang up. The next morning (Friday) I phone Teddy from my office and tell him I'm coming up there tomorrow and that I want to visit with him—"long time, no see" and all that. Teddy sounds like hell at the other end, hung over and speech slurry, but he agrees to the visit and that's that. It's settled. I'm coming up and I don't know what the devil I'm going to say to him. But I'll commiserate with him, if he opens up some. And if he brings up Aunt Katy, that *she's there with him*… Well, God give me strength.

🐦

I show up at Teddy's around three in the afternoon. He lives in a rancher in the same housing development as Betty. As I pull in behind his blue Falcon, I notice that his lawn is uncut. This isn't like Teddy, whose immaculate lawn care has practically been a religion with him.

He greets me at the door and ushers me inside. "Sorry about the mess," he mutters as I enter the living room. And it *is* a mess and so, for that matter, is he. Rumpled shirts, a pair of twisted slacks, and socks of various hues decorate the sofa and living room floor. Newspapers are strewn about. Dishes with remnants of ancient meals streaking them are on the coffee table, along with a three-quarters empty mug and a used glass or two. An open bottle of bourbon is on a table beside one of the arms of his recliner. As for the man himself, he's dressed in an open-neck white shirt (stained), a pair of black pants, and slippers on his otherwise bare feet. His clothes sag on him, and that's because he's lost a lot of weight since I saw him last. His eyes are watery and have deep circles under them. His once-trim crewcut has grown out and the short red hair is disheveled. He hasn't shaved today and possibly not yesterday either.

"Want a drink?" he asks, motioning limply in the direction of the bourbon.

"No, thanks," I say, pushing a wrinkled shirt to one side and sitting on the sofa. "I don't drink when I'm driving. Learned that the hard way once."

"Yeah, I remember," he says with a grin—the first sign of his old self that I see. "Your dad's poor car. Mind if I do?"

He doesn't wait for an answer and pours himself some of the whiskey.

"It's not like you to pay me a visit," he says, taking a drink. "What's the occasion? It's not my birthday or anything, is it?"

I tell him I'd heard about Doris leaving him and that I'm sorry and that I just wanted to see how he was doing.

"Well, you can see for yourself. Sort of obvious, really. I feel like hell warmed over. Like shit, if you must know." He takes another swig. "I don't blame her, though. What I put her through—it's my own stupid fault. The women, the booze, the fights…"

He looks off to the side, at a spot somewhere above the fireplace, not at me. I can see that he's holding back tears. Then he gets a handle on himself, looks at me through bleary eyes and smiles. It's not a happy smile, though. It's a grim smile.

"But I'm not alone here," he says. "Right after Doris left, someone else moved in. Didn't Betty tell you?"

I pretend not to know what he means.

"Sure, she did," says Teddy. "It's the damnedest thing. Do you believe in ghosts?"

"Ghosts?"

"Ghosts. Spirits of the departed, specters, spooks, phantoms…"

"Well," I say. "I grew up here just like you. Anybody living around

148

all those Neo-Gothic mansions up on the hillsides above town, and the old ruins out in the woods by the railroad tracks, and knowing the local lore, even in our own family, is going to be predisposed to give the notion some credence."

"English prof to the core," says Teddy. "Can't you just say 'yes' like a normal person?"

"Yes, then." I don't tell him I suspect that people who see ghosts are probably just seeing projections cast by their own troubled minds, and that those mysterious "things that go bump in the night" are probably caused by psychological disturbances in the heads of the living and not visitations from the restless dead.

He settles back in the recliner.

"Good," he says. "Guess who's moved in here? Betty told you. She said she did, anyway. Well, no need for suspense. Aunt Katy has come to stay. No, don't say anything. Let me get out the story first."

I nod and sit forward, clasping my hands between my knees and giving him my full attention.

"I first noticed something going on around here two days after Doris left," he begins. "It was the sound of someone moving around in the house at night. Of course, I never saw anybody when I got out of bed or my chair to check on it. Just sounds like footsteps occasionally, and sometimes like dishes moving in the kitchen. And then I noticed two things at about the same time. First, somebody seemed to be changing my stove settings. Don't laugh. I'd put the flame up to six, for example, then turn around to do something else and then turn back around to see it was turned up to seven. At first, I thought it was just my forgetfulness. But it was happening all the time and I'm not really all that forgetful. And then, there was the other thing. I kept seeing the shadowy figure of an animal moving past me—or, I should say, just an animal-like shadow. I never saw it directly or anything. I'd just be going about my business and, you know, just *catch* it dash by out the corner of my eye. Always just outside the full range of my sight. But I saw it over and over again. And, dammit, you know what I thought to myself when I saw it?"

"No. What?"

"That's Jacques, I thought. *Jacques.* Aunt Katy's dog. The one Uncle Bob had put down right after Aunt Katy's death."

149

Teddy pauses long enough to polish off his glass and pour himself another.

"And then it wasn't long before I saw *her*, too. Not directly, not ever directly. Just out the corner of my eye." He points an index finger at his eye as he says it. "Another shadow. A two-legged old lady shadow, if you'll believe that. And the sounds are still happening, especially at night. And then, I started getting dreams—*really vivid* dreams. And in them I'm right here, in this very room, face to face with Aunt Katy and she's talking to me."

"Talking?" I say in a low voice. "What does she say?"

"Well," Teddy goes on, "what she *says* I can't remember. And it sounds like it's coming from a distance—like maybe over a telephone receiver. I'm not sure what the exact sentences are, but I understand her. I mean *I understand her*. I know why she's here and I know why she did what she did. She's told me why... I don't know if I should tell you. Sounds really crazy. I haven't said it to anybody else, not yet..."

I see that his eyes are welling up again.

"It's all right, Teddy," I say. "I mean, good Lord, we're cousins. Go ahead and tell me." I sense he needs to get it out of his system—pent up guilt feelings, I suspect. He needs to spill his guts to somebody, and it might as well be me. He looks reassured at the encouragement.

"She comes to me every night now," he says. "In my dreams. And, you see, she's come here to *forgive* me—for what I did to her there at the family gathering after Dad's death. She wants me to forgive her for causing Dad's death. She blames herself for it and"—his voice drops—"also for your parents' deaths and for others as well. She tells me they were her doing. I tell her they weren't, but she won't hear it. When she was angry, she tells me, she brought about their deaths. She doesn't know how, but she knows she did and she's sorry. It's why she stood facing that wall at the gathering—it was a punishment she used when she taught school, and she was letting us all know that she had done something bad to others and that she was punishing herself for it right there for us all to see. And then, when I *abused* her there, she turned and, to show me that she truly regretted what she'd done, she *took that step...*"

And Teddy falls silent.

150

"That's a heavy thing for you to be carrying," I venture to say after some moments. "But you say she's *moved in*. Did you mean that? Moved in to *stay*?"

And now a new expression, an agonized look, spreads across Teddy's countenance. "Yes, that's exactly what I meant. And I *do* forgive her, and I *do* accept her forgiveness, but..."

"You don't want her staying here," I finish for him.

"No, God help me, I don't. I'm just as afraid of these things as anyone else would be in my place. And... it's the guilt, you see, and the sadness that comes over me. She needs to leave me in peace now. I want her..."

"To go," I say. "I see."

I don't tell him I think it's his compounded guilt that's really plaguing him, maybe even refining him in the long run. The shade of Aunt Katy, I have little doubt, is his own conscience taking on this particular form. Maybe there's something therapeutic in it. I can't say. But I take a risk and offer him some advice.

"Perhaps you should tell her to leave," I suggest. "She needs to move on—to heaven or Purgatory or wherever souls are supposed to go after they depart. She shouldn't be hanging around here. She's told you she's sorry, and you've let her know you're sorry too, and now it's time for her to move on. So, tonight after I go, tell her or ask her, please, to leave. Do it however you can. I'm sure, if she's come here to patch things up, she'll understand."

Teddy looks up over the fireplace again. He sits like that for a full two minutes at least. I watch him, an earnest expression on my face, thinking I've just done the right thing for him.

"I'll do that," he says, turning his gaze in my direction. He looks brighter, more hopeful. "You're right. We've made our peace. We're on an even keel now. So, that's what I'll do. I'll be kind to her. Should I ask the priest over?"

"I doubt Mr. Rich would know what to do about a ghost," I say. "He's low-church and preaches the gospel according to Paul Tillich. He'd tell you you're being medieval or something and then want to send you to an analyst. If I were you, I'd just tell Aunt Katy, between you and her alone, to move on to her rightful place and then see what happens."

151

We part on that note, and I urge him to do some "normal" things to get himself back on his feet. Clean up the place, mow the lawn, go to work on time... that sort of thing. He might be fourteen years older than I, but I feel like I'm talking to a depressed teenager. He thanks me profusely, which embarrasses me, assuring me he'll have "that talk" with Aunt Katy that very night, and I head back south to papers that need grading.

🐦

That evening, in addition to being tense after my visit to Teddy, my arthritis flares up. When that happens, I have a restless night. So, to sleep soundly, I take two sleeping pills along with a handful of aspirin tablets. I mention this only as a possible explanation how it is that I don't hear the phone ring downstairs in my townhouse after midnight, which I'm told later it did. I'm in a deep sleep at that hour and nothing short of a major earthquake can wake me up.

The next morning, I drive into D.C. to attend the Solemn High Mass at St. Paul's on K Street. In those days, still young enough to be enthralled by two solid hours of Anglo-Catholic worship, with its clouds of incense, gaudy panoply, and the music of a men and boys' choir, I make my way to the one church I can always depend on to give me that fix. I'm back home around two-thirty. No sooner am I back, jacket off and tie loosened, than the phone rings.

It's Betty and immediately I can tell that all is not well. Her voice is shaky and a bit hoarse.

"Peter!" she says. "Finally! I've been trying to get you for hours. Where have you been?"

I tell her and ask what's wrong.

"Teddy," she says, and it sounds to me like she's catching her breath, like she's having a difficult time keeping calm.

"What about Teddy?" I ask. "I just saw him yesterday and..."

"Yes, I know," she interrupts. "He told me. Last night. When he couldn't get you."

"Couldn't get me? When?"

"Last night," she says, sounding exasperated. "He tried calling. A number of times, he told me. He couldn't get through and gave up and called me. Must have been around one in the morning."

"I took sleeping pills," I explain.

"Well… are you sitting down? You might want to sit down before I give you the news."

I sit down and tell her I am.

Her voice drops and she says in a calming voice, as if she's trying to calm *me*, "Okay. You need to know that Teddy's dead."

That hits me hard. I can't reply immediately or even think clearly for a moment or two. I hear Betty breathing heavily on the other end and finally I recover my voice. I ask her in a whisper, "What happened? How…?"

"He hit a telephone pole. Down on Bonnie Branch Road. The police say he must have been driving seventy or eighty miles per hour. Hit the pole head on—nobody there to see it, apparently. The folks on Red Rock Farm heard the crash and phoned the cops."

"When was that?"

"Maybe an hour, two hours after he phoned me last night," Betty replies. "It's pitch black on Bonnie Branch that time of night."

"What was he doing out there at *that* hour?"

"I don't know," says Betty. "But I don't doubt it had something to do with why he called me and was trying to get you."

"Why *did* he call us?"

"Take a deep breath," Betty tells me. "He called me to tell me what you told him yesterday afternoon and that he took your advice. He took your advice and told—I know it sounds nuts—he told Aunt Katy she needed to leave the house. He said he did it as kindly as he could. He stood in the kitchen—apparently, she seems to have, er, *haunted* the kitchen more than other rooms in the house—anyway, he stood there in the kitchen and told her she needed to move on, go up to heaven or whatever…"

I hear myself inexplicably moan.

"Yes," she continues, "that's what he did. And then he said he fell asleep—probably drunk, is my guess—in his recliner chair. But then something woke him up."

I'm suddenly fully attentive to every detail Betty is relating to me, almost in a "hyper-reality" mode of attentiveness, as if I'm hovering over the events she describes and viewing them.

"Teddy heard things in the kitchen breaking—being shattered.

He told me he froze at first because the noise was so awful, but then he got up and went into the kitchen and there was glass and broken plates all over the floor. At first, he said, he thought they had merely fallen off the counter somehow, but then he saw that all the burners on the stovetop were on full. He switched off the flames and was heading out the kitchen door when he said *he saw her* in the middle of the living room, with Jacques beside her. Not filmy or transparent, but as solid as you or me. And she was looking at him in a hideous way—with rage and hatred. It was, he said, that look she got whenever she was in a fury, like with Uncle Harry before he died. He couldn't hear her, but her mouth was moving, Teddy said, like she was *damning* him. The voice seemed to reach him from a distance, but it was damning him. *Damning*—that's the word he used. And he said he knew there and then that there was no way in hell she was going to leave. He didn't know how he knew it, but he said he knew it. There wasn't the shadow of a doubt in his mind. She had moved in, and she wasn't budging..."

"And then?"

"And then, I suppose, he tried calling you and then he called me. And I told him I didn't know what he could do. Call a priest, maybe. And that was all. That was the last I heard from him. He did say— maybe I shouldn't tell you—he did say he wished to God he hadn't taken your advice—that he should've just let sleeping dogs lie..."

"I wish," I say, drained of all energy and feeling mentally pummeled. "I wish he'd followed my example rather than taken my advice..."

"Your example?"

"Not to drink and drive."

"That wouldn't have saved him," says Betty soberly. "You know that."

"Do I?" I reply.

"Yes, you do," says Betty. "I think we were probably right about her all along. Aunt Katy was never a person to be crossed. She always had the last word. Teddy could have been stone-cold sober last night and still the outcome would have been the same."

"You... you really and truly believe that?" I ask.

Betty doesn't answer. We both let the question hang there in the

154

ether. We say goodbye and I put the receiver down. And the question has hung there between us unanswered for sixty years.

Teddy—or what was left of him, poor man—was cremated and buried not many days after. He was buried next to his mother and father, less than ten feet from the ashes of Aunt Katy, under the copper beech.

# Sweets for the Little Demons

WHEN THE OLD WOMAN died in the summer of '62, it fell to her nephew to get her house and belongings in order. Walt Finch was the only son of an eldest son, and his father's single sibling had been his unmarried and childless sister, Agatha. After his father died, his mother having passed away three years before that, Walt took over the responsibility of caring for his aunt.

Not that he paid her constant attention. Indeed, he rarely paid attention to her at all, dropping in at her small home irregularly to see how she was getting by, and usually not staying for more than thirty minutes at a time, if that. She lived south of town, up on one of the surrounding wooded hills. The property behind her home ended abruptly at a cliff that overlooked the railroad tracks below and, beyond them, the flowing brown waters of the Patapsco. Walt had grown up hearing that "Patapsco" was an old Algonquian name meaning "backwater," and as a very small child he had thought matter-of-factly, as children do, that the "back" in "backwater" referred to the "back" of his Aunt Agatha's land. But that was many years ago now.

Walt lived in town and had a job at the local branch of the Commercial and Farmers Bank, and he considered driving out into the wooded countryside to see his relative on occasion an onerous obligation. He didn't like the old woman, to be honest. But being a moderately dutiful man, he did it whenever accumulated feelings of guilt induced him to do so just to make up for all those times he had put it off.

Walt was unmarried at the time of his aunt's passing, fortyish, balding, and not known either for his charm or imagination. He was practical, quiet, reclusive—if not ascetical—in his personal habits, a teetotaler, and his only intermittent pastimes outside his home were golf with a few friends from the office and sometimes a game of bridge with the same. He had been dating the same woman for nearly a decade, but neither, it appeared to the chatterers in town, seemed to have any feeling of urgency where nuptials were concerned.

So, Aunt Agatha had finally died, and now that the funeral was past and her body interred, it was left to Walt Finch to go out to her home and see what needed to be done there. The house had been left to him in the will, along with everything in it, and he had before him, he well knew, an enormous task. His aunt had been a notorious hoarder. Every room of the old place—at least every room *he* had ever visited, and they had been only the ones on the first floor—was filled with objects of all sorts. She had amassed and stockpiled quite a lot of furniture over the years, many of them family heirlooms, easily tripped over and in some rooms difficult to squeeze oneself around. Some were valuable antiques, and most of them were massive in size and weight. In addition, everywhere one turned there were heaps of books and papers and magazines, bric-a-brac and porcelain and framed pictures (hung and unhung), food containers (not all of which were clean, and which Aunt Agatha maintained "might be reused for something") and paper towels and saved grocery bags and just about anything else one could imagine a short, loquacious, round little woman collecting, storing, stacking, shoving into corners and closets, and pack-ratting. There was always a permeating atmosphere of moldiness and mustiness in the house, and Walt—who was unusually sensitive to such things—found the odor repellent. He quailed at the prospect of going through it all and breathing the air in those stuffy confines. But he knew his duty and set his face as flint, determined to get it over with.

As already noted, Walt set foot in his aunt's house as infrequently as he could manage. While she had been alive, he would drop by the home, situated on the cliff above the tracks, and stay for tea and the inevitable sweets. His aunt had been a diabetic, but she had never been able to leave off the sugar and, in fact, it was the diabetes that had killed her—mercifully before she had lost any limbs or her eyesight. It had harmed her cardiovascular system, and that had been the death of her. She had simply dropped dead in her kitchen one afternoon without any warning, her heart having given out. When-

157

ever he had visited her before that sad day, Walt would invariably pass through the dimly lit downstairs hallway, filled with so many objects that he could only maneuver his passage by squeezing through it sideways, and then on into the equally cluttered kitchen. His obligation fulfilled, he would exit through the same birth canal of a route, trying not to stub a toe or catch his shirtsleeve on anything along the way, popping out through the front door and careering toward the blessed relief of his waiting car. He had never, in all his forty years, been upstairs in her house at all.

When he was growing up, he recalled, his aunt had visited his parents in their home as their guest far more frequently than they had visited her. She had come during the holidays, and always for Thanksgiving dinner. At Easter, she invariably brought him and his brother baskets of candy, usually of the cheaper, most tasteless, and most sugary kinds. Only on rare occasions had his parents taken him to her home on the cliff. As a child, that cliff-edge had scared him. He had one particularly uncomfortable memory of himself repeating the phrase over and over, when he was quite small and had come too near it with his brother and had become deathly afraid that he would topple over the edge, "I don't want to be a dead soul, I don't want to be a dead soul…" He also had a recollection of his mother warning him and his brother about the cliff-edge each time they went to his aunt's, a warning that was repeated to them well into their teens. "I don't want you falling off," she would say on every single trip there—somewhat inanely, it now seemed to him. It had been that dangerous cliff near the house that had worried his parents where two rambunctious boys were concerned (not that Walt had ever been all that rambunctious), and why it was that they seldom took their boys there. Or so Walt was wont to believe.

Thinking back now on those large baskets of Easter candy and the other gifts of sweets Aunt Agatha had bestowed on them at other times, he was reminded of her own deadly weakness for things sugary. Related to that propensity of hers, probably to help her disregard her need for self-restraint, there had been an odd little phrase that she repeated so many times over the years that it was expected of her by all who knew her. Townsfolk called it "just one of her little ways," chalking it up to her whimsy and self-deprecation. Whenever her family, friends, and acquaintances heard the familiar words, they would smile indulgently or give one another a wink or a knowing glance from the corner of their eyes. The phrase was this. She would say, picking up a handful of candies (the quality never mattered to her) at a party or a gathering and stuffing them in her handbag, "I must take some of these sweets home for the little demons." She would do the same on shopping expeditions. She would purchase a bag of hard candies or cheap waxy chocolates or some other such stuff, and say to whomever was in hearing distance, "I must take some of these sweets home to the little demons." No one made much of it. Everyone thought—and Walt thought, too—that the old dear (or "old fossil," as he called her) meant to eat the sweets herself, and that this curious turn of phrase was just her version of giving a wink and a nudge to those around her. She had owned an enormous cat named "Buster" for some years, Walt mused, but cats (he was sure) don't have a sweet tooth. By "demons," then, she obviously had been waxing metaphorical, he assumed. She had only used the term as a euphemism for her own ungovernable craving. So it was that the "mystery" of the phrase was, in fact, not really a mystery for anyone. Everyone assumed that it was merely one of those fond memories of a departed person's little peculiarities.

And that assumption might have been the end of it for Walt had he not decided to spend a long weekend—from Friday night until Monday morning—going through his aunt's things. His plan was to brave the mustiness of the place and "camp out" in the house those few days, methodically compiling an inventory, noting what was there, what should be kept, what must go to the local landfill, what to the Salvation Army, and what should be sold.

"Your aunt certainly adored children," said Adelle to Walt, when he told his long-time sweetheart of his intention. "She must have regretted not having any herself."

Walt was reading the newspaper, and all he said was, "Yes, well."

They were seated side by side on his front porch, something they frequently did on summer evenings, and Adelle was knitting.

"I remember her at the school's Halloween parties," went on Adelle, who was an elementary school teacher. "She wore the same witch costume every year and brought treats for the kids."

She smiled, looking over at Walt, who glanced back at her and then back to his paper.

"Yes, well," he said again. "Old ladies are like that, I suppose. Probably the same awful treats she used to bring us."

Adelle ignored the sour comment, and instead went on with her reminiscing.

"She'd always pocket a couple handfuls of candy before leaving, making that silly excuse of hers." Adelle shook her head, still smiling. "What a funny old bird. And you'll go there tomorrow evening after work, then?"

"That's the plan," replied Walt. "I guess we'll have to cancel going out tomorrow night to see that new John Wayne Africa picture, but I really need to go over the premises and get the property sorted out. It's a godawful mess. Really foul. Mind taking a raincheck on the movie?"

"I understand," said Adelle. "The movie will be out for a while. No rush. But about your poor aunt, don't be too hard on her. She probably just couldn't keep the house in order, being all alone like she was. You do what you've got to do and get that place cleaned up—for her sake. It'll be over before you know it, and John Wayne and his rampaging rhino can wait. Just give me a ring or two while you're out there."

She set the knitting down in her lap and gazed dreamily up at the trees in the yard and the slanted rays of the setting sun shining through them, and said softly, "She really was a dear old thing. We're going to miss her. Such a bright, cheerful person. She brought a touch of sunshine everywhere she went."

"Yes, well," said Walt.

The following evening Walt packed his bag and made his way out of town to the home of his late aunt. Set well back among the trees, a stream running on its south side and the sheer drop of the notorious cliff about thirty yards from the backdoor of the house, it was a picturesque cottage, built in the early nineteen-thirties. It was not too large and not too small, with gingerbread trim about the exterior—just the right sort of home for a reclusive spinster with a sweet tooth, Walt had always thought. Like something in an Arthur Rackham illustration. She had seen to its outdoor upkeep, for decades hiring the same two workers to come out every other Saturday to tend to it. There were two stories for living space, with an attic and basement in addition. All told, it did indeed look invitingly cozy from the outside, but, once indoors, a visitor might be excused for feeling claustrophobic and a bit smothered by the musty atmosphere Walt so dreaded, packed with the stale accumulation of an inveterate hoarder.

As Walt unlocked the front door and stepped into the entranceway, he immediately felt overwhelmed by the task he had taken on. He stood there staring, nearly in a state of paralysis, at the piles and heaps and stacks of stuff on every side and the cumbersome furniture that cluttered the small hall. He tried to gauge as best he might the sheer agglomeration crammed into that space alone.

"Christ almighty," he muttered under his breath. "What a horror show."

He sighed loudly and resigned himself to his fate, wading through the oppressive paraphernalia toward the stairway that led upstairs.

"Well, I'd best get settled in for a long two days of pure, unadulterated hell," he said to himself gloomily. "Couldn't the old biddy have thrown out *anything* before she died? Saved it all for me. Thanks, Auntie."

Grumbling all the way, he ascended the stairs.

He had never been upstairs before, but he naturally assumed there would be a bed at his disposal, and, at any rate, he had brought along his sleeping bag (at Adelle's suggestion) because he dreaded the thought of sleeping in sheets that might have the house's ubiquitous odor permeating them. Once he reached the second-story landing, he made his way through the predictably cluttered hallway and found that there were three bedrooms. One of these was the master bedroom. A large poster bed was there, which he rapidly stripped of its linens—bedclothes just as malodorous as he had anticipated—and there unrolled the sleeping bag onto the bare mattress.

"That'll do nicely," he said to himself.

There was an adjoining bathroom, which was in some disarray with jars and toothpaste and brushes and pill bottles scattered about, but otherwise it was relatively clean. He put his toiletries down beside the sink and went out into the upstairs hall to have a peek at the other bedrooms.

Looking first into one and then the other, he was somewhat surprised to discover that both were relatively free of clutter. That was his first surprise. But there was a second, and it was one that he couldn't immediately take in fully. It certainly mystified and, in some deep place in his brain, disturbed him. Right then and there, he could not have said why it bothered him or even have framed a coherent question to suit the discovery. But there was something not a little troubling, he thought, to see that neither room contained a bed but rather that each room had in it one of two identical baby cribs. His aunt had been a spinster, after all, never wedded, and—it was assumed—never "with child." But here were two cribs and two rooms made ready for children: children's wallpaper, two mobiles above the cribs, a toy chest in each room, and a few old stuffed animals. What was he supposed to make of this, he wondered? Perhaps his aunt, he conjectured as charitably as he could, had once cherished some fond, unrealized hope, or maybe she had had infant visitors of whom he had known nothing…? Other, gloomier fantasies disturbed his thoughts for a moment, but these he dismissed with a shake of the head. Maybe it was just another manifestation of his aunt's propensity to collect and not discard anything that, as she was wont to say, "might come in handy someday." Surely, that must be the explanation.

Anyway, he was much too weary to give it any more of his attention at that moment. He shrugged it off for the time being, deciding to eat one of the prepared sandwiches lovingly packed the evening before by the reliable Adelle, and then turn in for the night.

Returning to the master bedroom after his meager meal, he began to look around and take stock of it. After all, he thought, I might as well start here as anywhere else in the house. A large marble-topped dresser with three broad, deep drawers and a mirror above dominated one side of the room. He pulled out the top drawer and started to go through its contents—folded garments, undergarments, a box of jewelry, and more. He pushed the drawer back in and pulled out the middle drawer. A sewing basket, three photograph albums, a large hairbrush, some pictures in frames... He couldn't help noting that these last were all framed photographs of children, none of whom he recognized.

He pushed the drawer back in and turned his attention to the bottom one. In it he found seven fat little brown books, all of them leatherbound, which he removed and set on the marble top of the bureau before pushing the drawer back in place.

What were these books, he wondered? They were uniform in design, each front cover identically embossed with a curious design depicting a rising sun with a grinning face and jagged rays that reached upwards and outwards above what appeared to be a table-land. The volumes had obviously been carefully kept. He opened one and began to examine the contents and discovered that it and the other six volumes were diaries, spanning the years from 1928 until just three days before his aunt's death, written in her old-fashioned, elegant cursive script, with pasted-in snippets from newspapers, clipped recipes, the occasional (usually quite poor) poem taken from a lady's magazine she had once subscribed to, and other items she had obviously wished to preserve, interspersed with reportage of the day-to-day events of her life.

He felt strangely moved. "Well, well," he murmured. "So, the old girl was a diarist."

Perhaps he was stirred inside because, like her, he also kept a diary and because he hadn't at all suspected that she had recorded her own thoughts and experiences. Perhaps, if he had reflected on that for a moment or two, he might have realized that that was because he never wondered much about her life at all. But he didn't reflect on his neglectfulness, but only concluded that maybe she had been a bit more like himself than he had ever realized. He almost forgave her in that moment for all the clutter she had left him to deal with. He went over to the bed, all seven volumes in hand, switched on the lamp on the night table, propped himself up on the abundance of pillows there, and began to read.

The diaries proved to be rather entertaining, he found, and even enlightening on some points of family history. She displayed in places, as he phrased it in his mind, a "wicked" sense of humor. There were more than a few incisive, unsparing observations of persons and situations set down, some of them savagely cutting in a witty, almost Wildean way. There were accounts of family foibles (including her own) and commentary on the social life of the town. Overlaying it all a coating of cheerfulness colored her outlook, though at times it was tinged with the sardonic. It made for lively reading. As he read, he became ever more aware, too, of just how much his aunt had delighted in the company of children. Page after page detailed her activities with them—sometimes she assisted with school parties and outings, read to groups of them at the local library, and paid visits to them at the playground simply to talk to them.

He read on for nearly three straight hours, becoming more and more delighted with these sunny descriptions of diurnal events and encounters, sometimes chuckling out loud over this or that witticism or sharp comment. He was truly warming up to his Aunt Agatha's hitherto unknown personality, flowing happily along on the stream of her bubbling prose (it was good enough, he was beginning to believe, to be published), when all at once he was unexpectedly brought up short.

It came as an unwelcome jolt, though in retrospect he realized it shouldn't have been wholly unanticipated after his inspection of the upstairs earlier. Had he not, after all, seen the two rooms just across the hall decked out for children? What jumped out at him and disturbed his peace of mind was a single line, deep in the third volume, dated October 15th, 1941. It was to be, he soon discovered, the first of many like it, and the first to use that all-too-familiar phrase, "the little demons." It was the first indication in the diaries that there might have been something *not quite right* with the psychology of his aunt.

The sentence simply read: "The two adorable little demons have arrived." And it was followed by another sentence, equally disturbing: "I have prepared their rooms and I'm so happy to have their company here at long last."

"The two adorable little demons," Walt repeated to himself. "*What* two little demons? *Demons*? Who talks about children like *that*? *What* children?"

Sweets for the Little Demons

A sense of unease asserted itself in his mind and, with it, a sudden chill seemed to penetrate the walls of the room as well. Or was it just his imagination? He got out of bed, crossed over to the bedroom door and shut it tight. Then, as an afterthought, he also turned the latch and locked it—though why he did it, he couldn't have explained even to himself. He returned to his sleeping bag and to the little books scattered on the mattress there.

He flipped through the pages more rapidly now, scanning them with his banker's eye as he might a ledger. Now he saw, again and again, that the phrase "the little demons" recurred with increasing regularity. He found himself searching through the entries solely to pick out the phrase amidst the recipes and clippings and the details of an old woman's daily celibate existence. To his frustration, the phrase was never explained in them. There was nothing to indicate to whom or to what it referred. Just the phrase itself, again and again, popping up here and there.

"Those two little demons," burbled one entry, "are exceedingly precious. How very thankful for them I am!"

Another read: "I returned home from the children's party laden with sweets for my two little demons, and how ecstatic they were to greet me. They love their sweets and—I am wont to entertain—their adoptive 'mama' as well."

And another: "I tucked the little demons into their new cribs just moments ago, and now I'm finally off to my own bed after an exhausting day downtown."

"So, they *did* sleep in those cribs," murmured Walt, "whoever they were."

He read on, becoming drowsy as the hour was now late. He was just about to shut the fourth volume—the entries were now those of the early nineteen-fifties—when, all at once, his eye caught the abstruse phrase yet again, but this time his aunt's "tone of voice" in the short passage containing it struck him as conspicuously ominous. What he read was:

"The little demons are outside my bedroom door, and I have had to lock them out. It's for their own good. I am beginning to realize that I've been spoiling them terribly, and now what was once received by them gratefully as a treat has become their daily expectation. They want their sweets, and today I simply haven't any, and they've been howling for them for the past two hours now. I hope they will wear themselves out and go to sleep (if they sleep—sometimes I don't think they do). But they've become so demanding of late! I hate to do it, but I really have to be more firm with them."

Walt turned the page, and three entries later he found this alarming passage:

"What am I going to do? They're at it again, outside my door as they were a few nights ago. They're shrieking horribly and tearing at it like little furies. A real din. I must deal with this if I'm ever to have order around here. I don't want to do anything drastic, I really don't; but tomorrow—I resolve, I mean it—it must be back into the trunk for them. I haven't had to resort to this measure in a good long while. I may hate myself for doing it again—I know I shall!— but it's for their own good. I can't have them behaving like savages in the house. So, the trunk it will be. Just as a measure. Maybe it will pacify them, and we'll have some harmony restored around here."

Walt shut the book with a snap and sank back against the pillows.

"The *trunk*?" he whispered to himself. "The trunk of her car? No, that's ridiculous... What on earth is she talking about...?"

But he was so tired now that his eyes drooped even as he put these questions to his swimming brain, and he couldn't continue to read or even think straight. Unsuccessfully trying to stifle a deep yawn, he reached over and turned off the bedside light. He went to sleep almost immediately.

Undoubtedly, he might have slept soundly the remainder of the night, but something woke him not many hours later. He checked his traveling alarm clock with the luminous dial and saw that it was ten past four. What had disturbed his sleep, he wondered? A noise? Everything seemed quiet, apart from the usual night noises. He strained his ears. A shaft of silvery moonlight fell across the foot of his bed. Outside he could hear the rustling of leaves in the breeze and the tree frogs chirping—the nocturnal sounds of summer, but nothing more. Yet—no, wait—he did hear something stirring above him, something in the attic directly overhead, just a slight scratching sound and a shuffling and then a clumping sound, like a shoe being dropped.

166

It must be squirrels, he thought, relieved. It would have been just like Aunt Agatha to leave the attic window open, letting the pests get inside. He would deal with it in the daylight hours, he determined. For now, he was going back to sleep. However, still awake and still unavoidably listening, he heard the clicking of small feet scuttling about, reminding him of cats' claws for some reason. After a few minutes, and with one last muffled thud, as if the clasp of a lid had latched shut, the scampering sounds ceased. And soon he was fast asleep once more.

The next morning saw Walt up early. He worked steadily through the day, taking stock of the basement first and then the first floor, making notes, cataloguing, deciding where each item was to go, and taking breaks only to eat and twice to phone Adelle for some welcome conversation. Evening descended after hours of relentless sweaty, dusty toil. Having accomplished enough to feel satisfied with his long day's efforts, he finally permitted himself the sybaritic indulgence of showering, and then watching some television in the living room before ascending the stairs at ten o'clock to retire.

However, this short-lived sense of satisfaction and achievement ended abruptly when he reached the upstairs passageway. He stopped in his tracks and stood staring at the threshold of the master bedroom's door. There, bunched into an untidy ball, was his sleeping bag.

"What on earth...?" he said aloud.

He quickly collected himself and gathered his sleeping bag, carrying it with him into the bedroom. Once inside, he switched on the light and saw immediately that things were not at all as he had left them that morning. His clock was lying face down on the night table and its face had been cracked. His suitcase was lying open, and it had been rummaged through. The light in the adjoining bathroom was switched on—although, he thought, maybe he had forgotten to turn it off after his shower. The seven brown volumes, though, were apparently untouched, still where he had left them on the foot of the bed.

He slung his sleeping bag back onto the bed.

167

"Damn squirrels," he muttered, although how squirrels had managed to ball up his sleeping bag, he could only dimly conjecture. "Well, it's got to be squirrels. Yeah, that's got to be it. Although, God, I hope," he added as a new thought struck him, "that it wasn't a fox…"

He cursed himself for not remembering to go up into the attic during the day and shutting the undoubtedly open window there. He went out into the hall to the foot of the narrow stairway that led up to the attic. Peering up, he saw that the attic door was wide open, but it was pitch dark up there and he had no desire to stumble around in a space sure to be as cluttered as the rooms below. Besides, he didn't have a flashlight and he hadn't seen one among his aunt's items downstairs.

"Oh, hell, I'll leave it till tomorrow and hope nothing else gets in tonight," he said resignedly. Going back into his bedroom, he shut the door behind him and locked it. "Damned if I'll have squirrels getting in here," he grumbled, although he wasn't sure that the squirrel or even the fox theory quite reassured him.

After squirming into his sleeping bag atop the bed, he picked up in the volume of his aunt's diary where he had left off on the previous evening. This time, as he read, he felt no sense of warmth in its pages, and his aunt's sunniness seemed now to have been eclipsed by something large and dark and anything but cheerful. Likewise, the atmosphere in the house, while he scanned the pages, seemed to become foreboding to him, as if something were creeping up slowly on him invisibly from the corners of his room. The night sounds outside the window were not unusual, nor were the sounds in the house other than the kinds that old houses make—wooden creaks and piping groans. Yes, he thought, and something else perhaps too. He pushed the latter feeling aside as the product of a stimulated imagination and pressed on with his skimming of the diaries.

In them now were constant references to "the little demons" and the "sweets" his aunt brought to them each day. He had read for more than an hour when he realized with an inner jolt that, from his calculations, the "little demons"—whatever they were—had been in the house for the shocking length of eighteen years by the time his aunt had come to write this profoundly troubling entry:

168

## Sweets for the Little Demons

"The little demons are not satisfied tonight, although I put handfuls of sweets in the trunk for them. I thought that the trunk would mollify them. It was the last straw—the same drastic measure I've taken many times before and which used to work so well to quieten them. I hoped it would pacify them and that they would leave me be. I simply can't give them all my attention. I can't. Other things demand my time, not just these little devils."

Walt could make very little sense of it, but it sent a chill down his spine to read that entry, nevertheless. Something abnormal had been going on in this house, something psychologically off-kilter. It didn't help now that he began to recall scenes from *Psycho*, which he had been fool enough to take Adelle to see when it had come out. But something had evidently become unhinged in his aunt's mind. Of that he was left in little doubt. But what it was that had come unglued in her, he hadn't a clue. Had the old woman lost her marbles without anyone outside being aware of it? Had she been recording real, objective occurrences in the home or were these the delusions of an addled brain?

"They are howling like bobcats and scratching on my door in a terrible frenzy tonight," Walt read a few pages later. "They refuse to go back into the trunk, no matter how much I order them to—I doubt they can even hear me shout at them over the ruckus they're making in the hall. I did vow to love and cherish them, I know; but sometimes I regret ever having let them into the house. One would swear I hadn't disciplined them at all. The candy spoiled them. Too much sugar in their little systems. I need to cut back."

"The trunk, the trunk," repeated Walt. "What trunk? Where?" And then he thought of the attic.

And as he did, he heard it.

At first, it was only the sound of two soft plops on the floor above him, followed by a scampering sound, just like the night before, like cats' claws or...

"Squirrels?" he asked the empty room shakily.

The scampering could now be heard descending the attic stairs to the passageway outside the locked bedroom door—and they were definitely footfalls and definitely coming from above, scuttling and scurrying, and now they stopped just outside his door. He tossed the book in his hand to one side and sank down deeper into the sleeping bag, clutching it as if it could save him from drowning at sea.

And then the scratching began—clawing, more like, as if by the claws of something or some *things* larger, much larger, than squirrels.

A fox, after all...? He tried to persuade himself it was no worse than that, though that was bad enough. Could it be a bobcat, though? His aunt had written that a bobcat had been loose in the vicinity back in... when was it?... he wracked his brain... back in 1939 that was... But something else, something way down in his gut, told him different—told him, in fact, that whatever his aunt had meant by her "little demons," this noise was... *them*. And who were *them*?

The scratching on the door was now accompanied by rude thumps, as if the creatures were kicking at the base of the door— and he could see the door vibrate from the blows.

That wasn't the worst of the horror, though, for now he heard voices. Feral voices, wild voices, chattering voices—at least two in number, he felt sure. They sounded like tomcats or, more frightening for him to take in, like screaming, raging, petulant children— their voices horrid, wailing, and mingled with a guttural snarling. Walt held the pillows over his ears, so loud became the dissonance, and he closed his eyes so tightly that the tears flowed. He could feel his heart pound wildly, his body shake, and his head throb, and still the shrieking went on and on, penetrating the cushions pressed against his head, and now the voices blended and seemed to chant rhythmically...

The horrific yowling din went on and on for what seemed to him hours. He was huddled in a fetal position, witless, his muscles taut and cramped and wrenched until, finally, the sounds receded into what seemed like a great distance. He could still make out shrieks and whines, but now they came to him as if filtered through cotton, more and more faintly, and now they were little more than sobs and whimpers.

Once again, he heard the tiny footfalls overhead and the sound of something like a lid shutting and then all was blessed silence. Walt remained curled up in the sleeping bag until, at last, senselessness and fitful sleep overtook him.

When he came to his senses it was broad daylight outdoors, and the clock showed half past ten o'clock. There were no sounds outside the door, and nothing whatever to suggest in the quiet of that bright Sunday morning that anything had been amiss the night before. He wondered if, just perhaps, it had all been a nightmare, though an all too realistic nightmare—possibly induced by reading from his aunt's diaries and allowing his imagination to run amok. He slowly crept out of his sleeping bag, pulled on his pants and shirt, laced his shoes, and—ludicrously snatching up a hairbrush to use as a weapon, if it should come to that—he crossed to the door and slowly, hesitantly unlocked it and drew it open inch by inch, and peered out. Sunlight was streaming into the passageway. He could hear birds singing cheerily outdoors and all seemed right with the world.

He crept out of the bedroom and, grasping the hairbrush more tightly, he bent down to examine the door for scratches or other marks of violence.

"Nothing," he dared to say aloud. "It must have been a dream... a nightmare. Still..."

He gazed at the stairs leading up to the open attic door. "I'd better get to the bottom of this damn squirrel problem..."

He stealthily ascended the steps to the attic. His heart was pounding again, nervously, apprehensively.

"Nuts," he grumbled, irritated at himself.

Despite the reassuring sight of sunlight flooding the attic through a tightly closed window, he was still feeling shaken as he entered. The closed window told him immediately that the problem wasn't squirrels or any other invasive wildlife.

Unlike the first floor and the basement, the attic was relatively empty. Relatively empty, that is, save for two exceptions. The first was a wide scattering of candy wrappers in every direction, thousands of them by his estimate, many of them in piles of noticeably large size, like so many hillocks and mounds. They carpeted the

171

floor and crunched and scrunched under the soles of his shoes as he advanced towards the second of the two exceptions.

And that was a large, accommodating *trunk.*

He stood over it for a few moments, feeling a tingling sense of dread creep over him, beginning at his scalp, and running down his spine and the backs of his legs like so many spiders. The trunk was large and black, battered and old, and he knew that it must be *the* trunk of his aunt's diaries. It was a deep trunk, crotch-high, and its lid was shut. He tested the latch on it and found that it was unlocked.

Walt swallowed hard, and then ever so carefully and hesitantly he lifted the lid with arms extended—as if he feared that something might leap out at him from it. He was prepared to leap back if need be. Steeling himself, he looked down into the depths of the now wide-open trunk. As he did, he felt a wave of nausea rise up inside him.

There, partially covered in candy wrappers, lay two diminutive withered, leathery forms, both carefully wrapped in baby blankets, their heads having been laid carefully on soft pillows—two lovingly preserved, dead infants, long dead, their eyes empty and their mouths open. And protruding from their blackened foreheads, each boasted two tiny horns.

# They Fly Forgotten

T O SOMEONE POSSESSING an imagination shaped by fairy tales or medieval legends, it might suggest a great grim giant seated above the town, austerely surveying it—a sober gray eminence constructed of ashlar granite, with two rose-window eyes peering down on the closed and boarded-up brick railway station beneath it. Below the railway station, a forsaken relic of livelier times, brews the turbulent brown flood of the Patapsco. The gray eminence, the giant—in reality, a church—situated on its high hill just south of the town's main street, is on an incline so steep that access to its entrance is by way of two ascending concrete stairways with cast-iron railings. These matching stairways ascend their separate ways up to corresponding doors set on either side of the church's rectangular central tower. The only other way into the church is through a rear entrance, just off a small parking area there. The tower is crowned by a tapering steeple. The edifice's architecture is eclectic, a blend of Romanesque and Gothic elements. When it was first built, it was the only Roman Catholic parish between Baltimore and the city of Frederick. Babe Ruth, as a plaque just inside the east entrance commemorates, was married there in 1914. In short, it has a history.

In 1963, the church had been standing watch on that hill for precisely a century and a quarter, and Father Augustine McManus, the pastor, was making grand plans for a celebration to mark the anniversary. A parish centenary had been celebrated back in 1938, but that was more than a generation ago. A multitude of world-changing events had transpired since then: a world war, a war in Korea after that, an escalating war taking place currently in Vietnam, the Bay of Pigs debacle; at home, racial unrest, cities set aflame, agitated and disaffected youth, rapid changes in every sphere of society, and—little did he or anyone else suspect it at the time—with worse yet to come in November.

It seemed to Father McManus that, amid so much confusion in the modern world, it was his duty to draw his congregation's attention back to the stability of steady foundations and eternal sureties. If he could revive a few sustaining memories of happier days—when everything was less hectic, less frightening, less noisy—he would make the effort, even if it were only for the sake of a brief respite. He had an idea. A festival of thanksgiving for the church's one hundred and twenty-five years might provide a needed reassurance amid the gathering storm. It might even kick off an extended program of parish renewal. He entertained hopes that it might. The sisters who taught at the parochial school next to the church supported his proposal for a parish festival with enthusiasm. They in turn galvanized the schoolchildren, and the plans were set. The celebration itself was scheduled for a month hence, in November, on the Sunday after All Saints.

Father McManus was sixty-seven, balding, rotund, and red-faced. He was known for his many endearing qualities around town: his quick wit, his fondness for a stiff drink, for having a healthy appetite, for his propensity to puff on small black cigars, and for a curmudgeonly manner that most people found charming rather than off-putting. He had been the church's pastor for twenty-one years and it didn't look like the Archdiocese was likely ever to assign him anywhere else—which was just fine with him. He had never harbored a desire to be a bishop or a cardinal or to be made a monsignor. He liked being right where he was, doing what he was doing. He liked the town. He liked his people. He was proud of the fact that his church was the only one in town with a mixture of races attending it. Assistant priests had come and gone over the years, but he had remained, steady as a rock. In 1963, he was the only Roman Catholic priest left in town. On the whole, he was well-liked by Catholics and Protestants alike, and by black and white alike.

He was satisfied in every respect, except for the unrest of the times. That he didn't like. He unapologetically preferred the past. He believed that the past, overall, had been better. Not the long past, that is, but the near past—the turn-of-the-century past, the past he dimly recalled from his own childhood. Old was good; new was, if not exactly bad, constantly intrusive, and unfailingly annoying. As is often the case with older people, he missed earlier times. He regarded the years of his youth through a filtering lens. And why would he not? They had been happy days for him, simpler times; those bygone years were, in a sense, his home country. He knew he could never return to the home country that had spawned his most idyllic memories, but he couldn't help but love those memories— even if that meant playing down the less felicitous aspects of that age. The tawdry, the ugly, the bigoted parts were brushed over in his mind with a thick coat of nostalgia.

He was, however, by all accounts, a kindly priest, and never more so than when he was hearing confessions. He was understanding and helpful, never carping, rarely reproachful. He regarded the sacrament of penance as a form of therapy for the soul, not an act of judgment. He said that what he applied to hurting people was medicine, not a verdict. He wasn't a judge; he was a physician. He delighted, he said provocatively, in "priestcraft"—a term he self-consciously employed to tease his Protestant friends but was also, for him, redolent of truth. What he practiced carefully and thoughtfully was indeed a craft. He heard confessions by appointment and regularly on Saturday afternoons. As his congregants knew well, he could also reliably be found in the confessional every Wednesday between six o'clock and seven-thirty PM.

It was on a Wednesday, October ninth, at about half past seven, just as he was preparing to "close up shop" (as he put it), that he heard the strangest and most unnerving "confession" of his entire career. It wasn't, strictly speaking, a confession at all—he was always clear on that point when recounting the event later.

Father McManus had heard what he thought must be the last confession of the evening, that of one of the nuns who taught at the parish school. The sister had made her exit, and he was sure that he was alone in the church. Outside it was dark, and only the most essential of the electric lights were turned on in the sanctuary and nave. The single confessional box, which stood near the narthex, was the old-fashioned kind. A matching pair of doors led into the two small compartments on either side, one for the kneeling penitent and one for the seated priest. The compartments were divided by a wall with a grill set in it, obscuring the penitent's identity from the priest. Of course, in a small community like the one Father McManus pastored, the priest generally recognized the penitent's voice anyway, so anonymity was usually a pretense for both actors.

Father McManus had just stepped out of the confessional and removed his violet stole, leaving it on the chair inside. He left the confessional's small light switched on, which he would come back to turn off once he had secured the building.

He followed his usual routine. He first went directly to the two tower entrances and locked and bolted them. He next made his way down the length of the nave, past the twinkling votive lights—red before the statue of the Sacred Heart, white before the altar where the Blessed Sacrament was reserved, green for the statue of St. Joseph, blue for the statue of the Blessed Virgin. He genuflected before the tabernacle on the altar, then locked the vestry door off to the side of it. Then he made his way back down the side aisle to the confessional, intending to turn off the light still burning inside it, snap up his breviary and rosary, and depart through the unlocked back door. He would lock that behind him on his way out.

He stepped inside the box and just as he put his finger on the light switch to turn it off, he heard a movement on the penitent's side of the confessional. It was the distinctive sound of a person putting his full weight on the kneeler of the *prie-dieu* there—it always let out a familiar squeak when someone did that.

Father McManus was hungry. He hadn't eaten since breakfast. His greatest desire at the moment was to get back to the rectory and to the cold repast he knew had been left there for his supper by his housekeeper. So, when he heard the groaning kneeler in the next compartment, he felt annoyed. He silently made an Act of Contrition in reparation for his aggravation and dutifully seated himself, draping the stole once more about his neck. He figured he must have inadvertently locked in a parishioner he hadn't noticed in the dark church. He mentally readied himself to hear one more confession, prayed it would be short, and resolved manfully to endure the grievous pangs of hunger for an additional five or ten minutes.

"Hello," he said in his best pastoral tones. "I'm here. Please begin."

He listened and heard stertorous breathing next door, as if someone was struggling with some effort to speak. There were a few choking and sputtering noises, then a husky, whispering masculine voice got out some words he couldn't quite make out.

"It's all right," said Father McManus reassuringly, thinking the penitent must be nervous. "Take your time. Catch your breath. There's no urgency."

He said these last words just as his stomach rumbled loudly. It begged to differ.

There was some more choking on the other side, and then an unfamiliar voice said with a modicum of strength, "Are you there, Father?"

The priest said, "Yes, my son. I'm right here. How long has it been since your last confession?"

More choking. Then came the rasping reply, "I've never made a confession before."

Father McManus was surprised at this admission.

"What? Never? Are you Catholic, my son?" he asked.

"No, I'm not." There was a fit of phlegmy coughing. Then: "But my sister is."

Father McManus was nonplussed, but he said, "Do I know your sister?"

"Yes. You know her," intoned the man. The voice sounded stronger, but it was gruff and flat.

"Is this about your sister, then?" asked the priest.

There was a rustling sound in the next compartment, and the *prie-dieu* creaked as if the man were uncomfortable and was shifting his weight. This was followed by a few moments of dead silence. Then the man replied in his harsh monotone, "Yes, it's about my sister. I've come for her sake."

"Okay," said Father McManus, his curiosity roused. "I'm listening. Tell me what this is about."

"What it's about," the man said, "is the man I killed—the man *we* killed. My sister and me both."

Father McManus had heard confessions of all sorts over the course of several decades. In prisons he had been a confessor to murderers and others who had committed brutal crimes. He wasn't squeamish, even when listening to the detailed descriptions of the

177

most appalling acts. So, despite the man's frank admission, he maintained an even composure.

"Sounds to me, then, like you need to get something very serious off your chest," he said. "Go ahead. You say you killed a man? In fact, you said '*we*' killed a man—you and your sister."

"Me and my sister and also others," the man replied. "Others I stirred up to do the deed."

"Okay," said the priest. "Take it slow. Tell me what happened."

The sound of a loud thud was heard on the other side of the grill, as if the man had slammed his fist down hard on the top of the *prie-dieu*. The elderly priest's heart skipped a beat.

"We killed that boy," the man continued hoarsely. "We strung him up, is what happened."

"When did this occur?" asked the priest.

"Years ago—a long time ago," the voice behind the grill replied. "We were young when it happened. I'm not making any excuses 'cause of that, though. But we were young, and we were mad, and we weren't thinking straight. It was October—October of 1903. Sixty years ago, this very day."

This was followed by loud choking, part sob, part coughing fit. Father McManus worked his rosary.

Then the man in the other compartment continued. "We took him and hung him on the limb of a tree. It was a bunch of us who did it. Like I said, I'm not making no excuses. I'm just telling you straight, just as it happened. What we did was we stripped him of those fancy clothes he wore, stuffed his mouth with rags so he couldn't make no noise, and we beat up on him and kicked him and... other things we did, too. We even—we even—so help me, God—we even took out our knives and we cut parts off him while he was still living."

"Good Lord," said the priest under his breath, and aloud: "Go on."

"Like I said, we stuffed some rags down his throat to shut him up. We weren't planning to kill him—just rough him up. It all got out of hand. Someone got the idea to splash kerosene on him and throw a lit match on him, and that's what we did. I want you to know that my sister wasn't there for any of that. That's God's holy truth. She

178

wasn't nowhere around. So, she can't be blamed for what we did to him then and there. What we did to him physically, I mean. But that doesn't let her off the hook—because she helped kill him in her own way, just as if she was there with the rest of us and doing the killing with us. That's why I'm here."

Father McManus experienced a reduction of his appetite. The temperature in the confessional seemed to have dropped precipitously. He felt a chill run down his spine, causing his shoulders to bunch and twitch. He ran the beads rapidly through his fingers.

"How do you figure she was guilty for what you all did without her even being there?" he asked.

"Everything we did to that boy we did for her," the man said.

The priest said, "Who was it you killed?"

"Who we killed was a colored boy who'd come to town. His name was Methley Tanner. I say he was 'colored,' but he was very light skinned. He could've passed for a white man with a dark complexion. He'd come to town looking for work. He got a job, too—down at the hardware store."

"You mean Clark's Hardware—just down the hill, across from the railroad station?" asked Father McManus.

"That's right. Methley was a bright boy. I'll give him that. Always wore a coat and tie and a smart-looking hat. Always spruced up. Had a fancy accent, kind of snooty sounding. He read books and played the guitar. He was polite for the most part, but he was kind of slick and sometimes he got uppity. He didn't know how to stay in his place. He talked back sometimes. We put up with it, and maybe that was a mistake. Maybe if we'd've told him early on to watch his step, he wouldn't of got himself killed like he did. As it was, he wasn't much liked by the other colored folk neither. He wasn't fish or fowl if you know what I mean. He didn't fit in with the white folk and he didn't fit in with the colored folk. Sort of a lonesome type, a 'lone wolf.'"

The voice next door had now acquired a juddering quality that made the priest's skin crawl. He couldn't quite twig why it had that effect on him. He plowed on.

"Then what happened?"

"He got friendly with my sister, that's what happened," said the

179

man. "Or, to put it more truthful, she got friendly with him. And that wasn't all. A lot more happened besides—a *lot* more. He was a handsome cuss, 'lone wolf' or not. The girls noticed him. White girls, I mean. Like I said, he could've passed for white. He had himself a little mustache over his lip, and his hair was combed straight, all oiled up and parted down the middle, and he wore some kind of fragrance the girls all liked and commented on. A real slick type. My sister said he had *panache*. I didn't know what that even meant when she told me, but I didn't like the sound of it. It made me feel dirty somehow, like she was dirty to even notice him. I knew she thought he was good looking. I could tell by the way she looked at him. I hated that."

"You don't like colored people," Father McManus said. It wasn't a question.

"I don't *not* like colored folks," the man replied. "I just don't like them mixing with white women, even if they happen to look white. But, to go on, him making nice with my sister was just the beginning of things. And things got worse from there. My sister started going down to the hardware store by herself and talking to him on her own. I didn't say nothing to her about it at first, but I got worried. I started keeping my eye out. I didn't trust that fella, and—to tell you the truth—I didn't trust my sister neither. I won't put on airs with you. We weren't never rich white people ourselves—my father came up here from Tennessee to work in the flour mills before me and my sister were even born. We always worked side by side with colored folk and we all got along right well with them, so long as they and we observed the proprieties. Well, my sister didn't observe the proprieties and neither did Methley Tanner. They got their stars crossed if you get me."

"I guess I do," said the priest. "Then what happened?"

"One night my sister comes home in distress. Our parents had us late in life, so they're old and they don't see it. They can't tell she's all worked up about something. I see it, though. My sister and me were too close for me to miss it. She was fifteen then and I was seventeen. Anyway, she comes home after being downtown with her friends. Her clothes look a mess, her hair's all mussed, and I see she's been crying. I ask her what's wrong. I press her to tell me. She doesn't want to tell me. She cries, but I push and push. Then an idea hits me between the ears. It's an ugly idea. I feel dirty all over just thinking it. I ask her anyway. 'Does it have anything to do with that yellow son of a bitch, Methley Tanner, down at the hardware store? Was that who you were with?'

"She breaks down then, starts crying, and after I push her some more, she comes right out with it and tells me he tried to have his way with her. I take a gulp and use the word 'rape'—'Did he *rape* you?' I ask her. She just nods, all tearful like, looking angry and hurt. I make her tell me the whole story. She says she met up with Methley downtown, that she'd gone off with him to where he was boarding on the edge of town. She said she went along with him unsuspecting, and he got the two of them by themselves, and then he forced himself on her. She said she tried fighting him off, but he overpowered her. She couldn't hold him off."

There was only heavy breathing in the other compartment for some moments, but nothing else.

Finally, Father McManus said, "And?"

"And I got together some friends," came the gruff reply, "and I told them that Methley Tanner had *tried* to rape my sister and that we had to do something about it and teach him a hard lesson about what happens when certain lines get crossed. I didn't tell them that he *had* raped her—which was what I thought. Only that he'd *tried* to do it. I wanted to protect my sister's reputation, you understand. Anyway, I told you the worst already. We went out looking for him. We cornered him. He denied everything. We called him a dirty liar. We hit him. We beat him. We dragged him up Church Road, into the woods. We kept on beating him. He was in pretty bad shape by the time we strung him up. We hadn't planned on killing him, like I told you, when we started in on him, so help me God, but it got out of hand. We buried him up there in the woods. There was some talk around town about him going missing afterwards, but that's all. Nobody went looking for him. To be honest, nobody in town cared."

Father McManus started to say something, but the man interrupted him before he could get a word out.

"Wait. That's not the whole story. There's more. I told my sister

181

what I'd done, and then I presented her with what I'd found on Methley Tanner's clothes when we stripped him naked, just before putting that rope round his neck. I didn't look at what I'd taken out of Methley's coat pocket before we torched him. We burned his clothes later, and if I hadn't found them, I would've never known the truth. I don't even know why I did it—went through his pockets, I mean. Anyway, I just put them things in my own pocket. I couldn't look at them closely under the circumstances anyway. When I saw what they were later, under the light, I wanted to scream. I *did* scream. I felt like hell. I felt betrayed. I felt suckered. I started raving. I became enraged at my sister. I wasn't angry with Methley anymore—I was *enraged at my sister*. I ran home. I woke her up. It was late. Our parents slept on another floor. They didn't hear a thing. I showed her what I'd found. I told her I knew she'd lied to me, and that she killed Methley just as much as we had. She got hysterical. She went crazy because we killed Methley. She threw things. She threw up. She threw herself on the floor and started sobbing.

"'I didn't mean for you to go and do that awful thing!' she yelled at me. 'I didn't tell you to go and hurt him any!'

"I said to her, 'Well, what the hell did you think I'd go and do? You're my sister! You told me he raped you!'

"Then she looked at me with big wide eyes. She was horrified—I think she was horrified at herself. She grabbed her stomach and fell on her knees. She said, 'He *didn't* rape me.'

"I told her truthfully, because I'd seen what was in Methley Tanner's pocket, 'I know that now. I know he never raped you. I know you lied.'

"She said to me, 'I'm carrying his child. I've been with him lots of times. But it was my fault—not his. I led him on. He told me tonight it all had to stop, and he was going to leave town because it had to stop, and he was scared of what would happen to him and me if it went on. I was going to tell him I was carrying his baby. I'd only just found out, you see—I had all the signs. When he told me he was leaving, I blew up. I lost my mind. I hit him—I grabbed things and swung at him with whatever I got my hands on. That's why I came home looking like a mess. I was crazy mad with him.

Crazy mad. And when I saw you and you asked me what happened, I told you the first nasty thing that popped into my head.'

"I put my hand over her mouth. She stopped talking. I took my hand off her mouth.

"'So,' she said, 'you killed that innocent man. And I guess I killed him, too!' Then she started wailing again. I held her head and calmed her down best I could.

"I kept those things I'd found on Methley. They've been on my person, hidden and secret up till now, sewed in my coat pocket. But now I'm going to leave them right here with you. Don't mind the condition they're in. They're old."

Father McManus tried again to say something. Again, the man didn't let him.

He said, "I want you to show them to her. I want you to show them to her and I want her to confess to you what she did—what *we* did. I know she hasn't confessed it to nobody else but me. That's not good enough. Don't ask me how I know she hasn't confessed it. *I know.* I know *her,* and I've been watching her all these years. I already told you I'm not a Catholic. You can't help me. I made my bed and I got to lie in it. But *she* is a Catholic. She married a Catholic and became a Catholic and she's got to follow through with what she chose. Now her husband's dead. You buried him last month. You know who I mean. He never knew what she'd done. He never even heard of Methley Tanner, whose bones are moldering up in the woods north of town. She belongs to your church. You got a responsibility to her as her priest. So, I'm going now, and I'm leaving these things right here for you. They're in your keeping now. I've done my part. You're free to read the note."

Father McManus heard the creak of the *prie-dieu.* The man was getting up to leave. He could tell.

"Wait," said Father McManus. "Don't go. Have we ever met before?"

"You know my sister," said the man, his voice giving out now. He was wheezing. "You don't know me."

"But you live around here?"

"Not far from here."

Father McManus, of course, knew who his sister must be. He had only buried one man the previous month. But he asked anyway, "Your sister is Ida?"

"It is," choked the man.

"Wait," said Father McManus. "Hold on. The baby. What became of the baby?"

"She lost it," came the hoarse reply. "Her friend Mae took her to see somebody—an old woman she knew—who made a mixture for her to drink. I gave her the cash for the stuff, when she asked me, out of my own work money. She drank it and it made her frightful sick, but the baby got flushed out in the end. Our parents never found out. They thought she had the grippe."

"Dear God," breathed Father McManus, gripping his beads more tightly. "What's your name? I'll pray for you."

"Randall," the man said. "But don't bother. There's nothing you can do for me."

"Hold on a minute," said the priest. "I need to let you out."

"I'll go out the way I came in, through the back door."

The door of the next compartment opened and closed, and Father McManus heard the man's retreating footsteps. He got up quickly and went out of his booth, hoping to catch a glimpse of him. What he saw was the shadow of a man moving rapidly down the side aisle on the other side of the nave.

"Looks remarkably spry for someone who must be in his late seventies," the priest muttered to himself.

The dark figure disappeared down the short flight of stairs that led to the rear entrance. The priest heard the back door open and shut.

The priest looked in the compartment of the confessional where the man had been. There he saw a locket on a chain, tarnished and with a touch of rust on the clasp. There were initials engraved on the outside of it: I. C. He picked it up and pried it open, holding it under the light in the confessional. Inside the locket was a small photograph of a young, very pretty, dark-haired girl.

On the *prie-dieu*, there was also a withered, yellowed piece of letter paper that had been folded into a tight square. He picked it up. It smelled musty. There were dark spots of mildew on it. He put it and the locket in his pocket.

184

# They Fly Forgotten

"You're free to read the note," the man had said. Father McManus had every intention of doing so, but over at the rectory. First, he would need to brace himself with a stiff drink, fortify himself with his long delayed cold supper, listen to the day's news on the radio, and get around to it when he felt strong enough to face it.

🐦

Father McManus read the office of Compline every night before retiring. This night he ventured first to read the halved and quartered note that the man calling himself "Randall" had left in the confessional. He settled himself in his favorite armchair, now cozily attired in his pajamas and bathrobe. He no longer knelt to pray; his arthritic knees wouldn't permit it. A hanging votive lamp flickered just below the crucifix on the wall opposite him. In that comfortable position he felt he was now ready to face whatever message the limp, mildewed sheet of paper contained.

He unfolded it, noting the faded floral design along the borders of it—roses and violets. It was notepaper designed for a woman. A barely legible note was written on it in faded violet ink. It read:

*Friday, October 9th*

*My dearest darling Methley,*

*I half taken the liberty of sending this to you by hand. Mae at the hardware store knows about us and she's my good freind and I trust her plicitly, and you can trust her too. You can slip me notes by way of her too. She doesnt know what's in this letter so dont say a thing to her about it after you reed it. Its got to remane <u>our own secret.</u>*

*Dearest Methley, I half given you everything I half—my heart, my love, and my own verry <u>self</u>. I want nothing more than to be at your side always and be always <u>yours</u>, my dear heart.*

*I half verry exiting news to tell you and I must see you tonight. I hope you will think it exiting too. Please meet me outside the store this evening. I truely must tell you what I found out and now we got to make plans about it. I wood tell you here in this letter—I am so exited and scared too—but I dont want to write it down just in case some body else shuold see it. I think its good news and I hope you will too when you hear it.*

185

*Well, I got to go. I love you more than words can discribe. I will see you tonight.*

*Here with this letter is a gift for you. Mama gave me this lockitt and now I give it to you with something inside. Its a picture of me you can wear under your shirt next your big heart.*

*Always as always, love love love,*
*Your verry own Ida*

"Atrocious penmanship," muttered Father McManus to himself, "and she can't spell any better than kids today."

He gently refolded the letter and set it next to the locket on the small table beside his chair. Combined with the story he had heard earlier in the church, reading the note left him feeling profoundly sad. A fifteen-year-old girl, an unexpected pregnancy, a relationship with a young man that was unacceptable in that day and, frankly, for the most part still was; a rejection by that same man before she could tell him her "exiting news," anger, a sense of betrayal, a foolish lie, a false accusation; the fruit of the lie: a vicious murder, a self-induced miscarriage... Altogether, a story of misery and woe, malignant guilt and ulcerating secrets.

Father McManus picked up his breviary and read through Compline with a fervency he rarely felt. He prayed for the repose of the soul of Methley Tanner. He prayed for Randall. He prayed for Ida, whom he intended to go and see the following day. He knew that what the man had said to him in the confessional was right: it was his priestly duty to approach her with the matter, and try to bring her some comfort and consolation, to give her the opportunity of doing penance.

"I can't believe she doesn't feel any guilt," thought the priest, "even after all these years."

That night his dreams were ugly and unpleasant. He sweated and thrashed as they played and replayed in his head. A twisting hanged man, bleeding and naked, burning, tormented to death by brutal young men—over and over the scene was acted out in his mind.

What poor Ida must go through, he thought in his nocturnal restlessness. He imagined her as a fifteen-year-old girl, more innocent than debauched, frightened, foolish, unsure, hurt, confused,

186

carrying the weight of her brother's sin on her shoulders for sixty long years, her own sins going unconfessed. Poor woman, he thought.

Finally, in the very early morning hours, his fitfulness relaxed, and he fell into dreamless oblivion. He slept soundly until dawn.

Ida Crosby (*née* Cartwright), her white cat in arm, glanced through her living room window. She watched as Father McManus pulled up in his black Ford Fairlane and parked directly below. He had phoned her that morning and asked if he might pay her a visit at three in the afternoon. It was almost three now.

Ida lived on Main Street above the grocers. She and her husband, Daniel, had moved into the apartment barely six months before he had died suddenly of heart failure. He had passed away, in fact, in this very room where she now stood, in the very chair that Father McManus would soon occupy this afternoon. Before they had moved into town, she and her husband had lived and raised their four children on the outskirts of town—not far, in fact, from where Methley Tanner had once rented rooms. Rooms she could still vividly recall. That boarding house had burned down in 1917. Occasionally a memory of Methley would intrude itself, but she had learned decades ago how to banish that specter and get on with her present-day life.

Ida watched the priest climb awkwardly out of the car, toss the butt of his little cigar in the gutter and grind it under his toe, and then head in the direction of the downstairs entryway. He carried in one hand, she could see, a small black book and a purple stole.

"He's probably wondering why we haven't been to Mass since your daddy went to be with God," she said to her cat, mimicking a child's voice. "How're we going to tell him nicely we've gone back to the Methodists, Fluff-Puff? Hmm? You tell me. How?"

Fluff-Puff made a discontented noise and jumped out of her arms. Ida went over to the apartment door, and when she heard the buzzer, she hit the intercom and said, "Come on up, Father."

Fluff-Puff slunk off to places unseen to wait out this annoying encroachment on his domain for as long as it might last.

187

Father McManus had been dreading the visit. Ida had asked him on the phone why he wanted to come, and all he had said was that he had something rather important to discuss with her. He hadn't seen her since Dan's funeral. He knew she would assume he was coming over to find out why she had been absent from Mass. As he stepped over the threshold into the apartment, which smelled of lavender and cat urine (the cat's litterbox was just to the right of the door), he suddenly felt the urge to make hasty excuses and back out of the visit. To confront this diminutive white-haired old woman standing before him with the awful story he had heard the previous night suddenly seemed to him to be an unnecessary cruelty. Surely, he thought, she made her peace with God regarding those events a long time ago. Why drag her through it again? Let sleeping dogs lie and all that.

Instead, however, he heard himself say, "Hello, Ida. Thanks for letting me drop in like this."

"A cup of coffee, Father?" she asked, motioning him toward a doily-decorated armchair (the same in which her husband Dan had died).

"No, thanks," he said. "You go right ahead, though."

"I won't have any either," she said. "It's instant. It tastes like battery acid, to be honest. I don't know why I even drink the stuff."

She seated herself on a similarly doily-draped chair.

"Please," she said. "Have a seat. It's always nice to see you."

The last bit was a lie, though Father McManus didn't know it. She was one of the very few people in town who didn't like him, but she had managed to keep her distaste a secret. She especially disapproved of his enjoyment of a drink, and she didn't mind telling her circle of elderly lady friends that she thought he behaved "too worldly" for a man of God. Her dislike was one of the reasons she had gone back to the Methodist church. She liked the preacher there. He was straitlaced. His sermons echoed Norman Vincent Peale and *Guideposts* magazine.

They sat and chit-chatted casually for a few minutes. Ida said she had heard about the upcoming celebration at the parish. She lied again and told the priest she intended to be there.

"There's so much confusion nowadays," she said. "I don't know what the world is coming to. To no good, I suppose. Back in our day, growing up, things were a whole lot sweeter. People were gentler. We all got along nicely, and it was so much more quiet then. It'll be nice to have something like the parish celebration to take our minds off the present moment—something wholesome and old-fashioned for a change."

The priest looked at his hands and the book and the stole he carried. He felt the folded letter and the locket in his breast pocket.

"I'm here for a special reason," he said, coming directly to the point.

"I'm all ears," said the old woman, smiling theatrically. "Do tell me, Father."

"Well… please forgive me, but…" He reached into his pocket and took out the locket. He handed it to her. "Do you recognize this, by any chance?"

Her eyes grew wide for a moment, and she stiffened, then she just as quickly relaxed. "It's something my mother gave me many years ago. I thought I'd lost it. See? It has my initials engraved on it. How did you get it?" She opened it. "And here's me at fifteen," she added, gazing at the photograph inside.

He took the folded letter out of his pocket. He just held it in his hand along with the book and stole.

"This is hard for me to ask you, but I have to. Bear with me." Father McManus drew a long breath. "Do you remember someone named Methley Tanner? From years ago?"

Ida froze as if turned to ice. She stared at him unblinkingly, stunned.

"Who?" she finally got out. Her face was suddenly an emotionless mask. Father McManus thought she looked as if wheels were turning rapidly inside her head, as if she knew she had to come up with something fast—and couldn't.

"Methley Tanner," Father McManus repeated. "This would be sixty years ago. Back in 1903."

Now her face betrayed her. Her eyes darted. She looked cornered, like she couldn't come up with the right answer in a tough quiz. She looked away, avoiding the priest's gaze.

"Yes," she said. "I do recall the name. A mulatto boy who used to work at the hardware store down the road from the church, across from the B&O station."

"Maybe you recall a bit more than just the name?" ventured the priest. "I have reason to believe you may have known him fairly well in those days."

"Like I said, I do recall the boy, yes," she replied, sitting motionless and as erect as a fireplace poker. "He was a sort of... sort of *a friend* of ours. We all liked him. I mean my friends and I all liked him."

"I have reason to think," said the priest, "and I don't mean this to be impertinent in any way, but I have reason to think you might have been rather close personally to Methley while he was still alive."

Her eyes narrowed. Her two hands gripped the arms of her chair claw-like.

"What are you getting at? What are you implying?" she hissed.

The sound of that hiss took him aback. She just as quickly took control of herself and slackened her posture, unhooking her white-knuckled fingers from the chair's arms. She sighed long and loud. She appeared resigned to the fact that the priest *knew something*, and there was no way around admitting as much of the truth as would prove necessary to disclose.

"Okay, yes. I was quite fond of Methley, and we were friends. He was colored, but he was a gentleman. And smart. And talented. I liked him very much, to be honest."

"And he died young," Father McManus went on.

"How do you know all this?" asked Ida, looking back over at the priest's face. "Nobody these days remembers Methley Tanner. He went and disappeared. Nobody missed him then, and nobody remembers him now. Nobody could."

"Somebody remembers him."

"Besides me?"

"Besides you, yes."

"All right." She sighed again. Father McManus saw a hint of sadness creep into her eyes. "He died young. Much too young. But why are you asking me about Methley Tanner all of a sudden? What's he got to do with anything *now*—or anything with *me*, for that matter?

190

He's been gone for sixty years, as you said, and the last time I saw him I was fifteen—the age I was in this photograph."

She held up the open locket. The priest looked past the small photograph of the dark-haired young woman into Ida's eyes.

"I was just a girl," said Ida.

"Not *just* a girl," said the priest.

The sadness in her eyes had emboldened him. "Here," he said, and handed her the halved and quartered piece of yellowed, mildewed paper.

She took it, tremblingly. She put on her rimless reading glasses, which had been hanging by a cord around her neck. She slowly, apprehensively unfolded the paper. She wrinkled her nose, evidently in reaction to the musty odor it gave off.

She read. She caught her breath.

After some moments, she slowly removed her glasses and let them drop against her bosom on the cord. She looked directly into the priest's eyes. Her face was impassive. He couldn't read her. For a few long moments time seemed suspended in the room. At last, though, she let out yet another deep sigh.

"What am I supposed to say to all this?" she said, pointing at the letter she was holding. "What do you want me to say or do about it? Confess that, once upon a time, I was a fifteen-year-old girl who was briefly smitten with a colored boy? Well, all right, I was. I confess it. He was a good-looking, bright young man. He could've passed for white."

Father McManus said quietly, "But there was more to it than that. It doesn't matter to God what color his skin was—how pale, how dark. It didn't matter to you back then either, I think. It certainly doesn't matter to me. What matters is what happened next."

A hard glint appeared in Ida's eyes. "Who've you been talking to? You said somebody else remembers Methley. Who would that be? Where'd you get this letter?"

"Did you accuse Methley of taking advantage of you?" The priest continued, determined now to press on, to just get everything out in the open and over with. "I see you loved him. I heard he planned to leave and that upset you, and you reacted by doing a foolish thing. You said in your letter that you had exciting news to tell him.

191

Was it—pardon me for the indelicacy of my question—but was it *a pregnancy?*"

Ida went from parchment-yellow to pasteboard-white.

"How dare you?" The hiss came back into her voice. "You may be a priest, but you've got no business bringing that up to me, throwing it in my face like that."

"I'm bringing it up only because I care about you, Ida," said Father McManus. "I care about your soul. I care about Methley Tanner, who died so young and so violently. Hear me out, please. You did a very foolish thing. Not an unforgivable thing. You were angry and hurt, and you spoke out of your hurt. But you *did* accuse Methley of raping you—you did. I'm sorry to be so crude, but that's the unvarnished truth here. And your brother, Randall, took it upon himself to avenge your honor. So, he got together some of his friends. They found Methley Tanner, and they took him up Church Road, up into the woods there, and they tortured that young man and they hanged him. They burned him and buried him up there in those woods somewhere. And he's still up there. He's been up there in that cold ground, alone and forgotten, for sixty long years. And then you took some terrible concoction that caused you to miscarry your baby."

He stopped. He had hoped to see tears or some other sign of remorse on Ida's part, no matter how slight. But he saw nothing of the kind. What he saw instead was a woman of stone-cold resolve. He saw flashes in her eyes. He saw hatred and anger and bitterness. He saw her face go taut and froth bubble at the corners of her mouth. Her voice hissed at him from between tightly drawn lips.

"You goddamn hypocrite," she hissed. "Who the devil have you been talking to? Where'd you get this letter and this locket? I thought they were long gone, like Methley. Who asked you to come up here and throw this dirt you dug up in my face? Who's been talking out of turn, behind my back? It couldn't be Mae. She died years ago, and she wouldn't have done it anyway, even if she was alive. And that old woman who gave me the stuff to drink—she was dead and gone before the Great War started."

"What does it matter who told me?" said Father McManus. "What matters is that you confess it and receive absolution if you never have before. That's why I came. Not to condemn you, and certainly not to speak about it ever again. You were responsible indirectly for one death and directly for another. You accused someone of doing something they hadn't done. You bore false witness. You lied. You need to get that right before God. You need forgiveness before you die, to rid your conscience of all these evil things."

He was sweating. He was shaking. But he resolved to remain undaunted.

"Will you seek that forgiveness?" he asked.

Ida shot up from her chair—remarkable, Father McManus thought, for a woman of her years. She stood over him, trembling with a barely contained rage.

"Get out of here," she ordered, pointing toward the door. "Take these... these *things*"—and she flung the moldy letter and the locket in his direction, both of which he just barely managed to catch mid-air—"and get the hell out. I'll be honest. I've never liked you. I don't like your papist church. I only went there to make Dan happy. But I'm no papist and I don't need to confess to you or anybody except God. Do I make myself clear?"

"Yes," said the priest, rising. "You do. I'm sorry you feel the way you do. I'll go."

"You sure as hell will," said Ida.

He went to the door and opened it to leave but stopped at the threshold. He turned around to look at the old woman one more time. She stood rigidly in the middle of the room, glaring at him. He felt he owed it to her to inform her that it was her brother who had come to him, that her brother had cared about her so much that he had urged the priest to pay her this visit.

"If you'll tell me where I might find him, I'll let Randall know I tried," said Father McManus. "I'll let him know I gave it my best shot."

Ida's jaw dropped.

"*Who*?" she said, looking startled. "Did you say 'Randall'?"

"Randall," said the priest. "Your brother. I just caught a glimpse of him heading out the back door of the church last night. He told me the whole story in the confessional. He left behind the letter and the locket."

"You're a liar," said Ida. "You said I was a liar, but you're the liar."

Father McManus was surprised by the reaction.

"Isn't Randall your brother?" he asked.

"Randall's dead," Ida said. The tone of her voice was flat. The hiss was gone.

"No, no," the priest said. "I saw him just last night. He said he was your brother—Randall."

"Randall hanged himself thirty years ago," Ida said, distress showing in her features. "He hanged himself up in those same woods where he and the others hanged Methley. He's buried in the Methodist graveyard on the edge of town. Not far from here."

Father McManus grabbed hold of the open door to steady himself. He felt dizzy. Ida watched him. She looked almost as if she felt sympathy for him at that moment. Her voice was softer now.

But all she said was, "Please close the door on your way out."

The sober gray eminence of ashlar granite overlooks the town from the south. Far below, the river ceaselessly flows.

In poetry and art, the river is a perennial metaphor. "Time, like an ever-rolling stream, bears all its sons away; they fly forgotten, as a dream dies at the opening day." So wrote Isaac Watts. The current of the river courses along, always the same, never the same.

The old railway station, boarded and unused, stands above these waters. Its own mechanized flow has stopped. No one rides those rails now. It serves as a memory of "the good old days," gayer times, a happier era—or so Father McManus once thought.

The hardware store, still in operation in 1963, is right across the street from it. No one remembers that a young man named Methley Tanner worked there for a few months sixty years earlier, or that a fifteen-year-old girl who lived nearby was once in love with him. No one remembers that he was working there one day, and he was gone the next. No one knows that his bones are buried unmarked somewhere up in the northern hills above town. Buried, as the crow flies, directly opposite the great gray church with the needle-like steeple to the south.

It's a Wednesday evening. It's mid-October. It's twenty minutes past seven. Father McManus is in the confessional, reading his breviary and waiting for his next penitent. Outside, making her way slowly and painfully up one of the flights of concrete steps, grasping the iron rail with both her hands to steady herself, but determined to reach the entrance into the church, is a white-haired, frail old woman.

# The Spot on the Bridge

H E NEVER MEANT to kill any of them. Not Vicky, with her red locks; not Roxanne, with those rosy cherub cheeks of hers; not Brenda, with her funny lisp. He reassured his talkative, castigating conscience with the protestation of his lack of intent whenever it started to nag at him. It did that sometimes. It could be a terrible scold. But when it did, he calmed himself by reminding himself yet again that he really had had no other choice. Each time it had happened, he would argue with himself, he had genuinely regretted it afterward. He would return home and lock himself in his room and berate himself, after first carefully cleaning his hands and brushing off his clothes. Surely, his subsequent feelings of self-loathing and his repeated decisions to repent would count in his favor and stand him in good stead before the Final Tribunal.

Often his remorse brought him to tears. He knew he couldn't look upon little Shirley's image immediately afterward, sometimes for days. Looking away from her trusting gaze, he would put her framed photograph face down. Her picture was always placed on the chest of drawers near his bed, usually with a recently cut flower in a small vase beside it. But he couldn't bear to let Shirley see his shame. He knew, of course, that the eyes in the photograph couldn't really see him, much less see *into* him, but still… the thought of those bright eyes alight with merriment and that dimpled smile and that unruly mop of curls, and her looking so innocent and happy and ready to play, was something he just couldn't reconcile with his bad deeds until sufficient time had elapsed.

The incident would have to recede into memory's consoling distance, and then, in time, it would begin to seem to him that it hadn't really been he who had done those awful things. It had been a different person, led astray by the devil perhaps, who had done them. But happily, he was sure, the fiend had left him now—maybe for good this time. For the time being, at least, he was once more in sole possession of his wits. It was water under the bridge. He would turn over a new leaf this time for sure. He would resolve anew never, ever to do it again. It was just a matter of willpower, after all. His renewed resolve would then reinvigorate him, restore his hopes, and once more Miss Temple's picture would be put upright—it was a little shrine, really—and he would resume his daily existence just as before, his tears dried, his cares lifted.

Edwin worked at the post office, not as a carrier but as a clerk. To all intents and purposes, he appeared mild-mannered and "normal" (a term that frequently means "forgettable"). He was painfully aware of the fact that some of his coworkers called him "dull" and "humorless" behind his back. That knowledge hurt his pride. He liked a good joke, just like the rest of them—so long as the joke was in good taste. He was slender, he rarely smiled, and he was going gray around the temples. He sported a small bristling mustache. He dressed always in a black suit, always the dapper gentleman. He was a bachelor in his late forties. He lived alone in the same house in which he had grown up; he had inherited it when his mother died. It was set in splendid isolation out in the rolling countryside, not far from Ellicott City and the Patapsco River. His nearest neighbor lived more than a half-mile away and couldn't be seen for the intervening trees. Edwin enjoyed this remote location, far from the madding crowd and the post office, and there he lived alone in his own little world. There he could be a king.

And there, too, he made believe he hadn't killed those three little girls. But he had. On three occasions, over the span of seven years, something had stirred inside him, something he couldn't understand himself, a drive, a force, a voice that wouldn't take no for an answer. He called it "the urge." It would build up in him, slowly and persistently, this urge, this *tendency* that he both hated and found a dark pleasure in contemplating. It was, he told himself, really just a desire for *love*. He would soothe his conscience with that self-assurance. It had no desire to hurt or harm anyone, he told himself, even if it was a desire to possess. The idea of exercising power over another—someone defenseless and unable to resist—stirred him, though. When he was honest with himself, he couldn't deny that.

But wasn't that a characteristic of how a *man* loves? Romantic movies seemed to reinforce that idea. And wasn't he a *man*? Obviously, domination was part of it. He naturally sought someone he could love and possess, he also told himself, if only for a little while. That was a normal drive for a *man*. Yet, he also realized, nobody else seemed to understand these things in these insipid, abnormal times. People like him would never be understood—and this fact sometimes made him feel exceedingly sorry for himself.

Shirley, he felt, would have understood that much about him at least.

He always fell in love with the girls first. It was love that motivated him. And wasn't all love all right? Love covered a multitude of sins. Who could possibly gainsay the magic and power of love? He would spot one, then spy on her over an extended period of time—often for a space of two or three months. And it was always because he had fallen in love first.

He never meant to kill any of them. Or so he wanted to believe. He must believe that.

He had developed a method, the fine details of which are not important. But it involved ingratiating himself with them. He could be nice. He liked being nice. He might pass them by on the sidewalk as they played in a yard. He would wave and smile and say hi in the beginning. Over time, he would become a familiar sight to them. And then, by hook or by crook, after waiting and watching for as long as it took, he would find the perfect opportunity and persuade them to get into his car unseen. On one occasion, the little girl had come willingly. With the other two, he had had to work fast. He had used a blanket and rope on both occasions. And then he would be off, no one any the wiser.

Three little girls had disappeared without a trace.

Edwin alone knew where they were, a location near the river, wooded, that was unfrequented. There were three little graves there that nobody, except Edwin, knew about. He would drive his "guests" to this secluded spot. Later he would drive back home by himself.

There was a bridge that spanned the river between this out-of-the-way location and the location of his house, and there was a spot in the middle of the bridge which he dreaded to cross. He was never sure why he feared that spot on the bridge so much, but crossing it frightened him to the core. It literally made his heart flutter and his body quiver to do it. It felt to him—quite irrationally, he knew—as if he were driving over his own grave. Sometimes the terror of crossing the bridge caused him to shut his eyes and speed up at the same time. He would point the nose of his car straight and gun it at precisely that point where it scared him the most. But cross the bridge he must if he were to get home and wash himself. He always felt an overpowering need to wash afterward.

No, he hadn't meant to kill them... There was simply no other way to keep little girls silent. He felt that it was the most unfortunate aspect of what he had done. A necessity, true, but unfortunate. Although he had to admit to himself as well that, unfortunate or not, those girls hadn't been entirely guiltless, either. Oh, yes, they always seemed innocent and sweet in the beginning, but he knew better than to be gullible about that. He had had a staunch Calvinist upbringing, and he believed in "total depravity," and "total depravity" included little girls also. They shared some of the blame, maybe even more than just "some." But even with that caveat, he tried to convince his scolding conscience, he had derived no satisfaction from ending their earthly lives. He always did it swiftly and humanely. It did thrill him to do it, admittedly, but who wouldn't feel a bit of a thrill in such a moment? Surely, that wasn't an abnormal feeling to have, under the circumstances. Invariably there would follow the bitter days of remorse, when Shirley's picture would lie face down, and he would suffer and water his couch with tears.

The last time he had given into the urge had been in the spring of 1960. Two and a half years had gone by since then. But during that time, he had felt the urge rising within him again, pushing him, dogging him, inflaming his brain, intoxicating his imaginings.

What had stirred it to life again was a little blonde girl who lived in a large wood frame house, set back in a wooded area, nearly as isolated as his own. He had started watching her as she played outside almost every afternoon. She was most often alone, with her dolls or some other toys, yards away from the front porch.

Edwin would park his car just around the bend in the street and watch her as best he could from that vantage point, never for longer than ten minutes at a time.

He had fallen in love again. And there was no resisting love.

Angela was six years old and given to curiosity. Lately she had become fixated on her own name. It was on the evening of the day after Thanksgiving that she at last succeeded in broaching the subject with her mother and father, who she was certain knew everything worth knowing. She had been pondering the secret of her name throughout the week, and every time she had remembered to ask her all-knowing parents, something else—of lesser importance, of course, like school or a bath—had intervened and she didn't ask. Up until recently, she had just accepted the fact that she was "Angela," and that "Angela" was she. And then, almost as a revelation from above, she had made the connection between her name and the word *angel*. She now wanted her etymological suspicions confirmed by older and wiser heads. In the matter of angels, she was a true believer. She had learned about them at her parochial school, and her own father taught the Sunday School class she attended.

"Does my name mean *angel*?" she asked her mother, who was nursing her baby brother, Adam.

"Yes, it means *angel*, dear," her mother answered.

"Why?" asked Angela.

"Why what?" asked her mother.

"Why did you name me after an angel?"

"We called you that because you're our little angel. You looked like an angel to us."

Angela was puzzled by this, since no picture of an angel she had ever seen—certainly neither Saint Michael nor Saint Gabriel—looked anything like her, even if they did look just a little girlish. What angels looked like was another burning question she wanted answered. But for now, she took a different tack.

"But I'm not really an angel," declared Angela. "Not yet anyway. But Mama, will I be an angel after I die?"

Her father, who was seated in the living room with them, reading his paper, looked over it at the little girl and said, "What did you learn in Sunday School?"

Angela, sitting on the floor beside the hassock and balancing one of her dolls on her knee, said, "I don't remember. It was long ago."

"It was only back in September when we talked about angels," her father said. "You remember that. Jesus said we will become like the angels in heaven. We won't actually become angels..."

Her mother interrupted: "Don't confuse her, dear."

"You're a human being," her father continued unabated, "a little girl. Made of flesh and blood..."

"And guts," added Angela.

"And guts," said her father. "But angels are spirits, and they live forever. And someday we'll live forever, too. So, we'll be like them. But we'll always be humans, and they'll always be angels."

He was waxing pedantic again, Angela's mother thought. The poor longsuffering Sunday School class...

"Oh," said Angela. "So why did you name me 'Angela' if I'm not really an angel and won't ever be an angel?"

Her mother buttoned up her blouse and started to burp the baby. "Because, as I said, you made us think of an angel when we first saw you," she said.

"Hmm," replied Angela, not entirely convinced by this reasoning.

"And don't forget that you have a guardian angel," added her mother. "We say a prayer to your guardian angel each night before bed."

"Where's my guardian angel now?" asked Angela. "Here in the room with us somewhere?"

"Watching over you," said her father. "Guarding you. Everybody has a guardian angel."

"Everybody?"

"Everybody."

"Even bad people?"

"Even bad people."

"Hmm," said Angela, laying her doll flat on its back on the hassock. She looked unsatisfied.

Noting it, her father asked, "What now?"

"Seems to me bad people can't have good angels watching over them," said Angela. "And what about good people who get hurt sometimes… or die sometimes…? Do they have angels?"

Her mother and father knew that Angela must be thinking about Joan. There had been a fire, and Joan—who had been Angela's friend at school—had died in it.

Her father said gently, "When someone dies, their guardian angel takes them to be with God. I'm sure Joan's guardian angel took her to be with God and she's happy now."

Angela still wasn't satisfied. "And bad people? What happens to bad people when they die? Do they go to be with God?"

"That's a tricky question," her father said. "I believe they're judged and punished…"

"But do they have guardian angels?"

"Yes… but there are some things we won't know till we get there. I'm sure our guardian angels are watching out for us. Even when bad things happen, we have to trust everything will turn out all right in the end."

Angela was satisfied for the time being. She was still curious what her guardian angel might look like. She wondered if her angel had wings.

Before she went to bed that night, her mother knelt with her beside her bed, and they said their prayers. As they prayed the guardian angel prayer, Angela thought she saw something flutter past the window outside. She wondered if it was her angel. She pointed and asked her mother.

But her mother only said, "Goodnight, dear," and kissed her before turning out the light.

One Saturday morning, Edwin on a whim strolled past the house and spotted Angela in the front yard, bundled against the chill and seated underneath one of the large maples there. She was sitting there, her back against the bole of the tree, as if she were waiting for a visitor. He had been passing by the house from time to time for the past month and a half, and this was the first time he had ventured to do so on a Saturday morning. When he had first begun his method of ingratiation with Angela, he had just waved to her. As time went on, he made bold to say hello to her as he went along. If the little girl's parents were around, he would turn around before being seen and head back to his parked car. But usually, they were nowhere to be seen.

Now, of late, he had taken to stopping and chatting with Angela. He had asked her what her name was. She told him. He told her she had an enchanting name. He told her that his name was Danny. Usually, the little girl was active, playing with her dolls or running and jumping. She even had a hula hoop that she did her best to master. Edwin noted with some delight that she was alone most of the time. She had friends and cousins, but they lived too far away to come over and play every day. He had asked and she had told him that. He had said he was terribly sorry to hear that. He said he wished he was a little boy, then he could come over and play with her. But he never protracted their conversations. That wouldn't do. Too risky. He kept the exchanges short and sweet, very sweet.

But today she was outside alone and sitting beneath that tree. Waiting. Waiting for him? Edwin shook his head. No, he thought, that was unlikely—it was Saturday, after all, not the usual weekday afternoon. Besides, it would be much too good to be true. He didn't want to dare to hope such a foolish thing. But there she was.

He steeled himself inside and strode over to the edge of the lawn, not far from where the little girl sat.

"Hi there, Angela," he said to her.

"Hi there, Danny," said Angela.

"What are you doing today?" asked Edwin.

"Oh, nothing," said Angela. "Just sitting."

Edwin blushed a little, but he nerved himself to say, "Are you waiting for someone?"

"Maybe," said Angela.

Edwin came closer. "Maybe you were waiting... for me...?"

"Maybe," said Angela again. "You do come by a lot, you know. You came by yesterday, too."

"That's because I like you," said Edwin. "It's always nice to see you. You're fun to talk to. Where are your dolls this morning?"

"They didn't want to come outside today," said Angela. "It's too cold for them."

"Ah," said Edwin. "Well, that sounds kind of lonesome for you."

"Nah," said Angela. "I knew *you'd* come."

Edwin's heart skipped a beat at that remark. "Y-you did...?" He was flattered. He felt himself blushing.

"'Course," said Angela.

The urge began to bubble up inside him. He was sure that she liked him, too. Did he dare to hope...? Could this be the day...?

He said, "Well, I'm a pretty nice man, Angela, when you get to know me, and I like you very much. That's why I like to come by and see you. And you say you were... waiting for me? Really? Is that true?"

Angela got up and came over to him. "Sure," she said. "Why not?"

Edwin's heart pounded. He put out his hand.

"How about a walk down the lane together?" The words just popped out of him before he knew what he had said.

She took his extended hand. When she did, he got a big lump in his throat. He could feel himself begin to perspire. This was almost too easy. She was so unexpectedly trusting that it made him feel a little uneasy. He was used to expending more effort. It had even been a struggle on two occasions. But there was no struggle this time. It was complete acquiescence without hesitation. It gave him something like the jitters. But he wasn't going to look a gift horse in the mouth.

"Yes, let's take a walk," she said.

He really couldn't believe his luck. He glanced over at the house. There was no sign of life. Not even a car in the driveway. No one was watching. The parents, he surmised, must be preoccupied and at least momentarily inattentive, and the absence of the automobile suggested that Angela's father was off somewhere on an errand. Edwin had her all to himself. And since the house stood virtually by itself on this part of the lane, there was no one else in view who would even see him with her.

He trembled. He tried not to let it show, but Angela noticed.

"Why are you shaking?" she asked. "Are you cold?"

"Old war wound," lied Edwin. "Makes me shiver sometimes."

"That's sad," said Angela. "You were in the war? My daddy was in the war. You got hurt?"

204

"Yes," Edwin replied, crossing his fingers behind his back with his free hand. "I was very brave."

"Did you ever kill anybody, Danny?" asked Angela, all innocence.

"What?" said Edwin, visibly disturbed. "Kill anybody? No, I never... I couldn't ever..."

The question left him shaking more than before.

"I'm glad you didn't kill anybody," said Angela. "Where are we going?"

Edwin was relieved to change the subject.

"Let's go over to where my car's parked and see what's in it," he said.

"Okay," said the little girl. "Let's do that. What's in your car?"

"Would you like to see?" asked Edwin, his face alight. "I really don't have anything interesting in it—just some tools and stuff in the backseat. But—I have an idea—how would you like to take a drive with me and see some nice sights?"

He fully expected the girl to resist and say no. That's what usually happened.

"Mama and Daddy told me never to go for rides with a stranger," she replied.

Damn, thought Edwin to himself, it's going to end up being another struggle, after all...

But then, Angela said, "But we're friends and you're a nice man, Danny. You never even killed anybody in the war. And I like car trips. I just need to be home by dinnertime."

This was unbelievable! It had never been so easily achieved before. Edwin almost swooned. They walked hand in hand around the bend in the lane and there was his car, a dark blue Chevy Impala.

"Well, there's our chariot," he said as gaily as he could.

Angela let go of his hand and ran over to the passenger's side.

"Can I sit in the front?" she asked.

"You sure can," replied Edwin, elated. "Anything for the little angel."

"That's what my name means," said Angela.

"I know," said Edwin, opening the door for her to climb in. He excitedly ran over to the driver's side, put his key in the ignition, and within seconds they were driving along.

205

Edwin kept it chatty. "So, Angela," he said, "what are your dolls' names?"

"I have three dolls," replied the little girl. "One's named Vicky. She has red hair. One's named Roxanne—she's the naughty one—and one's named Brenda."

With the mention of those three names, Edwin almost swerved off the road. He felt his palms itch and get sweaty. He started to cough uncontrollably. He took a handkerchief out of his breast pocket and covered his mouth with it.

When he had recovered from the coughing fit, he said hoarsely, "Those are very nice names."

Vicky, Roxanne, and Brenda had been the names of those other three girls. He felt a wave of nausea pass through him. She couldn't possibly have known that, he assured himself. It was just a crazy coincidence... but what a crazy coincidence. Quite unexpected and unnerving.

"Where are we going, Danny?" asked Angela.

"Oh, I thought we'd just take a spin," said Edwin. "Maybe down to the river and back. How's that sound? There's a nice, pretty area by the river just off the road a ways, near the woods. You'll like it. Lots of squirrels and chipmunks."

He conjectured that, if she was going to become worried or frightened, now would most likely be the moment. Suggesting a trip to the woods with a strange man should surely set off alarm bells even in a little girl's head, assuming her parents had raised her properly. But if he could just get past this point, the point of suggesting the destination... well, it should almost certainly be smooth sailing after that.

"That sounds nice, Danny," Angela said.

Edwin was simultaneously thrilled and aghast. He really couldn't believe what he was hearing. No fear, no trepidation—Angela simply evinced an absolute, trusting willingness to go along with his suggestion.

He wondered what in heaven's name was wrong with her parents. Didn't they know there were dangers out there in the big world? That little girls were vulnerable and should be protected? Didn't they love their child enough to watch out for her? Were they irresponsible dullards? Merely warning her not to take rides with strangers was hardly enough to prevent…

He winced. He vigorously shook his head to clear his mind. He felt a headache coming on. He sometimes had a headache right before…

Well, dammit, Angela's parents would just have to learn the hard way, he concluded. He wouldn't pity them. They didn't deserve to keep their little girl if they were this culpably stupid and careless. It enraged him just to think about it.

But he turned on the charm, despite his furious thoughts. Smiling, he said to Angela, "Tell me about your mother and father."

By now they were getting close to that single spot along the route that Edwin dreaded for reasons he couldn't explain even to himself: the middle of the narrow bridge that spanned the river. He always drove as quickly over it as he could, just to put it behind him fast. He knew it traversed the deepest part of the river. He invariably saw the same scene in his head every time he drew near to it—the vivid picture of himself veering madly over the side, trapped in his automobile, plummeting into the racing waters below, and sinking down, down, down in the icy and total blackness of its depths, the car flooding while he panicked and thrashed in desperation to escape his car, his tomb… and then nothing. Oblivion.

The horror of that vision never failed to force his foot down hard on the gas pedal.

The little girl meanwhile was talking nonstop about her mother and baby Adam, how baby Adam cried a lot, how baby Adam smelled bad when he messed in his diaper, how her mother nursed baby Adam…

They reached the bridge. Edwin wasn't paying any attention to Angela's babbling. He shut his eyes tight and gunned the engine. Angela let out a scream. Edwin opened his eyes just in time to avoid swerving into the left-hand lane and into a pickup truck approaching from the other direction. He swung the Chevy back into the right-hand lane just in the nick of time. He started shaking like he had the palsy—he had never come so close to a head-on collision before.

The man in the truck shouted something vulgar out his window at him and waved a clenched fist as he went past.

Angela sat quietly in her seat for a few minutes. Then she started talking again.

"Daddy works at Koppers Corporation," she said, as if nothing much had happened. "He's a businessman. He works in Baltimore. I don't really know what he does, but he's very important, and he was in the war, too, and he was a captain…"

Edwin turned off the bridge, still feeling shudders wrack his system. But he managed shakily to say, "Really? That's interesting…"

Angela said, "Yes, and he teaches Sunday School on Sundays, too."

"Always the best day to teach Sunday School," said Edwin.

Not much further now, he thought to himself. Then they would be together and out of sight of the rest of the world.

"Yes," Angela went on. "He teaches us what Jesus taught."

"Oh?" said Edwin. "And what does your daddy tell you that Jesus taught?"

The side road was coming up on his right. Just a few more seconds.

Angela said, "Oh, stuff like 'love your neighbor as yourself' and 'a city set on a hill can't be hid' and 'watch out for wolves in sheep's clothing' and 'let the little children come to me'—although the Bible he reads out of says, '*suffer* the little children to come to me,' but Daddy says that 'suffer' doesn't mean 'suffer' like hurting somebody—he says God doesn't want little children to suffer, but rather, he says, that 'suffer' didn't always mean 'suffer' like, you know, pain and stuff, but it used to mean 'let,' as in '*let* the little children come to me.'"

She took a deep breath.

"Anything else?" asked Edwin.

He turned the car down the side road. The place was just up ahead. His special place.

"Oh, yes, lots more," said Angela. "Like Jesus also said that little children's angels in heaven 'behold the face of his Father in heaven.' Jesus said the angels watch over children and get mad if somebody hurts them."

Edwin began to be a bit uncomfortable with the direction her rambling was going. But now he was off the road and pulling into his special hidden cul-de-sac, surrounded by the woods. There was a small muddy clearing there, eminently suited for parking unseen.

He stopped the car.

"And, you know, *Edwin*…" went on the little girl.

Edwin snapped to when he heard his true name spoken. He glanced over at the little girl, but she was looking away from him and out her passenger's-side window.

Her voice continued, but now it sounded oddly older than the voice of a little girl, and what she was saying was well beyond the language he would have expected from a six-year-old.

She was saying, "Jesus said that anyone who harmed one of his little ones would be better off having a millstone strung around his neck and drowned in the sea."

With that, she opened her car door, jumped out, and ran in the direction of the woods.

Edwin sat behind the wheel for a few confused moments, stunned. Then he also opened his door and got out, coming around to the front of the car.

Angela was standing now on the outskirts of the woods, looking into their depths. Edwin stood where he was and stared at her back.

"I… I'm Danny," he called to her, his head now aching savagely, his eyes blurry from the pain. "Not that other name you just called me in the car. Danny. Remember?"

She turned around. Her voice was deep, husky, unnatural.

"No, Edwin," she said. "Your name is *Edwin*. You can stop telling lies now. Your time has come, and all this"—she waved her arms in a sweeping gesture—"is over."

Edwin took a few steps nearer and stopped about six yards from her. The urge was gone, but in its place, he felt a different urge. It was the stripped-down, bare, uncomplicated urge to murder—just murder, nothing else—and then run like hell.

"Look," he said, restraining a mounting rage as best he could, "you need to stop playing these stupid, unfair games with me."

He savagely kicked a stone in her direction. "And don't you ever call me a liar again, you nasty little slut."

He started to froth at the mouth. He couldn't control the fury.

"Didn't your lazy, good-for-nothing parents ever teach you *any-*

*thing*—like how to behave like a good little girl and talk politely to grownups—to your betters? Where are your manners? Come over here and I'll teach you some manners, you brat."

He stopped. He felt like he was going to cry.

"I mean, did you lure me out here just to taunt me? You just can't trust girls—any of them! You're all alike! I should have known that by now…"

His voice became a moan.

"No… no… I'm sorry I said that… Please… I'm sorry. I didn't mean it. Come on over here. Let's make up and be friends again. It's just that I don't like being taunted."

When she didn't budge, his voice became petulant and peevish.

"Come on, Angela. Stop this right now." He stamped his foot. "You know how I tried to be nice to you. You saw how nice I was. You're not even all that pretty. But I took you for a spin anyhow. I thought we were getting to know each other pretty well, too, getting to be friends…"

"Speaking of friends," said Angela, "there are some friends of mine here. They're coming. You might remember them when you see them."

As she spoke, there emerged from the woods behind her three more little girls, all about Angela's age. They came up and stood shoulder-to-shoulder beside Angela.

"You remember Vicky," Angela said to the now thoroughly terrified Edwin, gesturing toward one of the little girls. "The one with the red hair."

Edwin shook his head.

"She was the first," said Angela. "Seven years ago. And here is Roxanne…"

She gestured to another of the girls.

"Five years ago. No, stop shaking your head, Edwin. Don't pretend you've forgotten Roxanne. You said you loved her, after all. And here is Brenda. Just two and a half years ago."

Edwin fell to his knees. He buried his face in his hands.

"Look at us," commanded Angela, her voice growing even deeper in tone. "Get your hands away from your face and look at us."

Edwin slowly lowered his hands and looked up. He felt nauseous, he felt his bladder go. His headache intensified and made him wince with pain.

The pale November sun was sinking in the west. The shadows were growing long. Edwin began to whimper. Angela approached him and stopped just a few feet in front of him.

"It's over, Edwin," she said. "The earth can no longer bear your weight."

There was a rush of air, blowing through the bare branches of the trees, scattering brown leaves everywhere. He could hear the waters of the nearby river surge—they seemed to seethe and rage. The other girls came forward and all four stood over him, looking down at him as he began to grovel in the mud.

Edwin had been moaning and mumbling unintelligibly. But then, suddenly, as if quickened by an electric jolt, he stood bolt upright and faced his tormenters. He screamed at them.

"I'd kill you all again, if I could, you vicious, miserable little hussies—oh, yes, I would. Don't you think I wouldn't. I enjoyed killing you. I did! I admit it! You think you're all so very, very good—well, I know what you are... I see through you... I always hated you..."

"Enough!" commanded Angela.

Edwin suddenly found he couldn't speak another word. Something had seized him by the throat, or it felt that way. He put his hand up to his Adam's apple to check, but no hand gripped him. Yet he felt as if one did. He choked and spluttered.

"Appearances are deceptive," said the girl. "We're not who or what you think we are. Those three girls you harmed are no longer here. Their brief sufferings are forever past. Yours are only just beginning. Look at us!"

Before his eyes the four figures began to shimmer and flash with a brilliance that burned Edwin's eyes. They seemed to expand in stature, looming over him like giants. At that moment, the wind whipped up again with an even greater intensity than before, the earth seemed to rumble beneath him, the river's flow sounded deafening in his ears.

And then Edwin jumped up and fled.

He dodged to the left and around the front end of the Chevy. He pulled out his keys, leapt into the driver's seat, fumbled with the

211

ignition, and within a matter of seconds he had backed up, turned around, and—spraying mud behind his back wheels in the direction of the four giants—tore out of the area, the gas pedal pressed to the floor.

Edwin drove like a madman, running the Stop signs, the wheels squealing and shrieking like condemned souls, tearing up the pavement.

Ahead of him was the intersection, where he must turn sharply to the left to cross the narrow bridge. *The bridge...*

His heart was racing faster than the car, his head was splitting, he was foaming at the corners of his mouth—which was all his mouth could manage. The intersection came up. He turned sharply onto the bridge, almost tipping the car up on its two righthand-side tires, leaving burnt rubber marks behind him on the asphalt.

He was on the bridge.

Below it he saw the wild, roiling river. He saw the frenzied current rushing uncontrollably. It was overflowing its banks.

If he could just get over the bridge, put it behind him, behind him for good—his brain was in a muddle—if he could just get over the bridge, then—then everything would be all right.

But there was *that spot*—that dreaded damned spot. It was coming at him fast.

He'd just have to brave it, like he always had before—well, not "brave" it exactly, but get over it quickly. He squeezed his eyes shut. He pushed his foot down on the gas again hard. The car surged forward.

And then a rush of wind came against the side of the car with a wallop and seemed to lift it. The car veered. Edwin, his eyes closed so tight the tears trickled, felt as if he was airborne. For one giddy moment he felt his stomach flutter wildly.

It almost made him laugh.

🐦

The Monday morning paper had it on the front page. The headline read:

**Dead Man Pulled from Patapsco Identified**

# The Spot on the Bridge

The sub-heading read:

**Three bodies found in woods may be related to tragic accident**

A photograph of Edwin appeared below the byline.

Angela caught sight of the photo as her father was immersed in reading the report. It was seven-ten in the morning and the family was seated at the breakfast table. Adam was in his highchair, smearing jam all over his face and the chair's tray with gummy fingers. Angela was still working on her poached egg and toast, dressed for school. The adults had eaten their breakfast hurriedly and were finishing their coffee. Angela's father dropped her off at the parochial school most mornings before heading to his office in Baltimore.

"I know him!" Angela cried when she saw the picture of Edwin.

"You know that man?" her father asked, looking somewhat troubled as he said it. Angela's mother looked quizzically at her husband.

"Yes!" exclaimed Angela. "That's Danny! Why's Danny in the newspaper? He's my friend."

"Your *friend*?" Her father glanced at her mother worriedly.

"Yes, yes," said Angela. "My friend. Danny. He walks past our house every now and then and stops and talks to me sometimes. He's a nice man."

"It says here his name was Edwin," said her father.

"Are you through with your egg, dear?" Angela's mother asked. "If so, go upstairs and brush your teeth. It's almost time to go."

"Yes, ma'am," said Angela. "But I want to hear about Danny when I come back downstairs."

And she left the table.

"Read this," said her father to her mother when she had gone. "But don't tell Angela about it—and keep the paper out of her sight."

Angela's mother took the paper. "Why? What's this all about?"

"Well, you remember that freak storm late Saturday afternoon, the one that hit while we were all still at your mother's and knocked out the power for a little while…?"

"Yes, of course."

"Well, this man's car went over the side of that narrow bridge over by Sewell's and he drowned."

Angela's father put his finger on Edwin's picture. "This man—the one Angela just told us she knew."

"Oh, dear," said her mother, "that's a sha…"

"Maybe," interrupted her father. "Maybe not. You see, if you read on, it says the police backtracked the route of his vehicle to where he was before he went over the side of the bridge. An out-of-the-way spot in a wooded area. And here's the really bad part—someone was there and showed them three graves, open graves, and in them were the remains of three little girls who've gone missing at different times in the last few years."

"Who was this 'someone' who was there and showed them these graves?" asked Angela's mother, scanning the article.

"Nobody seems to know," her father replied. "Apparently, it was getting dark, and every description of the person seems to differ— no one seems to agree even about the sex of the person. And then the individual—he or she—just disappeared, couldn't be found afterwards."

"And Angela knew the man who died?" her mother said, looking as worried now as her husband.

As she said this, Angela returned.

"Tell me what happened to Danny," she demanded. "Why's he in the paper?"

As gently as they could, they told her that the man had died in a terrible accident. Angela hung her head and looked sad.

Then she brightened up and said, "I guess it's okay he's dead."

Her father looked at her, nonplussed. "How so?"

"Why is it 'okay'?" asked her mother.

"Because he had a guardian angel," she said. "I'm sure he's look-ing after him."

She looked up and then back down. And then she asked that question she had been longing to ask them for days.

"What do our guardian angels look like?"

Her father breathed a sigh of relief. Here was a question he would rather deal with than the news about Edwin.

"You remember what Father McManus said about Saint Peter's guardian angel, don't you?"

The little girl shook her head.

# The Spot on the Bridge

"Well," her father went on, "when Saint Peter was released from jail by the angel, his friends thought that Saint Peter wasn't really Saint Peter, but that he was Saint Peter's angel. You remember that now, don't you?"

Angela nodded. "Yes!" she suddenly exclaimed. "So, if Saint Peter's angel looked like Saint Peter, then that means *my* angel looks like *me*!"

"I suppose so," replied her father. "At least, sometimes maybe your angel looks like you, and maybe at other times your angel looks more, well, angel-like. Not that I know what that looks like myself.

"Anyhow, young lady, it's time for you to get to school and for me to get to work."

# Bone Fire

*'Is not He just, that all this doth behold*
*From highest heaven, and beares an equall eye?*
*Shall He thy sins up in His knowledge fold,*
*And guilty be of thine impietie?*
*Is not His law, Let every sinner die:*
*Die shall all flesh? What then must needs be donne,*
*Is it not better to doe willinglie,*
*Then linger till the glasse be all out ronne?*
*Death is the end of woes: die soone, O faeries sonne.'*

> Spenser, *The Fairie Queene*,
> Book I, Canto IX, xlvii

THE ARM EXTENDED upwards out of the earth. The rest of the man had been crushed and mangled and re-mangled, irretrievably flattened and packed down by the treads of the column of tanks into the oily mud and among the loose stones of the unpaved mountain road. Notwithstanding, the arm from elbow to fingertips remained untouched and sticking straight up. It seemed to beckon to him, waving and swaying slightly in the cold mountain air, as if the man were still animated in some occult fashion, although his body had long since been pounded into an elongated red stain on the earth. Worse, inexplicably, his imagination interpreted the arm's appearance as possessing an indicting purpose and motivation—it was not only beckoning to him, he felt, but also *accusing* him.

The dead man seemed to invite him to join him there in the sludge, in the filth, in death, *because he deserved it...*

Herbie Shaw awoke in a sweat, his bedsheets twisted down around his ankles. He was jittery, his mind submerged in the blackest mood and disoriented. This dream and others like it assailed him from time to time; they were dreams and they were also memories. He must learn to accept that they would haunt him on occasion, his doctors had told him, but they would come and go, and life would go on. They were part of the ongoing strain, but he mustn't worry. Time and experience would dull their impact—or so he had been assured. It was this same mental strain that caused him to seek safety whenever he heard thunder roll in the sky, or to hit the city sidewalk face-down when the noise of a jackhammer or a backfiring vehicle took him by surprise. The war did this to survivors. Everyday noises were transformed into the deadly, nerve-wracking sounds of battle.

His head began to clear. He forced himself to get out of bed, and soon he was attending to his daily morning routine as if the dream had made no lasting impression on him. He showered, shaved, breakfasted, and set about the few chores he had to take care of before he could make his escape. He had definite plans for the evening, a bit of a getaway. In preparation, he spent the early hours after noon packing his knapsack. And sometime between the monastic office of None (three o'clock) and the start of Vespers (five o'clock), he set out for his planned destination.

Sister Constance looked up from her reading and saw him coming toward her from the direction of the groundskeeper's house on the hill opposite the convent.

"Where're you headed off to, Herbie?" she called to him. She was seated in a rocking chair on the raised platform just outside the barn, a .22 rifle laid across her knees. That item and her surplus army boots went incongruously with the traditional black nun's habit she was wearing, with its medieval wimple. She was charged with the oversight of the convent's vegetable garden, a job for which she was eminently qualified.

Herbie Shaw looked over and waved to her. He cut through the rows of growing vegetables and came up to the raised platform, stopping just below it. From where he stood, he could look her straight in the soles of her boots.

"You look terribly dangerous up there, Sister," he said. "What's with the BB gun?"

"Groundhogs," she replied. "They're cute, but they're pests. And it's not a BB gun."

Herbie laughed. "Just kidding. But I didn't know you were prone to violence."

"I'm a farm girl from Missouri," Sister Constance said with a smile. She adjusted her horn-rimmed glasses as she said it. "I'm protective of my crops. And there isn't a firearm I haven't used at one time or another—except for that heavy-duty equipment you boys used in the war."

Herbie saw that she had a book open, propped atop the rifle on her knees. "What're you reading?"

"It's called *Freedom and the Spirit*—it's by Nikolai Berdyaev. You know, the Russian philosopher."

"Never heard of him," said Herbie. "Any good?"

"It's pretty engrossing, I must say. So," she said, coming back to her original question, "where are you heading off to on this fine sunny afternoon with your backpack on your back? I see you've got your sleeping bag with you, too."

Herbie Shaw had been staying on the convent grounds for the past two years. He was living over in the groundskeeper's house, set in the meadow at some remove from the convent proper. George, the groundskeeper, was a widower and getting long in the tooth, and over time Herbie had become his assistant. In fact, it was a kind of ongoing therapy for him.

After graduating from college with a degree in journalism in 1950, he had been employed at the local newspaper in Catonsville. That had lasted for ten years, and then, all at once and quite unexpectedly, everything had come crashing down for him. The war finally caught up with him, and he was hospitalized for an incapacitating depression. Memories had come flooding back into his waking life and dreams—recollections of horrors he had endured daily overseas a decade and a half ago, that he had managed to press and push and pack down hard under the surface layer of his soul. But they wouldn't stay buried—he found that out the hard way. They broke free through the crust and erupted and overwhelmed him. He had come close twice to committing suicide. Both times he had managed to pull himself back from the brink. Then, finally, embarrassingly, one day he had collapsed at the office, in plain view of everybody, breaking down, weeping, and babbling incoherently until he had been hauled out by unsympathetic men in white uniforms before his stunned co-workers.

To make a long story short, in the months that followed he underwent electroshock and other treatments. Eventually he was released from the hospital as a "success story." Perhaps it really had been a success story for the doctors who treated him, but for Herbie the stigma of having been treated at a "mental institution" made it difficult for him to find new employment. He had had a humiliatingly public "nervous breakdown," something that stigmatized a person ever afterward and made most employers hesitant to hire when they noted it on the record. Such an "unsteady" employee was deemed a risk. And during his long stay in the mental hospital, Herbie's old position had been filled. It was made crystal clear to him when he went and inquired at the paper about picking up where he had left off—although they had been outwardly nice about it, even solicitous concerning his welfare—that they wouldn't be needing him back.

A lifelong Episcopalian, he had long been acquainted with the Sisters of All Souls, a religious order in the Episcopal Church, and he began attending their daily Masses and Vespers. This proved a balm to his soul. He grew to love the place, with its beautiful grounds, and he quickly became friends with many of the nuns and with the chaplain. Soon he was helping George with odd jobs. Not long after that, George's wife died, and Herbie was invited to come and stay and make a few bucks in the process. The next two years had passed quickly. During that time, he became a fixture around the place, a handyman who tackled all sorts of jobs pleasant and un. He discovered, despite his training and years of journalism, that he was truly content just to be a handyman. And George, cranky and peevish as he could be, wasn't poor company.

Most important of all, he had found a girlfriend. She was a darkly beautiful young woman whose diplomatic family had moved from New Delhi to London, and then from London to Washington DC. Her name was Draupadi, after the female protagonist of *The Mahabharata*, and he was very much in love with her. He had met her, of all places, right there at the convent. Raised entirely in London and Washington, she had developed into a modern young woman with Western tastes. She wasn't a Christian formally, but she had come there in search of a silent place to make a retreat. They had met. They had "clicked." And the rest had fallen into place. That was a year ago, and Herbie was now on the verge of proposing to her. He knew she would say yes. His modest income was no barrier. She had higher standards than merely the pursuit of material acquisition. She had told him so many times. He also knew he would have to approach Draupadi's father and observe certain proprieties, but Draupadi had already assured him that she had her father "wrapped around her little finger," and he would do anything she asked.

But there was an attendant matter that lingered in the back of his mind, that nagged him and gnawed at any prospect of happiness he might conceive of sharing with Draupadi. Try as he might, he couldn't shake it. It was this, and this was crucial: he knew the things that he had done in the war, how horrible they had been, many of them inexcusable. Worse still, he worried whether Draupadi could excuse them if ever she came to hear of them. Could he expose her to his tormented life, healed though he felt himself to be? Could he ever tell her the unvarnished truth? He thought of her as an innocent, like some babe in the woods, where real horror was concerned. Could she handle the true state of his haunted mind? Because, although he knew that what he had done in the war was past and unchangeable, but also that he had subsequently changed and become a better man, yet perhaps he was only deceiving himself; perhaps the passing of time would reveal to him and to those he loved that, in fact, he was no better now than when he had done those abominable things years before. In short, did he love Draupadi enough to protect her from himself?

Such thoughts caused him anguish periodically, if not constantly. He felt he could resist them, and he usually did successfully. But they would return to plague him, often unexpectedly. He knew, before ever he proposed to Draupadi, he would have to resolve this matter in his heart. For her sake.

"I'm going down to the riverside," Herbie told Sister Constance. "George has things well in hand up here at the moment, so I'm going to camp out overnight and come back in the morning."

220

He didn't tell her he wanted to be alone down by the riverside just to think things through regarding Draupadi and his—*their*—possible future. It didn't matter. The nun seemed to know exactly why he was going anyway.

She said, "We all like Draupadi, you know. Such a nice girl and so smart. She's the one who got me reading Berdyaev, by the way." She waved the book, as if to confirm this stunning revelation.

"George will be moving soon to go live with his brother," she went on. She looked off to one side, avoiding Herbie's eyes. "Has he told you?"

"He has," said Herbie.

"Reverend Mother was saying just yesterday you might be persuaded to take his place. The house is for the groundskeeper..." She paused, then looked back at him. "And his wife, too, if he's married... and his family," she added, with a wink.

Herbie felt himself blushing. "Well, you know, Sister," he started to say, then stopped and laughed with embarrassment.

Sister Constance suddenly stood up from the rocking chair. Berdyaev tumbled off her lap. She was looking intently at something beyond Herbie. She raised the rifle to her shoulder and fired. Herbie swung around to see a large brown groundhog loping off in ungainly fashion into the tall grass on the other side of the vegetable patch.

"You missed," he said to Sister Constance.

"I just fire over their heads," she replied. "Can't bring myself to kill the blasted things."

She set the rifle down.

"So, where're you going to camp out, then?" She knew, as all the community did, that Herbie loved being out in the woods and enjoyed solitary camping from time to time. The convent grounds were surrounded on three sides by the wooded hills of Patapsco State Park.

"I'm taking that path over there"—he pointed toward the trailhead leading into the woods not many yards from the barn—"downhill to those ruins alongside the river. It has a stone hearth and part of a chimney standing—you've seen it—and it's perfect for building a fire. Good dry area, too. Weather's supposed to be okay tonight, as well. There's no rain in the forecast."

Sister Constance sat back down in the rocker, after first scooping up her book.

"I wouldn't camp in that place," she said. "Anywhere else would be better. I don't like those ruins. In fact, nobody does. There are stories about it. People say they've seen and heard strange things down there."

Herbie laughed. "Well, I'm not too worried about that sort of thing. I've heard some of those stories myself."

"Still, I'd go somewhere else, if I were camping down by the river," she said. "I don't know about you, but I believe some places have an evil presence about them—something that's just not right. And that spot gives me the willies."

"You know me, Sister," said Herbie. "That sounds a lot like a challenge. And I couldn't pass up a challenge and still call myself a man, could I?"

He saw that the nun wasn't convinced by his bravado.

"Look," he said, with more seriousness in his tone. "I spent my nineteenth birthday in a foxhole in France in far more terrifying circumstances than overnighting down by the river with a nice, cheery bonfire close by."

"Do you know what that word 'bonfire' means?" asked the nun, her eyes narrowing as if she were making a fine point. "It means *bone-fire*. That's a fire that's fueled by bones."

"I thought 'bonfire' meant 'good fire'—*bon* fire," said Herbie.

"Common mistake," replied Sister Constance. "No, it refers to an old Anglo-Saxon custom that was practiced as autumn was setting in. Of course, it might refer to the burning of heretics, too..." She looked thoughtful for a moment. "But it definitely means *bone-fire*. Remember that while you're sitting there in front of the hearth feeling all 'cheery.' Anyway, you're a stubborn fellow. Just don't say I didn't warn you."

Herbie laughed again, shouldered his pack, and started in the direction of the trailhead. "I don't have any bones to burn, except my own, and I'm not letting go of those. I'm off. See you tomorrow, Sister," he said.

He went a few paces toward the trailhead, then looked back. She waved to him as he entered the woods.

222

# Bone Fire

The trail was a downhill slog all the way. The day was warm, but not as unbearably humid as summer weather in Maryland can be. The sunlight percolated here and there through the thick canopy of leaves above him, but otherwise he was in an ancient wood that could be dark enough in places even at midday that one had to look hard to avoid tripping over an exposed tree root or stubbing one's toes on jutting rocks. The forest here had its dangers—copperhead snakes, for example—and inconveniences such as poison ivy, but Herbie was an experienced woodsman and knew what to do when faced with natural predicaments and obstacles, and he always carried a first aid kit in his knapsack.

Only once along the way did he think of that dead man's arm extending from the mud, seeming to beckon to him. It was at a spot along the trail that always reminded him of that passage through the Vosges Mountains where he had first seen the remains of this unknown soldier, for whom expediency had left no opportunity for a show of respect. He had had no choice at the time but to march past. But as quickly as the memory had come, causing his heart to race for an instant, it dissipated again. He wouldn't let it bother him, he determined. He was doing the thing he loved, after all.

Camping and hiking were his hobbies, and solitude was something his soul craved from time to time. It had pleased him to learn that Draupadi understood this need. She had a similar desire at times to be "alone with the alone." Sister Constance had informed him, in one of her many didactic moments, that that phrase, which he had heard somewhere and adopted as a sort of mantra, had originated with the medieval Sufi poet, Ibn Arabi—whoever he was.

As he descended the trail, which could just barely even be called a trail, he rehearsed in his head the words of proposal he hoped to say to Draupadi. He wanted them to be eloquent and memorable. He also rehearsed what he would say to her father. No doubt her mother would be sitting silently nearby on that occasion. He tried to picture both scenes in his mind as he climbed over fallen limbs, scrambled over mossy rocks, waved at a blacksnake hanging from the bough of an enormous oak, and worked his way painstakingly down to the gray stone ruins that lay not far from the riverbank.

Those ruined walls were, he had been told, about two hundred years old. They had once been the site of an inn for those travelling by river on business. It had been a large inn and the remaining walls formed a large rectangle. In places the walls were waist-high, in others nearly as high as his head, and at one end there stood imposingly the remains of a fireplace and chimney. It rose nearly nine feet in height, and it was overgrown with ivy. It had, nonetheless, a suitably contained recess perfect for building a fire. He had tried it out on a walk one afternoon just to check it out, knowing he'd be back to make it his camp some evening. That prospective evening would be tonight.

Herbie had heard the stories about this old, abandoned place. Supposedly, one tale went, a German family had lived there and run the inn. The family's name, aptly enough, had been Sauer. They had been run out of Pennsylvania for some criminal act, had come south to Maryland, constructed the inn on this spot by the river, and set up shop. As with most stories of this nature, it was said that the Sauers robbed their customers and had even murdered a few. More dastardly still, they had practiced magic they had brought over with them from "the old country." It was said that they summoned a dragon to rob their neighbors and bring them the booty. They paid the dragon with the carcasses of their slain customers. This sort of dragon, apparently, was more of an elemental spirit than a fire-breathing reptile. The story ended with the tavern being burned to the ground by irate folk from the town, the Sauer family hanged and buried in the surrounding woods, and their bodies staked through in their graves just for good measure.

However, as Herbie well knew, there were no visible signs that the building had ever been burned, there were no historical records of a family named Sauer ever having lived there, and no doubt the rest of the tale was bunk, too. It was great for scaring the kids around a campfire but bunk all the same. Likewise, he thought, with all the other stories about strange sights and sounds encountered there. And there were many such accounts—spectral creatures, weird human-like singing echoing through the woods, lights that flickered, laughter and groans from unseen presences... As he had told Sister Constance, ruins like this one always had their ghost stories.

224

But Herbie had also seen real horrors. He feared the hauntings in his memories and dreams far more than any possibility of a haunting by restless phantoms. The latter he would endure with relative ease, he felt sure, but the former caused him to cringe in mental agony whenever they assailed him. And they did assail him in unguarded hours. When someone has seen war at its worst—the truly terrifying, in other words—a fear of things preternatural doesn't hold much of a candle to it.

It took him about forty-five minutes to reach the ruins. Beyond it flowed the Patapsco. An open stretch of dirt and pebbles lay between the edge of the woods and the waterway. Just within the borders of the wood were the ruins, in plain view of the river, its walls exposed in places and covered with vines and creepers in others. The old hearth and half-demolished chimney had ivy clinging to it, but otherwise the space for building a fire was dry and clear of plant life.

Herbie set down his backpack and unrolled his sleeping bag in front of it. His first job now was to gather enough kindling and firewood to keep a flame alive or at least smoldering through the night. This he set about doing, after first taking a long swig from his large canteen. Luckily, the weather had been dry for the past week and so he wouldn't have to contend with trying to start a fire with wet wood.

This chore completed, taking him another forty-five minutes or so, he stretched himself on top of the sleeping bag, pulled out a paperback thriller by Alistair MacLean and tried to concentrate on the story. But he was too woozy in the warmth of the day to do it, and soon he was napping, dreaming contentedly about Draupadi.

When he awoke, he saw that the sun was on its way down, the amber light of the day's last rays gleaming through the open spaces between the trees and casting long shadows. The overall effect on him was one of melancholy and a feeling akin to nostalgia, but nostalgia for what exactly he would have been hard pressed to say. A sense of beauty, he remembered having read somewhere, was linked to sadness. He suddenly recalled that it was Poe who had written about it. He might no longer be an active journalist, but at least his college education hadn't been entirely for nothing.

He set about building the fire. When it was merrily burning in the fireplace, he pulled from his knapsack a small frying pan, some bacon and beans, and his thermos of coffee. The coffee was still steaming hot. He made himself what he considered a good outdoor dinner and ate it while the twilight turned to pitch blackness. He had also brought along a Coleman kerosene lantern and a large Tiger Head torchlight, and with these and the light of the campfire he wasn't without sufficient illumination. He lit the Coleman lamp, lit his pipe with its flame, rinsed out his pan with a little water from the river, and sat smoking and listening to the night sounds in silent reflection. Fireflies appeared with their fairy lights. An owl hooted eerily somewhere in the depths of the forest. Frogs sang in the river and treefrogs in the trees. He occasionally heard the scurrying of small unseen feet outside or along the walls. They didn't alarm him. He felt peaceful and his thoughts, as ever these days, dwelled lovingly on Draupadi. The rising moon was full this night and the flowing river, brown during the day, was now a silvery amber in its glow. He threw another sizable branch on the fire, removed his boots, stripped down to only his undershirt and khaki pants, and crawled into his sleeping bag. Within minutes he was asleep.

In that state, the peace he had felt while still awake abandoned him. His dreams became nightmares—the sort he dreaded most. They were a series of memories. Memories of battle and bloodshed. They came rushing over him in a stream of images and fragments of images.

He was in a foxhole, in the mud. He had emptied his bowels and bladder in his pants. The shelling was seemingly endless and deafening. The shell-bursts stunned him, jolted him, shredded his mind. His ears rang painfully. It was night. He was bleeding from a wound in his arm. He was soaked to the skin and freezing cold. The rain had been heavy. He was kneeling in icy water. To his left lay the wasted body of his friend Wilson. Half his face was gone. His chest was obliterated. His lungs were hanging out. To his right was the other occupant of their foxhole, a new guy named Jerry. He had taken shrapnel in the neck. Also, dead. Herbie had only met him yesterday. Herbie was doubled over, shaking, crumpled up, gripping his BAR. He'd vomited on himself.

226

The scene changed. Now it was day. Herbie was running up a hill toward a pillbox. Another soldier flung a grenade through one of its apertures. It blew. Herbie had the flamethrower. He ran in and unleashed it on the Germans inside. He heard their screams. A few of them ran out of the pillbox. Herbie let loose again. Flames full in their faces. He watched them burn. He felt dead inside.

The scene changed again. Herbie held a pistol. A German, the last man in his foxhole, had his hands raised. He was begging for his life. He was crying. Herbie didn't care. He fired three bullets into his open mouth. Revenge for Wilson and for that new guy Jerry. He couldn't take prisoners anyway. He didn't care, he just didn't care.

Another scene: dead German soldiers, bloated to the point of bursting their buttons, faces blackened, the stench, a pig noshing on the guts of one of them...

And then that American soldier who had been knocked down in the road by a tank and run over so many times that he was only an elongated red smear in the mud, one arm still intact and stiffly reaching up from the sludge as if pleading for a helping hand...

The cascade of images was relentless. One crowded upon another. Herbie tossed and twisted and moaned in his sleeping bag. The scenes tumbled and roared and surged through his brain.

Then suddenly, with a choking, almost sobbing gasp, he sat bolt upright. He was drenched in his own sweat. He had kicked his sleeping bag down past his knees in his restlessness. The procession of memories still paraded through his mind—he could still see them, hear them, taste them, smell them, feel them.

And yet, they weren't what had awakened him. Something else had.

He couldn't at first say what it was, but something was *wrong*. Not just in his head, but all around him. Something palpable. He felt it before he saw and heard it.

The fire had died down to glowing red embers. He leaned over to his Coleman, fumbled with a match, and got it relit. It was only then that he realized that everything around him was altered.

Three details struck him simultaneously. First, that he was wide awake. He wasn't half dreaming. He wasn't hallucinating. He was, despite his midnight throes, entirely clear-headed, all his senses

alert. At the same time, secondly, he saw that his physical surroundings had changed. The hearth was still where it had been. All his
effects were still about him just as they had been when he had laid
himself down to sleep. But now, where there had been only ruins
before, he found himself in an enclosed space—he was, in fact,
inside a four-walled, roofed structure. It was as if a building had
grown of its own accord all around him, sprung from the fallen
walls of the ruins.

And lastly, clearly audible beyond these seemingly rebuilt walls,
he could hear what sounded like children's laughter.

For an instant he froze, then he grabbed the Tiger Head torch and
cast its strong beams in every direction. Four constructed walls
indeed now surrounded him, yellowish-brown in hue. He could
make out a staircase at the far end of what he realized was a room,
leading up to what must be the floor above. To his right, there was a
door, tight shut. He looked intently in the direction of the staircase—and for a moment he could have sworn that he saw the waving, swaying arm of his nightmares rising from the ground near it.
But when he shone the light in the direction of the apparition, it
dissolved in the steady beam.

He cast the light upward. The ceiling was low. It sagged. He stood
up, and his head came to about a foot and a half below it. The
atmosphere was musty and damp and oppressive. Just being in it
and breathing it in seemed to weigh his soul down. The setting in
general drained and depressed him, compounding those feelings of
fear and guilt and misery his dreams had already induced. His state
of mind was less one of surprise at the transformation that had
occurred than a mood of desolation and despondency. More than
that, he sensed that there was something truly malignant in that
environment. Something living and watching him and possibly
cruel. Another intelligence besides his—gloomy, grim, possessing
intention, possessing malice.

There was a single small window that looked out in the direction
of the river. It was from there that the sound he took to be children's
laughter could be heard. With apprehension he stealthily moved
toward it, anxious that his movements should not stir to action the
evil presence he felt within the room. He couldn't imagine what sort

of scene would meet his eyes, but he steeled himself to peer through the glassless window to see the source of the sounds.

What he saw confused him.

In the bright moonlight outdoors, he could clearly see what appeared to be more than a dozen children cavorting on the river-bank. Along with their laughter and cries he heard bells tinkling, and some of the dancers were singing. It sounded like a nursery rhyme, but he couldn't make out the words. It could have been another language than English, for all he could tell. All the figures looked grayish in the moon's radiance, although Herbie could see that their clothing was really of various colors when their prancing and gamboling allowed the light to reveal them more plainly. Their movements were erratic, with some of them leaping over others, some rolling and jumping and tumbling like a circus act, and Herbie almost laughed despite the strangeness of the scene and his unnerving predicament. At the same time, he hadn't lost the oppressive sense that something or someone was in that room with him.

The mixture of emotions—fear, depression, incredulity, the ability to be momentarily amused, all present in his mind at once—was nothing new to him. He had been a soldier with a soldier's training. He had already trudged through hell and even added to its evil. He had come through it intact—well, almost intact. He thought again of Draupadi. Even now, in this uncanny new situation, he thought of her. Whatever was going on, he was determined to get back to her. Nothing, he swore, would prevent that. Regarding his present state, he didn't ask himself why. He pushed questions like that right out of his head. Again, his soldier's training wouldn't permit it. No fuzzy thinking allowed; all imponderables kept at bay. He would face the situation directly, just as it presented itself, stowing away whys and wherefores until he had dealt with it.

He flashed the beam of his torchlight through the window toward the group of children. As he did, they turned, froze, and stared in his direction. He could hear them murmuring to one another. He heard more laughter. Then some of them began to push others in his direction, as if wanting somebody "to go first." He switched off the torch, thinking they might be more inclined to come his way if there weren't a dazzling light blinding their eyes. What he hoped to achieve by getting their attention and inviting them in this way to advance toward him, he couldn't have explained. He acted on the spur of the moment, without any definite plan. Despite his lack of a clear rationale, however, it worked. The entire company started moving toward the window as one body.

As they drew closer, he realized with a new sense of wonder that they weren't children at all. Their faces were grotesque and old; some were quite wrinkled, like creased leather. They were of both sexes. They were no longer laughing or singing. Their earlier merriment had disappeared entirely. They drew closer and closer, and there was something about them that now struck him as grim and unpleasant.

At the same instant, he heard something stir behind him. But he didn't turn around. He was too taken with the creatures advancing toward him. Then, at a distance from the window of four or five yards they halted, and one of them—he looked like their leader, appearing to be even older than the rest—advanced all the way up to the window and stood looking up into Herbie's face.

The top of his head just came to the windowsill. He was ancient and wizened, crinkled and beardless, but he moved with the flexibility of a child. He and Herbie locked eyes. As they did, the former reached into a pocket of the shirt or jacket that he was wearing— Herbie couldn't decide which it was—and extracted something that caught the light of the moon. The two of them continued to look directly at one another. And then the man spoke.

He didn't speak with his lips. Rather, he somehow spoke inside Herbie's head. Herbie could hear him loud and clear, and when the voice spoke it shut out all his other thoughts. This impression of being mentally invaded was accompanied by the freezing sensation one occasionally has while consuming something ice-cold on a summer's day, that soreness and cramping just behind the ears.

The voice said: "I see who you are. I see what you are."

Then it fell silent for a few moments as the man outside looked even more intently into Herbie's eyes.

Then the voice went on: "After everything you have done, do you believe you have a right to marry her?"

Herbie reeled back from the impact of the question. He had to grab the windowsill with both hands to keep himself steady. He started to say something but couldn't find the words.

"You have slaughtered and destroyed," the voice went on. "You have burned and stabbed and shot many men. Am I not right about that?"

Herbie hesitantly nodded his assent. He felt compelled to agree.

"You did not always kill in order to defend yourself," the voice said. "That might have served as some justification for your deeds. No, I see you killed in spite and with hatred. You have killed for revenge. And then, after better men than you were killed—men you called your friends—you shamelessly left your honorable slain comrades behind and came crawling back to your own selfish comfort and peace. No recompense was paid by you for what you did over there. Decent people here had no idea what sort of man had come back to live among them. Now you know what sort of man you are."

For the first time since he found himself in this whole horrifying scenario, Herbie felt fear. Not the fear of the strange surroundings, of the building that had suddenly reared itself up around him, not the strange ancient "children" before him, not even the "presence" he felt so close behind him in that stifling room. This was the same fear he had felt when he had collapsed on the job but intensified a hundredfold. It was the fear that had accompanied his debilitating depression, for which he had been hospitalized and treated with experimental therapies, which he had already survived once and didn't want to face again. It was the fear of self-disclosure, the revelation to himself—yet again—of the monster he housed inside him, that he knew himself to be. Added to that terror now was another, even worse one: the possible loss of Draupadi. Because, he knew, the little man wasn't mistaken. Did he have some sacred right to marry Draupadi, innocent of any knowledge of the murders he had committed, all the brutality he had unleashed? He had confessed it many times, over and over, both alone and to more than one priest, until he had finally come to hope that, by some grace, he had really been forgiven. The confidence that he had been, after long agonizing years, had finally come to replace the nagging guilt he had felt previously.

But now, with the words he had just heard, all that confidence

231

suddenly drained out of him, left him high and dry—in despair and scared to death.

The voice spoke inside his head again. The assembly outside still stood stock still, as if staying to see what would happen next.

"You know you would dishonor her to marry her, sullied as you are. Without the taint of you, she shall remain inviolate. Did you really believe that all those things you did could be forgiven? All the killing? Not one of the lives you took can ever be restored. Not by you. No blood can atone for your atrocities—or more to the point, *no one else's blood* can atone for them."

There was a pause, as if allowing these terrible words time to sink in. Then: "So, what should you do about it?"

Herbie shook his head. "I really don't know," he managed to mumble.

"You're not being honest with yourself. You know the answer. You've known it for a long time. You even tried bravely on two occasions to do the right thing. But you stopped yourself. That was cowardly of you. That was ignoble of you. You know that now. I believe you do. I will give you your opportunity here and now to amend your cowardice."

The man reached up and placed the object he had taken from his pocket on the windowsill before Herbie's eyes. Herbie gazed down at it. The light of the moon showed plainly what it was: a knife, about six inches in length. It looked rusty. Perhaps, thought Herbie, it wasn't rust but dried blood.

"Have there been others?" he asked hoarsely, staring at the blade.

"There have," the voice replied. "You're not the first. You won't be the last, either. But with us here you won't be alone." He waved a hand sweepingly toward his companions.

Herbie's mind was in a fog. He felt dazed.

"Should I go down to the riverside, then?" he asked.

"That won't be necessary," said the voice. "We tidy up. And no one will ever know. But come along now. You know it's for the best. Do it quickly. Get it over with and spare her. You will be giving her a happier life than you could ever give her otherwise. As it is, you have nothing but pain and sorrow to give her. It wouldn't be fair to her to weigh her soul down with your evil past."

232

There was logic in the argument, Herbie thought, and somehow, he couldn't come up with any logical counterargument. It all seemed to make bitter sense. There was plausibility in the man's words. His past *was* troubled. Draupadi would be better off without him. Who was he trying to kid, anyway? Everyone he knew, who had trusted in him, who didn't know all that he had done, would be better off without him. He had known before now that there really was no way out for him. No way out, that is, unless perhaps—

Slowly, tremblingly, Herbie took the knife in hand. He backed away from the window, grasping it, still not turning around, still sensing the ominous presence in the room with him, not wanting to face it. He didn't possess the will to fight; he had no inner resources with which to resist his despair. Whatever strength had been in him had drained away. It had ebbed out as the grotesque little man spoke. All his soldier's training had—without any warning or awareness of it—abandoned him as well. He couldn't stand up to the brute logic of the act before him.

He knelt down in the middle of the room, facing the window and the full moon. With his right hand he put the keen edge of the blade against his left wrist, prepared for the rapid thrust and slice. He said a prayer. He asked God for mercy. He resolved himself.

Outside he could hear the voices murmuring. He heard the congregation begin to ring their bells. They started to sing. It was atonal and unsettling.

He shut his eyes. The blade was poised to open his vein.

Suddenly something slammed into him from behind. He fell forward on his stomach, the wind knocked from his lungs. The knife flew from his hands and clattered against the wall under the window. Something had gripped and was pressing down both his shoulders. It felt like two large, rough claws, pinning him to the earth. He heard his undershirt tear under the sharp nails of the unseen feet. His face had been forced against the floor. A tremendous weight pushed down on his back; something was lying on him, squeezing him so tightly he couldn't catch his breath. A hot, moist, reeking breath enveloped his senses, miasmal and suffocating. The body—and it *was* a body—scrubbed his back sore with what felt like a coarse, hard, bumpy, almost serrated underbelly.

And throughout the ordeal the atonal dirge continued unabated.

Then there was a new, violent sensation. Wet, slavering jaws had clamped themselves to the back of his head, causing him excruciating pain. He tried to shout for help. He couldn't. He thrashed about as best he could to free himself, but he was too firmly clamped by the claws and held to the earth. A rough tongue moved against the crown of his head, as if tasting it. The creature's maw began to suck with tremendous force, as if it would pull Herbie's brain from his skull. The suction was terrific. The skin of his head, from his temple to the nape of his neck, was pulled taut. He thought his eyes might pop out from the tautness of it. The strain was unendurable.

The atonal noise reached a crescendo beyond the window. Herbie managed to cry out once for help—it was all he could manage. Then, as his head felt as if it might be pulled apart at the seams, he suddenly heard—or, rather, felt—a *pop* between his ears, as if something had come free and been dislodged from the back of his head. With that, he lost all consciousness.

He went tumbling and spinning into oblivion.

🐦

It was morning when Herbie came to. That much he could see through bleary eyes. He couldn't see much else, given his prone position. He was still sprawled on his belly, his face in the dirt. He was sore all over. He painfully turned himself over onto his left side. He was facing the hearth. The previous night's fire was now diminished to a mound of ashes. His sleeping bag, twisted and tossed, lay in a heap beside it. He was no longer inside a building, but instead surrounded by the walls of the familiar ruins.

He pushed himself up into a sitting position. He was groggy and confused, but piece by piece he was able to put together in his mind all that he had encountered during the night. He remembered, and was appalled by, the heavy despair that had conquered him and subjugated his mental faculties. It seemed inconceivable to him now that it had dominated him as it had. That misery, he realized with sudden relief, had entirely fled. He remembered the "children," the little man, the knife, the enormous creature that had felled him…

Bone Fire

He rubbed the back of his head. It still hurt. He looked from where he sat for the knife, over in the direction he thought it had been dashed. There was no sign of it.

A leaden mist had spread itself over the river and through the woods. At least, it was a cool miasma, not like the broiling breath of the thing that had attacked him. He examined himself from the neck down, feeling his shoulders and back as far as he could reach. He saw bruises and scratches. His shirt was indeed torn and there was some clotted blood on it. So, he thought to himself, it was evident he hadn't been dreaming. It had all really happened. But—what exactly had really happened?

He could barely stand up, but he forced himself to his feet anyway. He was dizzy, but he steadied himself until the giddiness passed. He stumbled over to his backpack and pulled out his thermos. The coffee wasn't hot anymore, just lukewarm, but he didn't care. He poured it down his throat. He washed his face and head with water from his canteen. He had every intention to get the hell out of there, but he was determined not to give in to fear and flee, and not before he had made himself presentable for a return to the convent grounds. He dried himself off with the torn, bloodied undershirt, then put on another he had brought along and a khaki work-shirt over that. All the time he kept looking around him nervously, but without any show of panic—if *they* were watching, he wouldn't give them the satisfaction. He had held the sense of fear at bay throughout his ordeal, but now it was crawling around in his brain like a legion of ants. He felt unseen eyes observing his every move from every direction. He was determined that it wouldn't get to him. He steadied his nerves.

He put on his boots, he put on his cap. He rolled up his sleeping bag, packed his backpack, and was just getting ready to shoulder it, when he heard a twig snap and what sounded like a man clearing his throat behind him. He turned abruptly around.

There, facing him, was indeed a man. He was dressed in khakis, like Herbie. On his head was a brown slouch hat, and Herbie took him for a park ranger. He was tall, gaunt, and his eyes seemed to glint like steel from under the hat brim. He stood there in the gray river mist and looked at Herbie with an air of stern authority.

235

Beside him and a little behind him, shrouded by the fog and partially by a clump of bushes, was a great black dog. Or it looked
rather like a dog—it was larger than a Newfoundlander or a Mastiff.
But Herbie couldn't see it clearly and he wasn't sure he wanted to. In
that mass of black shadow, enshrouded by mist, he thought he
could make out two shining eyes.

"Good morning," said Herbie, in as friendly a tone as he could
muster.

"Camp here last night?" asked the man.

"I did," said Herbie, shouldering the backpack. "I was just setting
out for home."

The man and dog just stood in place, not moving a muscle. The
only part of the former that moved was his mouth when he spoke.
"You know," he said. "There are camping areas in the park. This
isn't one of them. It's off limits for campers."

"Sorry," said Herbie. "I didn't know that. Anyway, like I said, I'm
leaving. Believe me, I won't be camping down here again."

"Best see that you don't," said the man. His voice was low and
deep. "Could get you in some trouble. Could, in fact, get you killed."

"What do you mean?" asked Herbie. This kind of talk always
stirred up his fighting spirit—something he thought he had lost
forever the previous night.

"I mean what I said," said the man, still not moving, standing
like a statue. "There are poisonous snakes down here, for one thing.
Copperheads. And there are other things out here, too."

Herbie was still shaken from the night's encounters. He had no
desire to prolong a conversation with this martinet, as he saw him,
but he also resented being prodded along.

"What other things?" he said.

"*Other things*," the man said with emphasis. Then he added,
"Were you able to rest here comfortably last night?"

"No," answered Herbie ruefully, rubbing his chin, still sore from
being pressed unceremoniously to the ground. "I wasn't."

"That's not surprising—this isn't a place for resting comfortably,"
said the man. "Not for anyone who doesn't belong here. This is a
place for passing by quickly and leaving be. There is only one way
one might be permitted to stay, and that's clearly not why you tres-

passed here. Maybe you know that already. You got through the night. Be grateful for that."

Herbie moved in the direction of the trail. "I am, and I'm on my way," he answered.

He said it in such a way as to suggest finality. He didn't want to continue the discussion. He just wanted to be on his way. He wasn't even curious to know more about the locale or its history or its phantasms, even though he had gotten the distinct impression that this stranger could probably tell him all. But he had had enough.

He stepped through a gap in the ruined wall and onto the trail. He wasn't looking at the man and the dog now. He was looking straight ahead, in the direction of home.

"One moment. One more thing," the man behind him said.

Herbie turned around and faced him. The stranger and his beast stood in the same postures as before.

"Marry Draupadi," said the man. "Marry her and confide in her. She's not a child. Don't treat her like one. That's all I've got to say to you. Now, leave here. Don't fall sleep in this spot by the river again."

These words startled him, but without another word Herbie moved up the trail. He didn't question the man. He was too unnerved. He knew somehow that that was the last word he would hear from him, and he had better obey. He ascended the path, not wanting to look back. He was afraid of what he might see if he did. But, just where a turn in the path would finally obscure the ruins from his view, his curiosity got the better of him, and he did turn around.

The man and the dog had disappeared into the fog.

Sister Constance, her sleeves rolled up, her veil pinned back, wearing her blue gardening apron, was on her knees weeding. She paused to wipe sweat from her face. Raising her head, she caught sight of Herbie Shaw emerging from the woods. She got up and came to meet him as he walked in her direction.

"You look a bit frazzled, but fairly happy," she said cheerfully. "It looks like you survived, after all. Guess I was wrong to have worried about you."

Herbie smiled. He realized, much to his surprise, that he was indeed feeling rather happy, just as Sister Constance had observed. His head and shoulders still ached, but he was… happy. There was no better word for it. And other words echoed in his mind—"Marry Draupadi—marry her and confide in her."

He would go home directly and phone Draupadi. He needed to do it. Indeed, he needed to do it right away. He suddenly became conscious of the fact that his mind had been wandering and Sister Constance had been speaking, though he hadn't heard anything she was saying.

"So, did you?" Sister Constance asked again, trowel in hand.

"Did I what?"

She pretended to be exasperated with him.

"Did you see anything—you know, anything strange or spooky—down at the ruins last night?"

"No," he said, looking distracted. "Well, nothing to talk about."

ADDISON HODGES HART is the author of ten previous books, including nine volumes of non-fiction and a novel, *Confessions of the Antichrist*, published by Angelico Press. His most recent book, also published by Angelico Press, is *The Voyage of Life, The Sacred Vision of Thomas Cole* (2023), a work combining art history, philosophy, spirituality, and biography. A native of Ellicott City, Maryland, he has drawn on his own experience of that region in writing this collection of spooky tales. He currently resides in Norway. (He also has a lively, easy-to-access Substack page, The Pragmatic Mystic, that deals with topics related to his books.)

CPSIA information can be obtained
at www.ICGtesting.com
Printed in the USA
JSHW081530140623
43165JS00006B/52